SEGUE

RAY HOBBS

Wingspan Press

Published in the United States and the United Kingdom by WingSpan Press, Livermore, CA

The WingSpan name, logo and colophon are the trademarks of WingSpan Publishing.

ISBN 978-1-63683-071-1 (pbk.)
ISBN 978-1-63683-941-7 (ebook)

Printed in the United States of America

www.wingspanpress.com

This book is dedicated to Michael Bennett-Law and the Piccadilly Dance Orchestra, who ensure through their superb performances and recordings that the music of the Golden Age of the British Dance Band lives on.

As ever, I wish to thank my brother Chris, who acted as a sounding board for my ideas and helped fuel my enthusiasm throughout the writing of this book.

RH

Also by Ray Hobbs and Published by Wingspan Press

Published Elsewhere

Segue – an Italian term used in music to mean 'follows' or 'goes on.'

AUTHOR'S NOTE

It may be that some of you will be unfamiliar with at least some of the music referred to in this story, and for that I make no apology. As well as entertaining you, I hope, with a slightly unusual tale, it is my intention to introduce you to a musical idiom from long ago, that I have nevertheless enjoyed for many years. Music from the Golden Age of the British Dance Band is, after all, best enjoyed when it is shared.

Although the age to which I refer occupied little more than the decade that ended with the Second World War, the music is still available to be downloaded, or enjoyed on CD. For the ultimate experience, however, I recommend that you indulge yourselves in one of the truly excellent live performances by the Piccadilly Dance Orchestra. Alternatively, there are YouTube clips of the PDO as well as CDs that I heartily recommend.

Such is the fascination of the Golden Age for me, there are characters and references to characters in this story, who have appeared in no fewer than eight of my published novels. I mention this in the hope that those of you who are less familiar than others with my output will refer to the list contained in the first of these pages and, basically, indulge yourselves. I hope you enjoy them.

RH

SEGUE

1

The Trouble With Growing Older

Tradition is a sacred trust, and for that reason, much has been written and said about it. Some of those observations are worth remembering:

'All that is left to us is mere words. It is up to us to find out what they mean.' – Ibn Arabi, poet and philosopher.

'A tradition without intelligence is not worth having.' – T. S. Eliot, poet, essayist, publisher, playwright, literary critic and editor.

'No holiday is complete unless it begins at the Ristorante Monteverdi.' – Frank Morrison, composer, arranger, and bandleader, whose life was busy enough with the jobs he already had, without looking for more.

It was a tradition that had begun less than two years earlier, when Frank's daughter Kate had arrived home after her first term at the Guildhall School of Music and Drama, but as far as they were concerned, lunch among the summery landscapes of Naples and Sorrento and the rich and welcoming aromas of Italian cooking was now a permanent event.

It was unfortunate, however that this was the second such occasion to be blighted by bad news. The first had taken place ten months earlier, on the day that twelve elderly musicians had found themselves cold-shouldered by the organisers of a new, breakaway orchestra, and now, Kate had arrived home to learn that the New Albion Dance Orchestra, with which she'd been so keenly involved, was depleted to the extent that its continued existence was under threat.

'And all this has happened,' she said, scarcely able to credit the news, 'since Christmas. Just three months ago.'

'That's how it is with old age, Kate. Ill-health chooses its own time and target, and there's nothing we can do about it.'

With tears threatening, she said, 'When I think of that wonderful party we had in the ballroom at Christmas, it makes no sense at all.'

A waiter approached the table to take their order, and Frank said, 'I don't think my daughter's decided yet.'

'What?' Kate looked up, glanced at the menu, and said, '*Pollo al Prosciutto*, please.' It required no decision, because it was what she usually had.

'I'll have the same, please,' said Frank, 'and a bottle of the 'eighty-seven Verdicchio.'

'*Subito,* Signor Morrison.'

Returning to the subject of the band, Kate said, 'I'm sorry to be a wet blanket, Dad, but this has come as a shock.'

'Of course it has, darling,' he said, squeezing her hand because it was the most comforting thing he could do in public. 'It's only natural you're upset.'

'But this morning was the first I heard of it. I knew about Fred, of course, and that was awful, but I didn't see why the band shouldn't carry on without a guitarist.'

'It was only recently that things began to look bad,' he explained. 'Fred's death was a shock, but we were all set to soldier on, and then we lost Heather on violin when she got a new job and moved away. Then Stuart and Dennis on clarinet and alto sax had to bow out for health reasons. The final blow, though, was losing poor old Vernon. In one go, we lost an old friend, a superb clarinettist and a stalwart member of the band.' He broke off to taste the wine. 'That's excellent, thank you.'

'*Grazie,* Signor Morrison.'

When the waiter was gone, Kate asked, 'When's Vernon's funeral?'

'On Tuesday, at the crematorium.' Reflecting, he said, 'We seem to spend more time at those places than we do in the ballroom.'

'I'll go to the funeral, of course.'

'Good girl.' It would be the second time she'd attended the funeral of a band member. He smiled deliberately and said, 'Let's talk about something more cheerful.'

'Right.' She thought quickly. 'Have you got the *Decree Absolute* yet?'

'Yes,' he said, laughing in spite of himself. 'It came last week. The next thing is that the house has to go up for sale.' More seriously, he said, 'I'm sorry, I didn't mean to laugh. It was just your idea of something more cheerful.'

'Well, I came to terms with the end of my parents' marriage a while ago.'

'Poor old thing,' he said, squeezing her hand again. 'You've had some awful things happen in the last couple of years.'

'But,' she said, 'I've had a brilliant time at the Guildhall, and playing with the band was wonderful while it lasted.'

The waiter arrived with the main course. It was a convenient diversion.

* * *

Back at the flat, Frank brought the coffee into the sitting room as Kate emerged from the study.

'I see you've still got your rogues' gallery,' she commented, referring to the portraits of Wyatt Earp, George Custer and Billy the Kid.

'Of course. I couldn't work without them for company.'

She took a seat on the sofa and accepted a mug of coffee. 'Do you remember the lady who did the catering for the Christmas party?' she asked.

'The Candidate for the Promotion of Regional Produce? Yes, I remember her.' The last general election had taken place in 1987, but Frank still couldn't remember her name, so he always referred to her by her title as it appeared on the ballot paper.

'I've just seen her run up the road. She must be incredibly fit.'

'Let's hope so. She's running in the London Marathon next month, for cancer research. I said I'd sponsor her.'

For the first time that day, a slow smile spread across Kate's features, and she said, 'You fancied her at one time, didn't you, Dad?'

'What on earth gave you that idea?'

3

'Just the way you could never take your eyes off her when she was out training.'

'I was just interested. Anyway, she and her husband are back together, now.'

'Oh, bad luck, Dad.'

Frank wondered if any aspect of his life could exist without his daughter knowing about it. 'It would have been doomed from the start, even if she'd stayed single,' he told her, hoping that would put an end to the conversation.

'Why?'

Realising he'd hoped in vain, he said, 'Because she frequents the Black Bull, where she participates in a weekly session of the out-of-tune guitar, the Aran sweater and the hearty vocals.'

'Oh, poor old Dad,' laughed Kate. 'How did you find out about that?'

'I had a chat with her when Norman was in hospital, and I was looking after Ida. That was when I decided I preferred Ida's company.'

'And her taste in music, presumably.'

'Only just.' The memory of having to play 'You Are My Sunshine' endlessly on his trumpet over Ida's basket, had never faded. It was the only way he could stop her pining for Norman.

Kate's eyes had been searching the room, and now she asked, 'Are you still seeing Sarah?'

'Yes.'

'When I say "seeing", I mean….' If she knew what she meant, she was struggling to put it into words her aged parent might understand and not find too disconcerting.

'Do you mean "seeing" in a meaningful, one-to-one, beneath-the-stars, on-a-moonlit-night kind of way?'

'There's no need to take the—'

'Yes, I am, but she's attending to things at the college.'

'I'm glad about that. I mean that you're still seeing each other.'

Frank was glad, too, and particularly because Kate was happy with the arrangement. There'd been too much turmoil in the past few months, with her mother's fleeting association with an amorous and designing tax collector.

'Dad?'

'I'm still here, darling.'

'What are you working on?'

'I'm currently working on a TV series about a lawyer in Victorian times, and I have a meeting soon with a music editor to discuss a two-part film based on a novel I haven't read, so I can't tell you much about that one, but – watch this space.'

'But you're keeping busy. That's the main thing.' Satisfied with that, she finished her coffee, looked at her watch, and said, 'I suppose I'd better go and face the reception committee.'

'Brave soul that you are, but at least you can do it now on a full stomach.' Kate's grandparents had always been a daunting prospect; at least, 'Medusa' had. Her husband usually performed a supportive role, simply agreeing with every contentious word his wife snapped. Frank had occasionally wondered about the conversation that led to Helen's conception, but he preferred as a rule not to think about it, especially on a full stomach. 'I'll run you over there, if you like,' he said.

'Oh, will you, Dad? Thanks.' She picked up her coat and bag to go.

They left the flat and walked out to the car. 'I love this car,' said Kate, settling into the passenger seat.

'It's just as well, because I can't afford to change it yet.'

'Why not?'

'Because I have a big wife and a little family to support.'

Kate laughed. 'That's not fair.'

'No, your mum's only dinky. I don't know how she keeps her figure, but she does, and that's very much to her credit.' He turned into Whitechurch Road and drove the three miles that led to the house he'd shared with Helen until their separation.

'Dad?'

'Still here, Kate.' Her voice had an uncertain quality that hinted at a return to a previous topic, and he thought he knew what it was.

'Last year, when we came back from the ballroom....'

'Do you mean after the formation of the new orchestra?'

'Yes, and we found the old men sitting there....'

'I know. It was awful.'

'I asked you if there was something you could do. Do you remember? And then you had your brilliant idea.'

His suspicion turned out to be correct. 'I'm afraid the brilliant ideas cupboard is bare,' he told her gently, 'likewise, wherever it is they keep thirties-savvy musicians, but I'm still cudgelling my poor old brain.' He pulled up outside the house. 'If I think of something, I'll let you know. Meanwhile, I'll pick you up at two o'clock on Tuesday for the funeral.'

'Thanks, Dad. Love you.' She kissed him and let herself out.

*   *   *

Later that evening, Frank sat in his studio looking through the timing sheets for *Not Guilty*. Each day was the same for him, so there was nothing unusual about working on Saturday evening, except that he wasn't feeling particularly motivated. He'd sometimes joked that inspiration came through the letterbox in the shape of bills and tax demands, but even they seemed to have lost their motivating power for the time being. The culprit was the conversation he'd had with Kate at lunchtime, when he'd realised again the strength of her feelings. He shouldn't have been surprised. He'd learned that lesson less than a year earlier, when her reaction to seeing the elderly musicians cast aside by the new orchestra led him to form the New Albion Dance Orchestra.

He took the list he'd made a couple of weeks earlier. Vernon's name was still on it. That was how quickly fortunes changed. Taking a fresh sheet of paper, he made a new list. He lived his life by lists; his old trumpet professor had encouraged him to do it as a way of managing muddle-headedness, and it often worked. He needed all the help at his disposal.

Piano1

Trombones2

Trumpets2

Tenor Sax1

Violins3

Bass1

Percussion1

That made eleven players in all, which was fine in itself; a great many bands had consisted of fewer than that. The difficulty was in the variety of instruments, or the lack of it. Three fiddles at one end and a battery of brass instruments at the other would never work. In the band's early days, there had been an embarrassment of reeds, and now there was a paucity of them.

He remembered sharing the original problem with the members of what Kate called his 'rogues' gallery', and he looked up at them again. Both Wyatt Earp and George Custer gazed back at him imperiously and, as ever, it was impossible to see Billy the Kid's eyes clearly, let alone form an idea of what might be going on behind them. The photograph was called a 'tin type', although Frank hadn't a clue what that meant, except that photography had a long way to go in those days. All he knew was that Billy's expression was open to free interpretation. He looked again at the other two and, now that he thought about it, they looked more demanding than before. They might almost be saying, 'Come on, Frank, the problem's not insurmountable. All you need is another alto sax and two clarinets.' They were right, too. He and the others had been guilty of letting the horror get in the way of the facts. Reduced to the basics, that was the extent of the problem. The band still lacked a guitar and occasional banjo, but there were worse deficiencies, and a guitarist might come along one day. Meanwhile, they had to persuade three reed players to join them. It was something he could discuss with the others after the funeral.

2

ADVERSARIES AND OLD FRIENDS

Kate was waiting for him when he arrived and, having walked past the 'Miserymobile', as he'd dubbed her grandparents' Escort, in the drive, he knew why. She opened the kitchen door even as he set foot on the doorstep, such was her readiness to leave. Helen was behind her, so Frank gave her a cheery greeting.

'Hi, Frank,' said Helen quietly.

A familiar voice of disapproval came from the sitting room. 'Has he come for her? I don't know what he thinks he's doing, taking a young girl like her to an old man's funeral.'

Helen winced, and Frank gave her a sympathetic nod before taking Kate to the car.

'She's been impossible,' said Kate as she got into the car, knowing that her dad would realise she was referring to her grandmother and not her mum. She waited until he'd taken his place in the driving seat, and said, 'The marriage is over, but she still can't stop slagging you off. She knows the judge has approved the agreement, so there's no way you could diddle my mum out of anything, even if you wanted to, but she won't let it rest.'

'It's been happening for twenty-one years, and it's been so much a part of her life, the habit must be hard to break. Listen, darling, it goes without saying that you like to spend time with your mum, but they seem to have taken root in there, so if it all gets too much for you, remember you can always come over to the flat.'

'I'll remember. Thanks, Dad.' Now aware of an unexpected deviation in the normal route, she asked, 'Aren't we going to Beckworth Crematorium?'

'No, this one's at the local authority place in Boothtown Road.'

'Odd.' The Boothtown Road Crematorium was austere and less well-kept than that at Beckworth.

8

'Well, it's the family's decision.'

Kate opened the front of her coat and said, 'I'm wearing my orchestra dress again.'

'Yes, I noticed.'

'I couldn't think of anything else to wear. Some people turned up at Eddie Young's funeral in jeans and T shirts and trainers, and I thought that was really naff.'

'I couldn't agree more.' A Fiesta pulled out ahead of them, and Frank recognised the registration. 'It looks as if Sarah's giving Hutch a lift,' he said, enjoying the lightening of his spirits that he always felt when he saw Sarah. 'I offered to take him, but I think Sarah was coming over, anyway. She usually takes him shopping, midweek.' Hutch's deteriorating eyesight had led him to surrender his driving licence about a year earlier. Peering again, Frank said, 'In case you haven't already noticed, she's got young Dan with her as well.'

'Yes, it'll be good— Oh, dear.'

'What's the matter?'

'I was going to say it would be good to see everybody again, but it doesn't seem right to say that at a funeral.'

He smiled at her innocence. 'Respect is expected,' he told her, 'but misery is not obligatory. Anyway, things usually lighten up at the reception, as you know.' He joined the line of cars turning left into the crematorium, followed them down the winding drive, and finally pulled into the bay next to Hutch, Dan and Sarah. Kate's mood brightened immediately when she saw them and, as soon as they were out of their car, she hugged each of them, including Dan, who was visibly delighted. Frank struggled to keep pace with Kate's love life, but he suspected she had unfinished business with the young vocalist, so his presence would be a distraction from the reality of the ceremony.

'Who else has arrived?' asked Hutch, shaking hands with Frank.

'Just about everyone you can think of,' said Frank. 'There's even a few here from the new orchestra.'

'For a bloke who took life so seriously, Vernon was a popular chap.'

'Are you giving a tribute on behalf of the band, Hutch?'

'No, I've left this one to Norman. He's known Vernon as long as I have, and it doesn't do to hog these things.'

'No, you're right.' Frank looked around the busy carpark and, spotting the new orchestra's conductor, said, 'I see Michael Tattersall's here. If you've no objection, Hutch, I'd like to have a quick word with him after the funeral.'

'Why should I object? You're a grown lad.'

'I want to ask a favour of him. It could help us out of our difficulty.'

Hutch smiled, no doubt suspecting what Frank had in mind. 'Go ahead, Frank, but I think we'd better make a move.' The pall bearers were opening the back door of the hearse, and the funeral director was marshalling the family.

Frank offered Kate his arm and they took their place with Hutch and Sarah in the line of mourners.

Walking into the small chapel, Frank was disappointed to hear recorded music being played. He wasn't a devotee of organ music, but it seemed a shame that a professional musician had to take his last bow to a piped accompaniment of pop music. Still, as he'd told Kate, it was the family's right to organise the funeral, and that included the order of service.

The minister called on everyone to stand, which they did, although a few, who sported casual headgear in spite of the venue, seemed surprised by the request. Vernon was then borne in by four young men in shirtsleeves, presumably his grandsons, with the minister reading the sentences.

It was a curious service, the minister presenting a brief synopsis of Vernon's life, which reflected, presumably, on the little the family had told him. It was a sorry business, but then the minister said, 'I now call on Norman Barraclough, a lifelong friend of Vernon, for his tribute.'

Norman, who stood at a generous six feet four, was an imposing figure and an example to the sportswear-clad minority, dressed as he was in a double-breasted, worsted suit, an immaculate white shirt and regimental tie. Frank knew that his shoes would be polished like glass as well, but most of the congregation wouldn't be able to see them.

'Vernon and I had been mates since before the war,' began Norman. 'It's true to say we didn't always see eye to eye, mainly because I'm six-foot-four, and he… wasn't.' There was a chuckle, mainly from the band members, and he continued.

'We first met in nineteen… thirty-seven, I think it was, when Hutch and I were playing with Carl Duverne's Band at the Golden Slipper in Soho. Along came this little clarinettist, who told us that, like us, he was from the West Riding, in his case from Littletown, Liversedge. I remember asking him if everybody in Littletown was as little as he was, and he said, "No, but I don't suppose everybody in Cullington's as daft as thee." Well, that was me put in my place, but we got on like a house on fire after that, especially after we heard him play, that morning. He'd a jazz background, so improvisation was no effort for him, and there were times when we were left wondering how he did it, I don't mind telling you. It was a treat every time he picked up that clarinet.

'We played at the Golden Slipper until the war intervened, and I lost touch with Vernon for a while because we served with different regiments, but we met up again after the war. It was a different kind of music by that time, and it didn't really suit either of us, but it was a crust. Anyway, come the nineteen-sixties, when popular music really did lose its way, we managed to get employment as peris. That's peripatetic music instructors. We hadn't to call ourselves teachers, because we weren't qualified, but we did a good job, Vernon, Hutch and me, and we got a lot of youngsters off to a flying start.' He grinned at Frank and said, 'I can see one of them, now.' There was another chuckle when Frank raised his hand in grateful acknowledgement.

'Just when we thought we'd never play proper music again, Frank here, organised some of us into what became the New Albion Dance Orchestra, and Vernon took his rightful place as First Reed, thrilling everybody again with his brilliant improvisations, and not just that. Let me tell you about one particular incident that wasn't about music, but it tells you a lot about Vernon. We were making our way home from a practice, and Vernon had gone on ahead of us. Then we spotted him, confronting three yobs – I believe they're called "skinheads" or something daft like that – and they were giving an innocent young lady, who's now one of our band, a very nasty time indeed. Let me tell you, it was the kind of thuggish behaviour Vernon and I, as well as a lot of others, once fought a war to stop, and it was happening again. There were these three fit, young ruffians, all of 'em big enough to eat Vernon and, without any hesitation at all, he was squaring up to 'em. That's the kind of stuff he was made of. We joined him a minute or two later, and the problem was solved, but that's another story.

'We put down the music track of a film called *Hey, Young Fella*, last Christmas, just three months ago. It was possibly the pinnacle of our achievements, but just as important as that, as far as we're concerned, it serves as a fitting memorial to Vernon Waterhouse, the hot man on the liquorice stick! God bless you, little Vernon. We're going to miss you!'

Frank wasn't surprised to hear a sniff beside him, and he handed Kate a tissue.

The funeral continued, the curtains were drawn on the coffin to a highly inappropriate track, and the minister brought the ceremony to a close, after which the congregation exited to yet more of the kind of cacophony Vernon would have hated. Thanks to Norman, however, and Vernon's fellow musicians, his passing had been marked and his life honoured.

'Well done, Norman,' said Frank as they stood outside. 'Your tribute made all the difference.'

'I had to say something, Frank. That lot would have let him go with barely a mention.'

'Just a minute,' said Frank, who'd just seen Michael Tattersall through the crowd. 'I'll be back in a sec. I just want a word with Michael.'

* * *

When they arrived at the Pack Horse Inn for the reception, Frank and Kate spent a few moments with Vernon's daughter before joining the others.

'Hello, Kate,' said Sarah. 'I see Norman's tribute left its mark. Don't worry, you weren't the only one. He got to me, too, and I don't think Dan was far behind.'

'It was a brilliant tribute,' she said, taking Dan purposefully by the hand.

'It was very necessary,' said Frank, watching Kate and Dan go off together. 'Is it still on between those two?' he asked.

'I think so. I can't speak for Kate, obviously, but Dan's been counting the days.' She made way for Hutch.

'Sorry to interrupt,' he said. 'I just wondered if Frank managed to speak to Michael Tattersall.'

'Yes, I did,' said Frank. 'He's going to let me speak at the Union Branch meeting next Sunday morning.'

'Good lad. It'll be easier, now we're no longer at daggers drawn.' With his question answered, he said, 'Right, I'm going to circulate.'

'See you later, Hutch.'

'By that,' said Sarah, 'he means he's leaving us on our own. Can you come over tonight, or have you got Kate staying with you?'

'I don't know, yet. She's been suffering under Medusa the Gorgon, so I've told her she can come over to the flat if it gets too awful. I'll give you a ring later.' It was a shame, but there would be other times, and he was ever-conscious of the way the divorce had affected Kate.

Sarah looked at him in surprise. 'What's been happening? I thought the battle was over.'

'It should be. I'm satisfied with the settlement, and so is Helen, but a judge's ruling isn't enough for Medusa. In any case, she's made a life's work of slagging me off, to use Kate's horrible expression. If she stopped now, she'd have to cope with withdrawal symptoms. My latest crime, apparently, is taking Kate to an old man's funeral. She can't accept that Vernon, like everyone else in the band, was a friend, and age had nothing to do with it.'

'Maybe friendship is an alien concept to her.'

'I'm sure it is.' He looked at his watch and said, 'We must go.'

'So soon?'

'I'm afraid so. An estate agent's coming to value the house and put it on the market. I need to be there, but I'll ring you as soon as I know what's happening.'

* * *

Frank and Kate were there a good half-hour before the agent was due to arrive. Unfortunately, Helen's parents were also there, no doubt clinging steadfastly to the belief that Helen was incapable of coping without their aggressive input.

'I'm going upstairs,' said Kate. 'This morning was enough for me.'

It was significant that Helen made no attempt to check her. Instead, she said quietly, 'I think I've had enough, too.'

Frank could understand that better than anyone. 'I'll appeal to their better nature,' he said, not without a hint of irony. Helen simply winced and braced herself.

Frank found them waiting on the sofa. 'Good afternoon,' he said. 'You'll have to excuse us. We're expecting the estate agent at four-thirty.'

'We know,' said Helen's mother, always the first to speak. 'What do you mean, we'll have to excuse you? What have you done?'

He explained politely. 'We've asked an estate agent to value the house and put it on the market.'

'We know.'

It occurred to Frank that only Helen's mother could deliver those two words with so much belligerence. 'In that case,' he said, 'you won't need me to explain to you that a property sale is a private matter between those involved. That's why I'm asking you to excuse us.' In response to a blank stare, he explained, 'To leave us, in fact.'

Helen's mother switched her glare to her husband and then back to

Frank. 'How dare you?' she said. 'We came here today to see that our Helen gets treated fairly, and you're telling us to leave?'

'The divorce is settled, you can't change the terms now, and no, I'm not telling you to leave, I'm asking you more politely than you deserve, or even understand. Good day to you both.'

She made several attempts to stand up, finally accepting assistance from her husband, whom she nudged with her elbow, demanding, 'Are you going to let him get away with talking to us like that?'

'You want to remember who you're talking to,' said her obedient husband, somewhat lamely and managing, as usual, to avoid looking Frank in the eye.

'I'm not likely to forget either of you,' Frank assured him. 'Drive safely.' He watched them go through to the kitchen, where Helen had sensibly kept herself apart from the confrontation. Unfortunately, it was now her turn to hear her mother's grievances. He heard her insist yet again that they'd come on her behalf, only to encounter rudeness from that vile man. Knowing how reluctant Helen was to stand up to her, he joined them in the kitchen.

'Listen,' he said, 'you've been here most of the day, and all you've done is upset Kate and irritate Helen.' He opened the outside door in invitation. 'Now, go before you do any more damage.'

Protestations were still audible until the two closed their car doors and drove away, which was when Kate came down to ask unsurely, 'Have they gone?'

Helen assured her that they had.

'I thought I heard raised voices.'

'That was the result of your dad's diplomacy,' said Helen. 'Don't worry about it.' She gave them both a tired smile. 'Have you got anything arranged for this evening, Kate?'

'Dan's calling for me at half-past six.'

'Good,' she said, evidently pleased that one of them, at least, was going to have some pleasure after a trying day. 'You two go and have a good time.'

Frank was also pleased that Kate and Dan were still seeing each other. Dan was a shy lad, and as far as Frank knew, completely trustworthy. It also meant he could accept Sarah's suggestion.

3

THE NEXT GENERATION

Frank took his seat beside Kate in the assembly hall at Cullington High School, remembering the desperate plea he'd made after Bernard Taylor's van had been stolen with his drums and equipment, almost on the eve of the London recording session. He had another appeal to make, and he hoped he could count on the same spirit of friendship he'd found then.

Everyone was assembled by ten o'clock, and Michael Tattersall opened the meeting with Apologies for Absence, of which there were none. He worked his way through Minutes of the Last Meeting and Matters Arising, the Treasurer's Report, and Applications From New Members. Eventually, he came to Any Other Business, but before throwing it open, he said, 'I had a conversation with Frank Morrison last Tuesday, and I've invited him to speak to you this morning. Would you like to take the floor, Frank?'

Frank walked to the front and nodded his thanks to Michael. 'I won't beat about the bush,' he said. 'The band has a problem. Since Christmas, we've lost people through ill health and… worse. I know some of you were at Vernon Waterhouse's funeral on Tuesday, so you know what I'm talking about. Basically, we're short of a guitar, an alto sax and at least one clarinet. It's the reeds that are the main problem, because without them, we can't function. I just wondered if any of you single-reed players might fancy doing something different. If you do, you'll be very welcome indeed. Now, you'll need time to think about it, so I don't expect anyone to speak now, but if you do feel that you'd like to join us, you know where we'll be. We'll be going back to the ballroom after this meeting. Otherwise, my phone number is in the MU Directory.' He turned to Michael to say, 'That's all, Michael. Thanks for letting me speak.'

'You're welcome, Frank.' As Frank returned to his seat, Michael spoke to the meeting again. 'It's important that you understand,' he said, 'that there's no "them and us" situation, now. We demonstrated that last Christmas, so if anyone does feel like responding to Frank's appeal, there'll be no unpleasantness. In any case, I know there are some of you who, because of numbers, never get a chance to play with the orchestra. Maybe this is your opportunity to get involved in something.'

* * *

Norman, Hutch and Geoff Brierley occupied three of the buttoned leather armchairs in the lounge of the Wool Exchange Club while Ida made herself comfortable with her chin resting on the toecap of one of Norman's immaculate Oxford brogues.

'I see nobody's turned up yet,' said Geoff, a little unnecessarily.

'Give 'em time.' Norman told him. 'They'll be mulling over what young Frank said to 'em. It's a big decision an' all.'

'Yes,' agreed Hutch, 'it was easy enough for us, once we'd got used to being left stranded. Most of us had played dance music in the past, but the younger end will only ever have played classical.'

'I'm hopeful,' said Frank, arriving with three pints of bitter while Sarah brought the rest.

'Where's little Katie?' asked Geoff, looking around the room.

'She's gone somewhere with Dan,' Sarah told him. 'I expect they'll want to catch up.'

'I suppose so.' Geoff had no idea of the way youngsters conducted their affairs, but he nodded his agreement.

Frank took a clean ashtray from the table and decanted into it some of the half he'd bought for Ida. He put it down for her and watched her lap enthusiastically.

'What makes you hopeful, Frank?' asked Norman, laughing. 'Other than desperation?'

'I look at it this way. There are more than thirty musicians in the new orchestra, which was formed, if you remember, to provide pit orchestras for the amateur societies. Now, how big an orchestra can most societies afford?'

Norman had no need to think about his answer. 'A dozen or so.

Fifteen at the outside.' Reflecting, then, he said, 'Some of 'em struggle to find the cash even for a dozen.'

'Right, and how many shows go on at the same time, given that we have half a dozen societies in the area?'

Hutch answered for him. 'None. They take good care of that.'

'So, at any one time,' said Frank, 'no more than half of the new orchestra have a show to play for. That's why I'm hopeful.'

'Also,' said Hutch, 'how many of the new orchestra have ever done a professional recording?'

'That was a one-off,' said Frank, 'although if we can get a full band together again, who knows what might happen? *Hey, Young Fella* is due to be released later this year, and it could do us a lot of good.'

'At all events,' said Hutch, 'anybody who's been left out of the shows will most likely get a chance to perform if they join us now.' He turned as Bernard Taylor, the band's percussionist, approached the group.

'There's three of 'em come from the new orchestra, Hutch,' he said.

Everyone looked towards the entrance, where a man and two women stood uncertainly.

'We've come to see Frank,' said the man.

'And you're all welcome,' said Frank. 'What would you like to drink?'

'I'll get the drinks in,' said Hutch. Norman and Geoff pushed their chairs aside so that the newcomers could join the group.

With the matter of drinks dealt with, Frank said, 'I know David and Joanne. You're both clarinettists, aren't you?'

'I can double on alto sax,' said David, 'if that helps.'

'It certainly does.'

'So can I,' said Joanne.

'Excellent.'

The remaining member of the group asked somewhat shyly, 'Can you use a flute?'

'I'm sure we can. What's your name?'

'Zoe Harrison. I came to Cullington quite recently. I work at the High School with Rosemary Bentley, and she introduced me to the orchestra, but they already have two flutes.'

'Well, come and take a seat with the rest, because you've just found a home.'

'This feels like home,' said Joanne. 'I can feel the friendly atmosphere already. I came to the party at Christmas as well, and I thought the band was brilliant.'

The others expressed their agreement.

'Well,' said Geoff, 'happen we can get a practice organised now we're up to strength.'

'Next Sunday's as good a time as any,' said Hutch as he and Norman put down the drinks.

'We'll certainly do our best,' said David.

'What's worrying you?' asked Norman, as ever, more sensitive than most people realised.

'Only that some of us remember hearing the clarinet solo in 'Limehouse Blues' at the party, and now that Vernon's gone, it's a tough act to follow.'

'Vernon was a luxury,' said Hutch, 'but that doesn't mean the show's over because we haven't got a virtuoso clarinettist.'

Norman looked up from stroking Ida. He said, 'I have a suggestion to make.'

'You don't sound right confident,' said Geoff, and the others looked at him strangely, because no one had ever associated diffidence with Norman.

'Well, I don't want Frank to think he has to do anything out of loyalty or friendship, 'cause there's no question of that.'

'You've lost me, Norman,' said Frank.

'I know what's on your mind, Norm,' said Hutch, 'and you've nothing to worry about.'

Frank waited to be enlightened.

'It's Mark, my grandson,' explained Norman. He's keen, but I wouldn't want you to take him on just because of me, and he wouldn't want that, either.'

'Tell us about him, Norman,' said Sarah.

'He's an ex-Army bandsman, clarinet and sax, but he took a degree when he came out, and got qualified as a teacher. That's what he's doing now he's moved to Cullington. He's working as a peri.'

'I know him,' said Zoe. 'He comes to Cullington High, and he's excellent.'

'I can't see a problem,' said Frank.

'The thing is, the people who've just joined us,' he said, 'who, I have to say, are more than welcome, didn't need to audition, because you knew they were up to the weight. Now, I've spoken to Mark, and he insists on doing an audition for the reason I gave earlier, and I think he's right.'

'If that's what he wants,' said Frank, 'tell him to give me a ring.'

'Thanks, Frank.'

'It's no trouble, Norman.'

* * *

Frank was working on the score of *Not Guilty.* It had presented him with a problem, to begin with, in that it was set in early nineteenth-century England, and no particular musical style had suggested itself until he spent a little time listening to some piano pieces by John Field. Now that he had a style that seemed to fit the setting, he was able to sketch the main theme, and he was working on that when the doorbell rang. He saved his work and went to the intercom.

'Hello?'

'Hello. Mr Morrison? It's Mark Barraclough.'

'I'll be down in a minute, Mark.'

Frank had wondered a little about Norman's grandson, having only heard him mentioned briefly before Sunday's conversation and, when he opened the outside door, he wasn't surprised to see a smartly dressed young man, who was well over six feet tall.

'Hello, Mr Morrison,' he said, transferring his clarinet case to his left hand and offering Frank his right.

'Hello, Mark.' Frank shook his hand. 'Call me "Frank".' He led the way into the flat and took Mark's coat. 'Can I get you a drink?'

'No thanks, Frank. I never drink when I'm working.'

'Very professional.' He wondered how that kind of self-denial had gone down in the Army, but when he looked at Mark's build, he doubted whether anyone had ever been reckless enough to challenge him. 'Tea or coffee?'

'Not unless you're making one.'

'I'll put some coffee on.' He filled the kettle and measured ground coffee into the filter jug. 'That tie,' he said, 'the Coldstream Guards, isn't it?'

'That's right. My grandad would have disowned me if I'd joined any other regiment.'

'I only recognised it because Norman was wearing his last Sunday.'

'Oh, Sunday, yes. He was very upset about Vernon. They'd known each other a long time.'

'Yes, I know.' As well as his height, Mark bore some slight resemblance to Norman, but in other respects, he was very different. His speech was gentler, and his manner was completely unlike Norman's.

'I'm afraid I'm putting you to some trouble, Frank, but I have to audition. People do things for my grandad because of who he is and the way he is, but I couldn't rely on that.'

'I know, Mark, and he feels the same way.' Out of curiosity, he asked, 'Are you married?'

'Not now. I'm afraid my wife was less than understanding about my musical activities. She reckoned she was on her own quite enough when I was in the Army.'

'Bad luck. I'll just set the coffee filtering and then we can get started. He left Mark for a moment, to perform the necessary task and then returned to the sitting room to find him with his clarinet assembled. He was blowing air through it to warm it up.

'Take your time, Mark. There's no hurry.'

'No, I'm all right, Frank,' he said, fastening a reed to the mouthpiece.

'Come through to the study. What do you want to play?'

'Donizetti's *Concertino in B flat*, if that's all right. Just the *Allegretto*. My grandad says you're a good pianist, but if you prefer it, I'll play it unaccompanied.'

'I'll make the effort,' said Frank, taking the score from him.

'Do you know this piece?'

'I've heard it,' said Frank, preparing himself to sight-read the piano reduction.

He began the movement, and it was evident from the start that Mark was an excellent clarinettist, with a rich, clear tone, but he continued to the end, simply because he was enjoying the music so much.

'That was excellent, Mark.' He was about to pronounce himself satisfied, but Mark was all set to play again.

'Thank you. If it's all right with you, I'll play a bit of Gershwin without accompaniment, just to show you I can play popular idioms.'

Frank was already satisfied with Mark's performance, but he thought the next piece might be worth hearing. 'Okay.'

As soon as Mark began the trill on the low concert F, Frank knew which Gershwin piece he was going to play, and he closed his eyes to enjoy the *glissando* that led to the opening theme of the *Rhapsody in Blue*. It took particular skill, as the intonation had to be 'bent' between the keyed notes, so as to make the ascent stepless, and that passage alone would have convinced Frank of Mark's ability.

Resting his clarinet again, Mark said, 'If you like to give me a theme, I'll improvise on it.'

Frank laughed. 'Is there any limit to your talents?' Turning to the piano again, he played the first eight bars of 'All I do is Dream of You'. Immediately, Mark launched himself into a jazz improvisation that re-awoke memories of Vernon and confirmed Frank's earlier impression.

'That's enough for me, Mark. If you still want to play with us, we'll be delighted to have you.'

Mark was visibly pleased. 'Thank you, Frank,' he said. 'When's the next practice?'

'Next Sunday at ten o'clock in the ballroom of the Wool Exchange Club. Meanwhile, the coffee will be ready. Come this way.'

4

JUST LIKE OLD TIMES

When Frank called for Kate, he wasn't surprised to find the familiar Escort in the drive, nor was he at all taken aback when Kate came out to meet him before he'd even reached the door. He greeted her with a kiss and, noting her mood, waited for her to speak.

She put her violin case in the back of the Saab and took her seat in the front. When Frank got in, she said, 'It's just a pity I have to be back for lunch,' she said, 'but I couldn't leave my mum to suffer on her own.'

'That's very noble of you, darling.' Glancing at the dents and scrapes on the Escort, he said, 'You'd think she'd have learned by now to aim for the gap between the gateposts, wouldn't you?'

'She's hopeless, and she won't let him drive.'

'Maybe she's scared he might escape.'

Kate smiled at the thought, and said, 'She's growling now about finding something more economical.'

'More economical than an Escort? I wonder what she has in mind.' A Mini would possibly make it easier for her to negotiate gateposts.

'Maybe a two-seater broomstick.'

'Oh, Kate,' he said, laughing, 'that was naughty, but no one could blame you for it.'

No doubt by the association of opposites, Kate said, 'I haven't seen Granny Morrison for ages. I missed Mothers' Day, with it being so early, this year.'

'Penny and I took her out,' he assured her, still feeling the awkwardness of referring to his sister in that way. It had been at her suggestion that they dropped the 'Auntie' and 'Uncle', but Frank was old-fashioned. 'I'll tell you what,' he said. 'Let's have an extended

22

Morrison family lunch mid-week. That way, we shan't be rubbing shoulders with other Sunday revellers.'

'Could we?' The prospect evidently appealed. 'Maybe Penny could come too.'

'I'll ask her. It's not as easy for Tim to get away, now he's been privatised.' Reflecting, he said, 'Now I think of it, it wasn't all that easy before, but whoever took over the electricity board isn't as easy-going about flexible working as the old firm was.' He pulled into the Wool Exchange carpark, finding his usual place available.

'Who's that with Norman?' asked Kate. The two men were just entering the building.

'That's our new hot man on the liquorice stick, Norman's grandson Mark.'

'He's too tall to be a grandson.'

'He can't help it,' said Frank, locking the car. 'Anyway, they come in all shapes and sizes. Let's go and join them.'

They made their way into the Wool Exchange, greeting other members as they saw them, and climbed the imposing marble staircase to the place they'd come to think of as the band's home, and it occurred to Frank, not for the first time, that the paintwork of the Art Deco ballroom must be due for freshening up. Naturally, he would be horrified to see the place lose its Art Deco character, but he was only one member among many, so he kept his feelings to himself.

Kate spotted Dan and went over to talk to him before setting up. Meanwhile, Frank found Sarah. 'Hello,' he said, kissing her discreetly. 'I'm just going to the library to sort out some numbers.'

'I'll come with you.'

They went through the band room and then downstairs into the small library, with its dust-covered, manila folders that contained band parts.

'We'll have to make some temporary adjustments,' he said. 'Our new flautist can play second violin in Heather's place. I'm so relieved to have a full band again, I really don't mind.'

'Pass them across to me,' said Sarah. 'I can't choose them, but I can carry them.'

'Can you sing them? That's the important question.'

'I'll do my best.'

'Good.' He pulled out two of the vocal numbers they'd played in the past few months.

'While we're alone, Frank….'

'Mm?' He was blowing the dust off 'Memories of You'.

'Kate phoned me yesterday.'

'Yes?' He handed her the folder.

'Yes, she wants you to know something, but she's too shy to tell you herself.'

'So she told you so that you can tell me.' Frank had a feeling he knew what it was about.

'She didn't ask me to tell you, but I shall, anyway. It's about you and me.'

'I thought it would be.'

'Naturally, she knows what we got up to in London before Christmas, and after Christmas, too.'

'She said as much.' He'd found it embarrassing, so it wasn't surprising Kate did.

'Well, she wants you to know you've no need to feel awkward on her account if you and I have – she called them "sleep-overs" – at your flat.'

'I remember her criticising Helen for doing that with the Sheriff of Nottingham, but thanks for telling me, Sarah. It makes things much easier, I'm sure you'll agree.'

'Oh, I do.' In a casual double-take, she asked, 'Why did you call him that?'

'He worked in the District Council Finance Department.'

'Oh dear.' She smiled at the aptness of the label, and then asked, 'Did you hear the announcement, last week?'

'What announcement was that?'

'Oh, Frank, you do live in a burrow. I mean the announcement that the Poll Tax is to be abolished.'

'And not before time. Let's take these parts up to the band before they think we're doing that thing Kate was talking about.'

They re-joined the others, and Frank handed over the parts for 'Memories of You'. 'I think it's high time we appointed a band librarian,' he said. His suggestion prompted total silence, and some members even avoided his eye. 'Well, I don't see why I should have to do everything,' he said. 'I arrange the music, and despite my naturally self-effacing temperament, I stand in front. I really don't see why I should be the keeper of the band parts as well.'

'Neither do I,' said Bernard Taylor. 'I don't mind doing it.' His offer received a round of sheepish applause.

'Thank you, Bernard. I'm obliged to you.' Looking around, he said, 'I see the new people have organised themselves into first and second reeds. Will someone pass Zoe a copy of the second violin part, please?' When that was done, he said, 'Now, for the benefit of those who haven't played this with us before, I'll just say that we play it rather quicker than Benny Goodman used to. So, a-one, a-two, a one and two and....'

They were off. The New Albion Dance Orchestra was back in business. They played through the number, following it with 'I'll Never Say Never Again, Again', with Sarah singing the vocal refrain. Later, Dan joined them to sing 'A Nightingale Sang in Berkeley Square', and after several more numbers, for the final piece of the morning, Frank had chosen 'Limehouse Blues'. It was to be Mark's band debut.

It was an exciting, breathless number, an ideal band number, and the perfect platform for Mark. When his solo came, he remained seated, but improvised the most glorious *bravura* display, made even more entertaining for Frank when he saw Kate staring at Mark with her mouth wide open. The clarinet solo gave way to a high G on the trumpet, which Thomas Davies held for four bars until the rest of the band came in for the rest of the number.

'Mark Barraclough, ladies and gents,' announced Frank. 'Welcome to the band, Mark.'

* * *

Frank returned from the phone to tell Kate, 'I've just spoken to Granny Morrison and Penny, and we're going to get together on Tuesday. They're both looking forward to seeing you again.'

'Brilliant. Thanks, Dad.'

Elsewhere, Frank could hear Mark telling some of the band, 'I'm not a show-off, honestly, but when I get a break like the one in "Limehouse Blues", I sometimes get carried away.' Frank couldn't imagine anyone calling Mark a show-off. He found Joanne and David on their own, so he joined them.

'Frank,' said Joanne, 'we've just been saying how marvellous it felt, this morning, to be part of that glorious sound.'

'I'm glad you enjoyed it. Do you think you'll stay with us?'

'There's no doubt about it,' said David. 'It's a completely different experience from what we're used to. I think it's amazing that you formed the band after the new orchestra was formed.'

'We did,' said Hutch, joining the group with Zoe, 'but we've played that down since the coming-together at Christmas. Hopefully we've seen the last of the ill-feeling.'

'Oh yes, I didn't mean to rake over old coals. I just think it's amazing that you formed something like this from scratch.'

'We had a core of experienced dance band musicians in Hutch, Norman, Geoff, Bernard, and of course, Fred and Vernon,' Frank reminded him.

'And a potential bandleader and arranger with the ability to see potential when the rest of us could only feel sorry for ourselves,' said Hutch.

Zoe saved Frank further embarrassment by saying, 'I've been wondering if there's a special dress code for the band. I remember everyone was in evening dress at Christmas, but maybe that was because it was a special occasion.'

'It was a very special occasion,' agreed Hutch, 'but, apart from the Albion Street School tea dance, which is the only daytime gig we've played, we've only ever worked in overalls.'

Seeing the others frown in confusion, Frank explained, 'He means evening dress.'

'Aye, sorry.'

'You're forgiven, Hutch.'

'As you mention it,' said Hutch, 'we need to make a decision about band dress. I'll table it for the next meeting.'

Looking around the club lounge, Frank felt satisfied that the band was functioning again, both musically and as a group of like-minded friends. He hoped it would continue.

* * *

When he took Kate home, they were both surprised to find the drive empty.

'Well, blow me down,' said Frank. 'What's happened here?'

'Let's go inside and find out,' suggested Kate.

They found Helen in the kitchen amid the enticing aroma of roast beef. Her mood was less convivial, however, and she lost no time in telling them why. 'My mum waited until half-an-hour ago to tell me that the fibrositis in her neck and shoulder was so bad, they'd have to go home. After I'd gone to the trouble of preparing a roast, as well.'

'Bad luck, Helen.' Frank resisted the temptation to remark on the novelty of Medusa having a pain in the neck, instead of just being one. It was difficult to think of anything more meaningful to say, but Kate rescued the situation by saying, 'Dad could stay to lunch, Mum, couldn't you, Dad?'

'If I'm invited.' In truth, he was already seduced by the whiff of roast beef and the possibility of Yorkshire pudding.

Helen smiled apologetically. 'I'm sorry, Frank. It wasn't your fault, and you're more than welcome to join us for lunch.'

'I'd love to. Thank you, Helen.'

'I'm afraid I've nothing in the house to drink.'

'I'll get some wine,' said Kate.

'Good girl.' Frank took out a ten-pound note and handed it to her with the car key.

'I find it's easier to go along with it,' said Helen, clearly referring to her mother's narrow-mindedness. 'I don't usually keep wine in the house. I'm sure it would be noticed.'

'I know, but you're a big girl, now.' He left the rest unspoken. With her unsuccessful relationship with the Sheriff of Nottingham out of the way, it was more than likely Helen would meet someone else, and it would be a tragedy for her if her mother buggered that one up as well as her marriage. It was time to change the subject. 'Before we both forget,' he said, 'Kate and I are taking my mum out to lunch on Tuesday. I know it's not long since Mother's Day, but Kate wants to see her.'

'Oh, that'll be nice. How is she?'

'Same as ever.' Although she was now twice widowed, Frank's mother was quite indomitable.

'Give her my love when you see her,' she said, a little tentatively.

27

'She bears you no ill-will, Helen. She knows perfectly well what the problem was.'

Helen nodded sadly, and then returned to the present, opening the oven door and taking the joint out to rest it. 'How was your practice, Frank?' The change of subject was deliberate and probably necessary.

'Excellent, thanks. We've had a dip in numbers recently, but three new reed players joined us this morning, two of them from the new orchestra. Oh, and we have a flautist, as well.'

'I'm glad things are looking up again.' She took three dinner plates from the cupboard and placed them in the warming drawer of the oven. Almost without thinking about it, Frank took knives and forks from the cutlery drawer and set the table for lunch.

'We've got an apple pie as well,' Helen told him.

'Now, I really am glad I came,' he said, going back to the cutlery drawer.

'Are you still seeing Hutch's granddaughter?'

'Yes, but we've been discreet lately, because of Kate.'

'She'll be all right,' Helen assured him.

Happily, he was spared having to think of what to say next, because Kate arrived home with the wine.

'Thanks, Kate.' Frank took the car key, shook his head to refuse the change, and took a corkscrew from the gadget drawer.

'Kate and I spring-cleaned the house from top to bottom, yesterday,' said Helen. 'It's all ready for viewing.'

'Well done, both of you.' Just the thought of it exhausted him. 'In view of that, I'll take care of the paperwork when the solicitor starts generating it. I gather it's quite a performance, nowadays.'

'Yes,' said Helen, 'I'm glad we're using your solicitor.'

'He's ours, now we're on the same side,' he reminded her.

'Of course.' In spite of objections from Helen's mother, and in view of the mountain of work created by Helen's solicitor, they'd chosen the firm who'd acted for Frank in the divorce. Hopefully, the house sale would be more straightforward.

* * *

Later that afternoon, Frank returned to his studio to work on *Not*

Guilty. Before making a start, he addressed his confidant, as was his custom. 'It was an excellent lunch in friendly company, Wyatt, and it was very much as I remembered Helen's Sunday roasts and Yorkshire puds, but what's done is done.'

The great lawman appeared to agree with him.

'Yes, it was a tragedy, and it was neither Helen's fault nor mine.'

Again, Wyatt Earp lent his silent, solemn agreement.

5

SPOILING AND LOVING

Frank was making a rare excursion into the late nineteen-forties, by arranging Frank Loesser's 'Slow Boat to China', mainly because he liked the song, but also because it would provide Zoe with a flute solo. After her apologetic introduction, he thought it would be a pleasant way of making her feel included, and he was making good progress when the alarm clock reminded him that he had to pick up Kate and meet Penny and his mother. He saved his work and drove to the ex-marital home, cheered when he arrived, by the 'For Sale' notice fixed to one gatepost. It almost compensated for the Miserymobile on the drive. He could only imagine that Medusa's neck was improved.

He opened the door and, seeing no one within, ventured beyond the kitchen. In the sitting room, like two baleful judges, sat the in-laws from hell. 'Good morning,' said Frank. 'How's the fibrositis, Medusa?'

'As if you care, and I wish you wouldn't call me that. I've only your word for it that it's an old-fashioned version of "Mildred".'

'Carry on taking the pills, Medusa. Any change will be a welcome improvement.'

'I'm using an embrocation, if you really want to know.'

'Amputation? Why didn't I think of that?'

'I said "embrocation", you cheeky young devil. Tell him, Eric.'

'Don't be so cheeky, you.'

The situation wasn't without humour, at least from Frank's point of view. 'Do you know, Eric,' he said, 'with you two sitting there, and me standing here, I'm reminded of that painting of the Roundheads and the little lad, the one called *When Did You Last See Your Father?*'

'I'm surprised you ever had one,' snapped Medusa.

'I lost him when I was three, but I'm on my way to see my mother.' He looked at his watch. 'That's if my daughter's anything like ready.'

'Aye, well,' muttered Medusa in what passed for an apology in her language, 'happen I shouldn't have said that, but you make folk say things they wouldn't normally say.'

'It's just another of my annoying sins, Medusa, but hark, I hear footsteps on the stairs.'

'I'm sorry, Frank,' said Helen, coming into the room with Kate. 'We've been trying things on.'

'Don't worry about it, Helen. Eric and Medusa have been keeping me entertained.'

'Huh,' said the latter. 'Is that what you call it?'

'You did your best, and no one can ask for more than that.'

'That isn't what I meant. Tell him, Eric.'

Eric settled for an uncomfortable, 'Aye.'

As he opened the back door to let Kate and himself out, he heard Helen's mother say, 'That's probably why he's the way he is, all them years with no man in the house to keep him in check.' He gave Helen a reassuring smile and left the house.

When they were both in their seats, Kate said, 'You're skating on thin ice, Dad. She's bound to find out who Medusa really was.'

'I don't care. I'm not related to her now. Anyway, and more importantly, what were you trying on?'

'Some clothes we bought yesterday. We had to be a bit secretive about it, under the circumstances.'

'I know,' he said, pulling out into Bradford Road. 'You don't want to be accused of adopting my extravagant ways.' He remembered some of his offending purchases: a dishwasher, a coffee grinder, a separate telephone for the studio…. The list was endless.

'It's inevitable, really. I've never known anybody as tight as those two.'

'Penny wise, pound foolish,' he agreed.

'That's a neat way of putting it, Dad.'

'Thanks, but it's not original.' Wearying of the topic, he said, 'Enough of them. What's new at the Guildhall?'

'A lunch-hour recital next month.'

'So soon? Excellent. What are you going to play?'

'Brahms's *Sonata in A*, and Kreisler's *Liebesleid* and *Liebesfreud*.'

'Really?' He took a minute to assimilate the news and then said, 'Give me the details, Kate, and I'll be in the audience.'

'Will you come to London, just to hear me play?'

'I can't think of a better reason.'

It was more agreeable than discussing Medusa's worst traits, and they were both in a carefree frame of mind by the time they reached Granny Morrison's house.

'Penny's not here yet,' she said, greeting them.

'What a surprise,' said Frank. 'She was late for her own wedding, and she enjoyed the experience so much, she's been late for everything ever since.'

'Don't be awful, Frank. Take no notice of him, Kate.'

'He doesn't mean anything by it, Granny.'

'I know. Come here and let me look at you.' She gave Kate her periodic appraisal and said, quite predictably, 'You're still growing.'

Kate knew better than to argue, and she was spared having to respond, in any case, because the front door opened, and Penny walked in.

'Hello, everybody. I'm sorry I'm a little bit late.' She greeted everyone, treating Kate to an enthusiastic hug.

'You're only about half-an-hour late,' said Frank.

'Surely not.' Penny looked hurriedly at her wristwatch.

'Take no notice of him, Penny,' said her mother. 'You know what he's like.'

'I should,' she said. 'I've known him long enough.' Pulling a face at her brother, she asked, 'Shall we take my car? Last in, first out?'

To save time, Frank agreed, and they all went out to Penny's car.

'Where are we going?'

'The House on the Hill,' he told her.

'There had to be a musical connection,' she observed, 'in the absence of a western one.'

'That's "The Folks Who Live on the Hill", Penny.'

She turned to smile at him sweetly before releasing the brakes and joining the main road.

'How's your mum, Kate?' asked Granny Morrison.

'She's okay, thanks. We've been getting the house ready for people to come and look at it, so she's quite busy.'

'Poor girl. I know what hard work it is.'

Kate turned to Frank and mouthed, 'Girl?'

'These things are relative,' he told her discreetly.

Frank had chosen The House on the Hill partly because of its proximity to his mother's house and, in a very short time, Penny turned into the long drive and headed for the carpark.

He'd reserved a window table so that his mother could indulge in one of her favourite pastimes and admire the gardens. Horticulture meant nothing to him, but it had always fascinated his mother.

As they took their seats, Frank told them about Kate's lunch-hour recital.

'Oh,' said Penny, 'when is it?'

'The twentieth of next month,' Kate told her.

Penny leafed through her diary and found the date. 'Bugger,' she said with some feeling.

'Penny,' said her mother, 'I didn't bring you up to use that sort of language.'

'I know, Mum. It's all Frank's fault. He taught me to swear, and the reason I said, "Bugger" was because that's Open Day at the college. Kate, darling, I'm sorry. I'd have loved to be there, but Beckworth College of Art has other ideas.'

'Do part-time staff have to go to those things?' asked Frank.

'Are you demeaning my importance at that place, little brother? Actually, it's a contractual obligation. Otherwise, I'd be off to London like a shot.'

Kate patted her hand understandingly, and then the waitress interrupted the conversation by arriving to take their order.

Having ordered food and wine, Penny said, 'Let's come to an agreement, Frank. I'll do the wine and coffee if you do the food.'

'Fine.'

Referring to their earlier conversation, Granny Morrison asked, 'Why don't you ask Helen to go to Kate's recital, Frank?'

'That's a good idea,' said Penny.

Frank had been aware for some time of a Morrison family conspiracy to heal the breach between Helen and him. It was very touching, but what they had in mind was out of the question. Even so, it would be good for Kate as well as Helen if she could be there. 'I'll ask her,' he said.

'It'll be a lovely Fathers' Day treat for your dad, Kate,' said Penny, 'and your mum will enjoy it as well.'

'When's Fathers' Day?' asked Frank, whose calendar was usually featureless apart from birthdays and Christmas.

'The sixteenth of June,' Penny told him, having found the date again in her diary. I have to remind the boys about these things.'

'What about Mothers' Day?'

'I resort to dropping hints, Frank. Tim and the boys are as blinkered as you are.'

'Well, I think it would be lovely if Helen could go to Kate's thing,' said Granny Morrison, driving her point home, as usual.

* * *

The erstwhile in-laws were still at the house when Frank and Kate returned, a situation he now regarded as irritatingly normal.

'I expect Katherine's been spoiled rotten, as usual,' said Medusa, watching her granddaughter disappear to her room to change.

'She enjoyed the day,' said Frank, 'but not in a way you'd understand. As for being spoilt, I can tell you she wasn't.' He'd seen Penny slip some cash into Kate's hand when she paid for the wine, but that was nothing more than an affectionate gift.

'Didn't your mother spoil her? She usually does.'

'I think you should invest in a dictionary, Medusa. It needn't be an expensive one – you might even pick one up second-hand – and you might learn the difference between loving and spoiling.' He added helpfully, 'You'll find "loving" conveniently between "loathsome" and "low-down", two descriptions you should find meaningful.'

Her eyes suddenly became more fierce than usual, and the lines that radiated from her mouth grew more marked. 'You cheeky young devil,' she snapped. 'Tell him, Eric.'

'Yes, tell me quickly, Eric, because I need to have a word with Helen before I go.'

'Don't be so cheeky, you.'

'Well done, Eric. Goodbye, you two.' He found Helen in the kitchen, as usual. 'Helen,' he said, 'can you take three days holiday, next month?'

'What for?'

'Kate's got a lunch-hour recital on the twentieth of next month. It's most unusual for a second-year student to get one, so it's very important. If you can take the Thursday, Friday and Saturday, we'll have a day either side for travelling. Think about it and let me know so that I can book an extra room.'

'Won't it be expensive?'

'If I can arrange a meeting with Patsy Daniels at Orion Productions, I can claim at least some of it on expenses.'

'I don't know.' She looked nervously towards the sitting room.

'It'll give you three days' respite. Okay, you'll have to face the flak when you come home, but at least you'll be fresh.'

'It's important to Kate.' It was as if she were convincing herself. 'All right,' she said, arriving at a decision, 'I'll come.'

'That's the spirit, Helen.'

* * *

'Would you believe it, Wyatt?' Frank asked his long-term confidant. 'That tiny baby I held in my arms is going to give a lunch-hour recital at the Guildhall next month. I just hope that malevolent old bat keeps her nose out of it. She's quite capable of throwing a ladle into the works.' In case his choice of implement needed explanation, he said, 'I'm talking about the ladle she uses with her cauldron, you understand.'

The victor of the famous gunfight looked even more impressed than usual.

While it was on his mind, Frank picked up the phone and dialled Patsy's number. She had one of those trendy mobile phones that made contacting her easier than of late, and he was considering the possibility of getting one himself, when she answered.

'Patsy Daniels.'

'Patsy, it's Frank Morrison.

'Frank, were your ears burning?'

'Not so that I noticed. Should they be?'

'Yes, I just told my secretary I needed to speak to you. How's the score going for *Not Guilty*?'

'I'm making headway, Patsy. I need another couple of weeks, and speaking of which....'

'Speak on.'

'I'm going to be in Town from the nineteenth to the twenty-first of next month. Could we meet on the nineteenth for dinner?'

'So that you can claim the expenses?'

'You wrong me, Patsy. I'll only claim part of it.' He could hear pages being turned, which was promising.

'The nineteenth? I can do that. Where shall we meet?'

'How about Anstey's in Westmoreland Avenue?'

'Nice.' Presumably, she knew the place.

'My ex-wife will be with me, Patsy.'

'Oh? Or shouldn't I ask?'

'It's not as strange as it sounds. Our daughter, who's a student at the Guildhall, is performing in a lunchtime recital on the twentieth, and it's a special occasion, as she's only in her second year, so we naturally want to be there for it.'

'How marvellous! You must be very proud of her.'

'We are, otherwise, I don't think we'd be making the journey together. The *Decree Absolute* came through only recently.'

'Is your journey likely to be less than amicable, then?'

'No, there's no problem when her mother's not around to work her from behind. The in-laws have been the problem all along. At least, she has. Her husband's an unappealing character, too, but he just agrees with everything she says, when he's prompted.'

'Bad luck, Frank.' There was a pause, as if she were thinking about something else she had to mention, and then she confirmed his suspicion by asking, 'Have you heard from Anvil Productions recently?'

'The people who made *The Droitwich Diamond*? No, not since that one. Should I?'

'I thought you might. I'll give them a nudge, as they're now part of Orion. They're shooting another series set in the Midlands, and it sounds as if it might be right up your street.'

6

DATES AND DIPLOMACY

Sarah eased herself into bed again and snuggled up to Frank. 'I've just seen something downright weird,' she said.

'Mm?' He was only half awake. 'Don't worry, it'll look better when it's fully awake.'

'No, not that. I wasn't peeping, but Kate's door was half-open, and on my way back from the bathroom I could see the soft toys on her bed. I actually saw a one-armed dragon.'

He was now sufficiently awake to correct her. 'Dinosaur,' he said. 'It has two arms – forelegs, I suppose – but one is shorter than the other.' He turned over to face her. 'Good morning.'

'Good morning, Frank.' She kissed him. 'Was it a recognised species?'

'I don't think so. Her grandparents bought it for her when she was tiny, and it scared her silly. They probably bought it as a factory second, knowing their skinflint ways.' He screwed up his eyes until he was fully awake. 'I'll put the kettle on.'

'Go on, and then you can tell me how Kate came to terms with a mutant dinosaur.'

'Yes, I'll tell you in a minute.' Still yawning, he went to the kitchen and flicked on the kettle. While he waited for it to boil, he thought about the previous evening's conversation about Kate's recital or, more particularly, about Helen making the journey with him. Sarah hadn't actually said anything, but her misgivings were quite evident. Still, it was quite right that both parents should be at such an important event in their daughter's career, and she would have to get used to the idea. He measured tea into the pot, reflecting as he did so that Helen's parents would have disapproved. Loose tea and cups and saucers were a posh affectation, according to them, and the sensible way to boil water was to measure the exact volume of water required into the kettle to save electricity. He gave the tea a stir, poured it into both cups, added milk and carried them into the bedroom.

'Lovely man,' said Sarah. 'You did that on the first morning we woke up together. Do you remember?'

'Of course I do. It was only three months ago.' He disappeared for a moment and returned with the disabled dinosaur.

'Yes, you said Kate was frightened of it.'

'She was terrified. Helen was all for chucking it out once the Despicable Duo had gone, but its absence would have required explanation at a later date, so I had some thinking to do, and that was how this character came to be reborn and became one of Kate's favourite companions.' Placing him on the duvet, he explained. 'This is no ordinary appendicularly-challenged prehistoric lizard, you understand. He is Kevin the Kung-Fu-Saurus.' He felt Sarah shake, but he continued. 'He lives in a forest and he defends the weak and helpless. When the citizens of Toyland are threatened, the call goes out, "Send for Kevin! Only he can save us!" The wonderful thing is that, however often they send for him, he never lets them down.'

'Oh, Frank,' said Sarah, laughing but no less impressed, 'I bet he even has his own music.'

'Of course he does. I don't skimp on the job where my nearest and dearest are concerned.'

'No, I can't imagine you do.'

She became thoughtful, and he suspected something was troubling her, and he had an idea he knew what it was. 'What's troubling you, Sarah?'

'Nothing, really. I just…. What's your itinerary for London?'

'We'll travel down on the nineteenth and check into The President, where I've reserved separate rooms. That evening, we'll eat with Patsy Daniels, who fixed up the *Hey, Young Fella* gig for us; on the twentieth, we'll go to Kate's recital and have a celebration dinner with her in the evening. Then, on the twenty-first, we'll come home, Helen to hers, and me to mine. Does that set your mind at rest?'

'Yes, I was being silly.'

'You were,' he agreed, 'very silly. Look, Kevin's laughing at you.'

Ducking beneath the duvet, he produced a belly-laugh worthy of a martial arts dinosaur.

'He's still looking at me,' said Sarah. 'What's he thinking now?'

'He's thinking we have almost an hour before we have to get up, and being the sensitive dinosaur he is, he's going to turn his back while we forget all about parental duties and remember why we got together in the first place.'

'How very civilised of him.'

'And us,' said Frank, kissing her by way of encouragement.

* * *

When they picked Kate up, there was no sign of the Miserymobile.

'It's a bit early for them,' said Kate. 'Anyway, whose place did you two misbehave at last night?'

'I always say there's nothing quite like subtlety,' said Frank, 'and that bore absolutely no relation to it.'

'I stayed at your dad's place,' Sarah told her, 'and I learned all about Kevin the Kung-Fu-Saurus.'

'Not *all* about him, you didn't,' said Kate. 'Neither of you knows, for example, that I won a prize at school for writing a story about him.'

'I think that was a bit sly,' said Frank, who remembered being told about the prize during a parents' evening. 'If anybody should have had a prize, it was me.'

'Don't be silly, Dad. What would you have done with *Hans Andersen's Illustrated Fairy Tales*?'

'He'd most likely have set them to music,' said Sarah.

They continued on their way, encountering the Candidate for the Promotion of Regional Produce, who gave Frank a cheery wave as she ran in the opposite direction.

'Isn't that the person who provided the buffet for the Christmas party?' asked Sarah.

'That's her,' confirmed Frank. 'I'm surprised you recognised her after all this time.'

'She's quite an attractive woman.'

'But she's married,' Kate assured her, 'and she's a devotee of the out-of-tune guitar and the Aran sweater, so there's no competition.'

'There's no competition anywhere,' said Frank, perhaps a little tersely. Kate didn't know about the previous evening's conversation, or that morning's, but it was a subject he preferred to avoid.

'I hear you're giving a recital, Kate,' said Sarah, obligingly changing the subject. 'That's good going for a second-year student, isn't it?'

'Apparently. I think someone dropped out, and they had to find someone else in a hurry.'

'You're too modest.'

Frank turned into the Wool Exchange carpark, conveniently bringing the conversation to a close.

Hutch met them when they went inside. He seemed pleased about something, and they soon learned why.

'We're in business again, Frank,' he said. 'Now that we're up to strength, the Exchange Club are starting the social evenings again. I'll say more when we're all together, but it's good news, isn't it?'

'It certainly is.' The Club Committee hadn't wasted any time, and that was a measure of their commitment to the band evenings.

When everyone was ready, Hutch announced his news. 'They've suggested the twenty-first,' he said.

Frank had to interrupt. 'Sorry, Hutch. Is that the twenty-first of April?'

'Yes, is that a problem?'

'Only for me. If you'll stand in front, just for one evening, it'll be all right.'

'What's the difficulty, Frank?'

'Kate's got a recital at the Guildhall on the twentieth, and I don't want to travel back immediately. I've arranged to stay over and return the next day.'

Hutch was silent for a moment. Then he said, 'I appreciate your problem, Frank, and I'll speak to the committee, but if the date's been made definite, I'll have to stand in for you.' Turning to the band, he said, 'Meanwhile, we need to get a programme together, and we'll have to arrange some mid-week practices, as we did when we first started out.'

* * *

40

After the practice, Kate came to the bar, where Frank was about to buy a round of drinks. 'Dad,' she said, 'there's no reason why you shouldn't get the train back after my lunch-hour. If it comes to that, you could even give it a miss. Mum will be there, after all.'

'No, darling. The band will be fine with Hutch in front. I wouldn't miss your recital for anything, and I don't intend to disappear immediately after it.' She was looking around her nervously, so he said, 'Nobody's going to blame you for anything. As I said, they'll be okay with Hutch in front.' The steward came to him, so he gave his order. As he did so, he heard Dan say, 'I wish I could be at your recital, Kate, but I'll have to be here.'

'Suddenly, I feel like a wicked fairy,' she protested, 'spoiling everything for everybody.'

After he'd got the drinks in, he saw her talking to Sarah. Perhaps she could calm her down. Meanwhile, the job had to go on, and that meant helping Hutch and Bernard produce a programme for the social evening.

* * *

Kate had little to say on the way home, but she groaned when she saw the Escort parked in the drive.

'If it gets too much,' Frank told her, 'remember you can bale out at any time.'

She nodded, accepted a kiss and took her leave of them both.

'It must be awful for you,' said Sarah, 'leaving her to their tender mercies.'

'It's not good,' he agreed, 'but she's known them for twenty years, so she knows what to expect.' Looking at the clock on the dashboard, he asked, 'Lunch?'

'Why not?'

He turned round at the end of the avenue and headed for the Ristorante Monteverdi.

'Wasn't Monteverdi a composer?' asked Sarah when they arrived.

'Yes, but in this case, it's a reference to the green mountain on the sign. It's also Kate's favourite restaurant, so we always begin her holidays here. I like it particularly because I get preferential treatment.'

Ferdinando, the proprietor, met them at the door. '*Buon giorno, Signor Morrison e Signora.* No reservation? No matter. I find you a table. *Uno momento, per favore.*'

'I see what you mean,' said Sarah, laughing.

Ferdinando beckoned to them, and they took their seats at a table in the far corner.

'Is a dark corner, *Signor e Signora*, but the lovely *signora* light it up already.'

'Bless you, Ferdinando,' said Frank. 'You light the place up all the time.'

'Is kind of you to say so, *Signor*. Here is menu and everything is available.'

'Thank you, Ferdinando.'

'*Prego, Signor.*'

'Isn't he lovely?' asked Sarah, examining the menu.

'He's one of the many genuine people I'm fortunate enough to know,' said Frank. 'You know, when the awful day arrives, and Ferdinando turns up at the pearly gates, Saint Peter won't know which of them is the more welcome.'

'It's quite a thought.'

'And it's not the only one, if I read the signs correctly.'

Sarah sighed. 'You're priceless, Frank, and you're so right. I was thinking about poor Kate wrestling with her problem and coping with her grandparents as well. From what you've told me, they'd try the patience of a saint.' Before he could respond, she said, 'Because I can't imagine you marrying anyone who wasn't pleasant and engaging, I can only assume Helen is a lovely person, so how did she come to be born of those two horrors?'

'I've wondered about that, off and on, for the past twenty years.' He broke off when Ferdinando came to their table. He gave their order and requested a bottle of a Chianti he'd had earlier.

'Did you ever reach a conclusion? I mean, regarding the grandparents from hell?'

'No, I think there's probably a kind of specialist anthropologist who deals in that kind of mystery, but I must confess it's beyond me.' Thinking about the problem a little more, he said, 'Medusa has played a few dirty tricks in the past, but she excelled herself shortly after Christmas.'

'Do tell.'

'You see, Kate's no mathematician, but she's capable of subtracting the date of our wedding from her birthday and arriving at the conclusion that the wedding was timely. She must have realised that, but the malevolent old harpy made a point of telling her that I'd got her mother "into trouble" and that I'd "had to marry her", a crisis in which I featured as the greatest villain since Vlad the Impaler.'

'What a vicious thing to do. How did Kate react?'

'She told her she knew, which rather stole the old bat's satisfaction, but it set her off thinking, and she spoke to us about it. It was shortly after the Sheriff of Nottingham had gone on his way, so relations between Helen and me were rather better, and we handled it together.'

Sarah was still trying to come to terms with the kind of mentality that was capable of such an act. 'What did you tell her?'

'We admitted that we'd put the cart before the horse, not that it means a thing nowadays, but we told her that the important thing to remember was that she was conceived in love. It was true at the time, and nothing could change it.'

'Well said, Frank.'

'It was such a cruel thing to do to her so soon after the upset about the Sheriff. It was also after the party at the ballroom, when Kate was feeling so buoyed-up about things.'

'Why does she do these things?'

Ferdinando brought the wine, and Frank tasted it. 'That's excellent, Ferdinando. Thank you.'

Frank thought for a minute. The wine had come as an interruption, albeit a pleasant one. 'I'm the target,' he said, 'but she tries to get at me through Kate and Helen.' He shrugged. 'Other than that, it's anybody's guess how Medusa's mind works.'

'All right, Frank, let's forget about her for now.'

* * *

Later that afternoon, Frank received a phone call.

'Frank?' It was Helen, and she sounded like a woman under siege, as usual.

'What's the matter, Helen?'

43

'I'm sorry, Frank, I can't go to Kate's recital.' She was almost tearful.

'What's happened?'

'I just can't go. You'll have to do it without me.'

'You've been got at, haven't you? Medusa's done it again.'

'Don't say that, Frank. You don't understand.'

'I understand the situation well enough. The old bat's leaned on you so that you can't even go to your daughter's first recital.'

'I really wanted to, Frank.' She was actually crying. 'You don't know what it's like here.'

'I do.' Suddenly, he backpedalled. 'Don't worry. I'll speak to Kate and make it right with her.'

'She's in her room. She won't come down.'

He couldn't blame her. 'When she does come down, I'll speak to her.' As an afterthought, he asked, 'Are they still there, your parents?'

'No, they went home half-an-hour ago. I've just been working myself up to telling you I can't go to London.'

'Well, you've told me, so you can stop worrying about that. When the bricks are down, ask Kate to phone me, and I'll sort things out with her.'

'Okay. I'm sorry, Frank.'

'It's not your fault. Goodbye, Helen.'

'Goodbye.'

He replaced the phone and said to Sarah, 'You'll have gathered that Helen can't go to Kate's recital. The vicious old bag has doubtless put the mockers on it because she's convinced it would bring about a miraculous reconciliation between us, and everything she's worked for would be back to square one.'

'Oh, Frank.' Sarah sat beside him and stroked his hand. 'How's Kate taken it?'

'I'm not sure. The old teenage barricade is up, but whether it's because Helen's not going, or simply because the row got too much for her, I really don't know.'

'I have to admit,' said Sarah soberly, 'I wasn't altogether happy about you and Helen being away together, but when I'd given myself a talking-to, I realised I was being petty, and the important thing was Kate's recital. I'm sorry, Frank.'

'You've nothing to be sorry about, whereas that vicious old virago has plenty, if she only realised it.'

'What's her husband like?'

He wondered how he could describe Eric succinctly. ' "Little Sir Echo",' he decided. 'Do you know the song?'

'I think I've heard it.'

'He's her yes-man. She'll say, "Are you going to let him speak to me like that? Tell him, Eric." That's when he says, "Don't talk to her like that, you." He never says these things with much conviction, but he always does as he's told.'

'What a pair.'

'What a pair, indeed.' He kissed her, and it was developing into something even more promising, when the phone rang again. 'Don't go away,' he said, picking up the phone. 'Hello.'

'Dad,' said the second tearful voice of the day, 'Mum said you wanted me to ring you.'

'Yes, I did.'

'Is it about her not wanting to come to London?'

'It's not that she doesn't want to, Kate. She was very keen until... let's say until circumstances intervened.'

'There was an unholy row.'

'I can imagine it. Where's your mum now?'

'She's gone upstairs.'

'Honestly,' he said, attempting to lighten the conversation, 'you're like Cox and Box, you two. One comes on the phone, and the other goes into hiding. Mind you, it's not really surprising, considering what you've both experienced.'

'That's another thing, Dad. Medusa's found out who the Gorgon really was, and she's furious with you.'

'Good. Maybe she'll stop gunning for you and your mum.' It was a forlorn hope, but one of the kind that were inclined to co-exist with life, or so the proverb ran. 'On that subject, Kate, don't be hard on your mum. It's not her fault.'

'Isn't it?' She sounded sceptical.

'You know the situation. Your mum's been conditioned to do Medusa's bidding for forty years. She learned obedience as a tiny tot, watching the cauldron bubble and seethe, and listening to the muttered incantations and scheming cackles.' He detected a grudging laugh and continued. 'Forty years is a long time to acquire a habit. It would take a major disaster for your mum to defy Medusa, so instead of blaming her, just try to remember that, and you'll realise how sickened she must be by the turn of events.'

'Yes, I'll go and talk to her.'

'Good… for you.' He remembered in time not to say, 'Good girl.' His daughter was twenty and very much aware of it. 'All right, darling, let's leave it there, shall we?'

'Okay, Dad. 'Bye.'

''Bye, darling.' He put the phone down.

'You're a born diplomat, Frank,' said Sarah.

'Not really. I've just had lots of practice.'

* * *

Late on Monday afternoon, Frank received another call, this time from Hutch.

'Frank, the Club Committee evidently prefer to see a young, good-looking chap in front of the band. They've put the Social Evening back to the twenty-seventh, so unless you've got anything else lined up, you'll be in charge, as usual.'

'Thanks for telling me that, Hutch. After the day I had yesterday, I need something to go right.'

'I know. Sarah told me.'

'Just one thing, Hutch. I'll tell Kate they changed the date because they remembered that social evenings were always on the last Saturday of the month.'

'Good thinking, Frank.'

'Yes, if you can keep a secret, so can I.' He also had it in mind to speak to Sarah and ask her if she'd like to go to the recital.

7

Vicarious Jitters

Sarah climbed into the carriage and waited for Frank. 'I didn't know we were going to travel first class,' she said.

'It's a special occasion, Sarah, and I'm in special company.'

'Ah, you say the nicest things.'

'Also, do you remember the first time we went to London?'

'Of course I do, but I bet you don't. You were unconscious most of the time.'

'Some of the time,' he conceded, 'not most of it. I remember being seduced the night before the session, and the memory is so magical that I want to repeat it, but in more luxurious surroundings.'

'I won't argue with that,' she said, finding their reserved seats and slipping into hers.

'I also want to talk to you.'

'Oh good, I hate travelling in silence. What do you want to talk about?'

' "I Won't Dance".'

'I don't blame you. There isn't a lot of room in here.'

'The song "I Won't Dance", music by Jerome Kern, lyrics by Oscar Hammerstein, Otto Harbach, Dorothy Fields and Jimmy McHugh.'

'Now you're making sense,' she said, arranging herself more comfortably. 'Which particular aspect of all that do you want to discuss?'

'The possibility of you and Dan singing it, maybe not next week, but probably on the twenty-fifth of May, or whenever the Exchange Club decide to hold the next one.'

She narrowed her eyes in thought. 'Have you spoken to Dan about it?'

'No, he usually goes along with anything that's decided.'

'So I'm the difficult one.'

'Yes, but I thought that with three days together, I might talk you into it.'

'Okay,' she said cheerfully, 'I'll let you know on Saturday.'

'Good.'

'Tell me again, what's happening tonight.' By way of an excuse, she said, 'All the excitement about "I Won't Dance" made me forget what you said.'

'Tonight we'll be negotiating the traffic system imposed by the London Marathon, to meet Patsy Daniels of Orion Productions and Anvil Productions for dinner.'

'I'd forgotten about the Marathon being this weekend. I suppose they'll have the route cordoned off ready for Sunday.' Then on a more suspicious note, she asked, ' Are you meeting Patsy so that you can claim this on expenses?'

'Some of it. It's always a good idea to keep in touch with Patsy, anyway, because she's a generous source of work.'

'Is she very glamorous as well?'

'I'd say so, but with you in the same room she'd pass unnoticed.'

'I should hope so.' After a moment's thought, she asked, 'Have you known many glamorous women?'

'Quite a few, although I remember one in particular. She taught maths at my school.'

'You had glamorous teachers?'

'Only the one. The others were dowdy creatures.'

'A maths teacher, too.'

'She couldn't help that. She was born with the impediment.'

'Tell me about her.'

Frank thought hard. 'It was a long time ago,' he said, 'but I remember her as fair-haired, with limpid blue eyes, an hour-glass figure, and a honeyed voice.'

Sarah shook her head. 'I don't believe any of this.'

'It was a shame I was hopeless at her subject, because I'd have done anything to win her favour.'

'Oh, the pangs of forbidden adolescent love.'

'You can say that again,' he said regretfully, 'but it was short-lived.'

'Go on, you can tell me.'

He braced himself for the painful disclosure. 'She came into our lesson one day,' he said. 'It was just after morning break, and I noticed that, unknown to her, she was about to reveal herself in a way that would have been downright embarrassing. Ah, I thought in my naïve, fourteen-year-old way, this is my chance to be helpful and win her approval. "Miss Mapleton," I said, "your skirt is tucked into your knickers." The rest of the class laughed uproariously, but you should have seen the horrible look she gave me.'

'After you were so helpful.'

'And I wasn't one of those laughing. It was a while before I even considered another chivalrous deed, I can tell you.'

'Oh, Frank, I can tell you're still feeling wounded. Would a cup of coffee help?'

* * *

Frank introduced Sarah to Patsy, who asked, 'Didn't you sing on the *Hey, Young Fella* score?'

Surprised that Patsy remembered her, Sarah said, 'That's right.'

'You were very good, and so was the young man. What was his name?'

'Dan, Dan Bairstow.'

'Yes, where did you find him?'

'He's one of my students.'

As they took their places, Frank explained that Sarah taught at Beckworth College of Performance Arts.

'And you're spreading the word among the new generation. Wouldn't it be marvellous,' said Patsy, 'if there could be a real resurgence of interest in bygone musical styles?'

'I'm concentrating on one idiom, and that takes all my time and effort,' Frank told her.

'And you're doing an excellent job.'

They studied the menu and made their decision. Patsy said, 'If you're agreeable, Sarah, I'm happy to let Frank choose the wine, especially as he's paying… this time.' She spoke the last two words with emphasis.

'The Beaune 'eighty-one, please,' he told the waiter.

'The Beaune eighty-one, *Monsieur. C'est bon.*'

'Frank's name is associated in my office with expensive vintage wines,' Sarah,' said Patsy, 'but I usually overlook his weakness because he's worth it.'

'I've always said he gets away with murder.' Turning to Frank, Sarah asked, 'What do you imagine your in-laws would have to say about your taste in wine, Frank?'

'The same as they'd say about any poser who wastes money on posh, foreign muck. My ex-mother-in-law has deep lines radiating from her upper lip, caused by the frown she's practised over the years at my various shortcomings.'

Patsy nodded sympathetically. 'You've mentioned her from time to time, Frank, and I thought you were probably exaggerating, but now I just feel sorry for you.'

'She should soon be in the past, though, surely,' suggested Sarah.

'If only. She's like an infestation of ants: there wherever I look, irritating beyond belief, and damned nearly impossible to remove.' He checked the label on the bottle of wine the waiter brought to the table, and said quietly, 'I asked for the 'eighty-one.'

The waiter looked at the label and closed his eyes in embarrassment. 'I cannot apologise sufficiently, *Monsieur*. Do you wish to speak to the Maître d'Hôtel?'

'No, there's no need for that. Just bring a bottle of the eighty-one and we'll put it down to a lamp that needs replacing in your cellar.'

'I am very grateful to you, *Monsieur*. I shall bring the wine immediately.'

'Thank you.'

'Well done, Frank,' said Sarah when the waiter was gone.

'Well, it was an honest mistake, and there's no harm done. I know some people would have made an issue of it, but it does mean we'll get immaculate service for the rest of the evening.'

'And there are no prizes for guessing what your in-laws would have made of that,' said Patsy. 'However, on a happier topic, have Anvil Productions spoken to you yet?'

'Yes.' He broke off to check the second bottle of wine. 'That's right,' he said. The waiter drew the cork and poured some for him to taste. He scented the bouquet and tasted it. 'Excellent,' he said.

'Thank you, *Monsieur*. Enjoy the wine.' He poured some into all three glasses and left them once more.

'Anvil Productions phoned me to ask if I could take on a pilot and six episodes. They said they'd give me the details as soon as they could.'

'I must speak to them again,' said Patsy, 'but I'll tell you now that it's a sitcom about unemployed foundry workers who go into the odd-job business. It's not a terribly original idea, but the actors involved make it promising.'

'It's not even remotely original,' said Frank, 'but beggars can't be buggers.' He took a sip of his wine and closed his eyes in near ecstasy. Some things were beyond criticism.

* * *

A taxi drew up beside them, and Frank said, 'The Barbican, please.'

'Which end, guv?'

He thought quickly. 'The City end.'

'Right you are, guv.'

They got in and took the short journey to the Guildhall School of Music and Drama.

'Does this bring back memories?' asked Sarah as they entered the building.

'Not really. This is very modern. They've only been here... less than fifteen years. Anyway, I didn't study at the Guildhall.'

'Where did you go? I'm sure you told me once, but it's slipped my memory.'

'I was at the Royal College of Music.'

'Of course. I remember now.'

They found their way to the Recital Hall, where Frank's attention was arrested by a notice that read:

Today's Lunch-hour Recital

Features

Katherine Morrison, violin
and Nathaniel Palmer, piano.

Programme

Sonata No. 2 in A, Op. 100 for Violin and Piano
– Johannes Brahms

Liebesleid and Liebesfreud **– Fritz Kreisler**

A student standing inside the entrance handed them a printed programme. Grinning excitedly, she said, 'It's going to be fantastic today. Kate's just incredible!'

'It's kind of you to say so,' said Frank. 'I'm her dad.'

'Oh!' The girl gasped as if she'd just encountered royalty.

'Enjoy the recital,' he said. 'We will.'

They found two seats quite close to the front and waited.

'This is so exciting,' said Sarah. 'I can't begin to imagine how you must feel.'

'Very proud and just as nervous,' he told her.

Eventually, the auditorium filled up, a student, presumably the pianist's page turner, took his place and, at one-fifteen exactly, a door opened and Kate stepped up to the platform followed by the pianist. Kate tuned to the piano, and the Brahms sonata began with its gentle, waltz-like theme.

From the first, yearning phrase, Frank sat with his head bowed and his eyes closed, listening to the glorious music of Brahms and occasionally allowing himself a glimpse of the performers, a reminder that this violinist on the platform really was his daughter.

At the end of the sonata, he joined in with the enthusiastic applause for the two young musicians. Kate looked more relieved than pleased, and he could understand that. There was more technically demanding playing ahead of her, however, and he saw her take a deep breath before starting it. *Liebesleid*, or 'Love's Grief', called for tremendous tonal clarity and sensitivity of feeling, both of which were surprisingly evident in a girl of only twenty. Remarkably, Kate looked more confident now that she'd started. It possibly helped that the Brahms was behind her. The pianist seemed quite at ease, too, which was good. Frank listened to the gentle, aching phrases and recalled buying Kate's first full-size violin. He and Helen had gone into debt to pay for it, much to the in-laws' disapproval, but it was worth every penny, and he was hearing that quality now.

Liebesleid drew the applause it deserved, and the two went on to play *Liebesfreud*, or '*Love's Joy*'. The character of the piece was as jubilant as its title, and in total contrast to its predecessor, but Frank could relax. Kate was visibly enjoying the demands it made on her technique, and that continued to be the case to the very end, when she stood with her bow aloft, acknowledging her applause. Frank was pleased to see her shake hands with the pianist, and he took his share of the applause. Then, Kate looked at her watch and, after a moment's discussion, held up her violin and bow to ask for silence.

'Thank you,' she said. 'Thank you all very much. There's time for one more piece, and it's Paganini's *Twenty-Fourth Caprice*.' There was a cheer from the students, because the piece was always popular.

Frank listened to the encore happily and without nerves. Kate had risen above them, and that meant that he could do the same.

The applause was both passionate and prolonged, but Frank and Sarah were eventually able to weave their way through the departing audience and find Kate at the front. Sarah reached her first and congratulated her while Frank was still dodging excited students. As soon as he was free, Kate threw her arms round him excitedly, and he held her for several seconds while he kissed her repeatedly and said quietly, 'Kate, I'm so proud of you.' Then, conscious that she might feel embarrassed in front of her fellow students, he released her.

'There's someone else here who wants to speak to you, Kate,' said Sarah. It was the girl who'd given them the programme, and they were evidently on friendly terms, because the hugs continued.

'Dad,' said Kate, 'when we go to dinner tonight, can Dawn come with us?' Dawn was presumably the enthusiastic programme monitor.

'Of course she can. We're going to Anstey's. We were there last night, and it's very good.'

'And your dad's sure to get preferential treatment,' said Sarah.

Kate's mind was on something rather more practical. 'Dawn's third study is composition, but that's what she wants to do, so she really wanted to meet you.'

'I'm flattered. How do you do, Dawn? You're very welcome to join us tonight.'

* * *

'That was truly wonderful,' said Sarah as the train pulled out of King's Cross, 'Kate's recital and everything else. Mind you, I thought I'd have to call for first aid on your account, you were so nervous.'

'At the recital? Of course I was. I know what it's like, and I was feeling it for her.'

'I can understand that. I just thought I'd mention it.' After a little more thought, she said, 'Kate's friend Dawn's nice, isn't she?'

'She's lovely, a bit naïve, but they all are at that age.'

'You were naïve enough to think you'd find your way into Miss Mapleton's good books by telling her she'd trapped her skirt in the waistband of her knickers.'

He couldn't disagree with that. 'Yes,' he said, 'that was an ill-judged move on my part.' He noticed that she was looking thoughtful, so he asked, 'What's on your mind?'

'There was something else I had to tell you. Yes, I remember, now, it was about "I Won't Dance". I've thought about it and decided I'd like to sing it with Dan. I wonder also about "A Fine Romance" from *Swing Time*.'

'It's a terrific song,' he agreed. 'Would you like to sing that with Dan as well?'

'Yes, I can tell you that without having to think about it.'

'That's a relief. Now I can look forward to the dance in May.'

'We have one before that, next week.'

'The excitement is never-ending.'

8

Iniquity Challenged and Virtue Rewarded

Frank arrived home to find a phone message from Helen, left that Friday, telling him that the estate agent had booked two viewings for Saturday, and that feedback was expected soon. All that had happened in his absence. He had to know how the viewings had gone, but there was one matter of more immediate importance. He phoned Helen.

'Hello,' she said. 'Back so soon?'

'I got in a few minutes ago.'

'How was it?'

'She was superb, Helen. I was prouder than I've ever been, and you would have been, too, if you'd been allowed to go.'

'Don't start that, Frank.'

'All right. How did the viewings go?'

There was a hesitation, and she said, 'It's difficult to say. The first couple seemed quite impressed at first, and so did the others.' However positive they might have been, Helen didn't sound exactly optimistic. An unpleasant thought occurred to him, and he asked, 'Were your parents present when all this was happening?'

There was another hesitation, and Helen said quietly, 'Yes.'

'Have they found that they're allergic to their own home,' he asked, 'or are they just saving on the heating bills?'

'There's no need for that.' Her voice had assumed its long-suffering tone. It was a twenty-year-old difference, and one that was unlikely to be reconciled.

'I'll just have to wait for the estate agent's feedback,' he said, but it's going to be an uphill task, selling the place with those two drowning it in gloom and malevolence.'

'Oh for goodness' sake!' The phone went down, reminding him as usual that he was aiming at the wrong target. Helen was powerless when her parents were around.

He busied himself with the score of *Not Guilty*, taking the line that he would find out whatever decision the viewers had made the next day.

* * *

The estate agent phoned him shortly after eleven the next morning.

'I'm afraid there's been no offer, Mr Morrison. Both lots of viewers were impressed with the house, but....' He sounded embarrassed. 'I can only tell you what they said.'

'Go on.'

'The first couple told me the "vibes" were all wrong. The sale had apparently come about, they said, because of "an acrimonious divorce", and it was "a house that knew its own history". Those were their words, not mine.' There was the sound of paper being shuffled, and he said, 'Unfortunately, the second couple said much the same sort of thing.'

'Do you know who told them it was the result of a divorce?'

The agent hesitated. 'The second viewer mentioned a middle-aged couple, who introduced themselves as Ms Kent's parents.'

'I thought as much.' He could imagine Medusa rolling Helen's maiden name off her tongue. 'So they told the viewers about the divorce, did they?'

'I'm afraid so.' Still sounding embarrassed, he said, 'You know, Mr Morrison, I'm afraid selling the house is going to be very difficult if Ms Kent's parents are going to be around each time there's a viewing.'

'I couldn't agree more.'

'I'm sorry to have to say these things, Mr Morrison.'

'Not at all. I've been coping with those two for the last twenty years.' An idea came to him, almost out of nowhere. 'Do you think,' he asked, 'I could get a court order banning them from going to the house when there's a viewing?'

'I doubt it, and even if you could, it would take far too long.'
'In that case, I'll just have to think of something else.'

* * *

Frank called round after the practice on Sunday morning. As he suspected, the loathsome bothsome were already there, so he walked in and found Helen loading the dishwasher. Lunch was evidently over.

'Hello, Frank,' said Helen, 'I wasn't expecting you.'

'Pleasant though it always is to see you, Helen, I've actually come to speak to your parents.'

'Oh.' That one syllable was loaded with apprehension.

'I'd hide somewhere, if I were you.' She usually did, as she found exchanges between Frank and her parents extremely embarrassing. He went through into the sitting room, where he found Medusa waiting for him.

'I've a bone to pick with you,' she said, in her usual *en garde* tone.

'I've more than one to pick with you, Medusa, but I'm a reasonable man, so I'll let you go first.'

'I've found out who Medusa was, haven't I, Eric?' She accompanied her question with the usual thrust of her elbow.

'Aye, she has.'

'You cheeky young devil, calling me that.'

'Have you seen a picture of her, Medusa?'

'Don't call me that.'

'All right, Mil-dread. Have you seen a picture of her?' He hoped she had.

'No, but I've been told what she looked like, with snakes coming out of her head, or something daft like that.'

'Ridiculous,' said Eric, for once without prompting.

'It's not a flattering image, I agree, but as they used to say in her part of Greece, "If the snakes fit, wear them." Of course, they said it in Greek, and you wouldn't approve of that, because it's spoken by foreigners.'

Mildred plied her elbow again. 'What's he going on about, Eric?' she demanded.

'Nay, I'm blessed if I know.'

57

'I'll tell you what I've come here to tell you,' said Frank. 'I was in London on Friday, at Kate's recital, and she played magnificently. I couldn't have been prouder, and it was a great moment for her. There was only one element missing, and that was her mother.' Mildred opened her mouth to speak, but Frank held up his hand. 'No, you've had your turn. If you're honest, you know this already, but I'm still going to tell you that it wasn't Helen's fault she missed it. It was your fault, Mil-dread. She wasn't there because you wouldn't let her go. You were terrified that she and I might patch things up between us. Let me tell you, I bear Helen no ill-will at all; believe it or not, I still feel some affection for her, but there's not the slightest chance of reconciliation, with you spitting venom and Eric agreeing with you every time you bare your fangs. No, you'll be pleased to know that would be impossible, but something you need to realise is that in denying Helen that freedom, you caused your granddaughter severe disappointment and put your daughter in an impossible position into the bargain. Well done on both counts.'

'You impudent young…. Eric, are you going to let him get away with that?'

'Just you be careful what you say.'

'Be quiet, Eric. I haven't finished yet, and this concerns you both.'

Mildred attempted to get up. 'This is—'

'Sit still and be quiet, Mil-dread.' He admonished her with a stare. 'Yesterday, we lost two potential sales because of you two. There was no need for anyone to know why the house is up for sale, and to tell the would-be buyers that the divorce was acrimonious was a downright lie. Apart from the episode with the Sheriff of Nottingham, relations between Helen and me have been nothing but civilised. It could even have been called an amicable divorce, but no, you two had to vent your spleen, and in a situation that was none of your business, or the buyers'.'

Again, Mildred tried to stand. 'I'm not going to listen to this anymore.'

'Yes, you are. Be quiet and listen, because I'm going to tell you what's going to happen. You'll both stay away from this house when there's a viewing.'

'You can't stop us coming. We've every right—'

'You've no right at all. Now, I have a very good friend at the *Cullington Herald*, who's always on the lookout for a story, and if you come here again when people are viewing the house, I'll give him that story – with pictures.'

'What story?' Mildred's tone was rather less bellicose now.

'The story about the people who can't sell their house because of the misanthropic meddlers who chase buyers away with malicious lies.' He paused for thought. 'Now I think of it, such a story could easily help to sell the house. People might come out of curiosity to catch sight of the disagreeable duo, and take a fancy to the house in the process.' Frank knew no one on the *Herald*, but he reckoned the threat would be sufficient.

'Come on, Eric,' said Mildred. 'I'm not going to have our names in the paper because of this… *ne'er do well*.' As she rose unsteadily to her feet, she told Frank, 'You're too clever for your own good, you are. You'll come a cropper one of these days, won't he, Eric.'

'Aye, a right cropper.'

Frank flinched away from him playfully and waited for them to go.

When Helen returned from seeing them off, she asked anxiously, 'What did you say to them, Frank? My mother was in tears when she left.'

'Only because she's been bested. I just told them some home truths. Suffice it to say, they won't interfere with any further viewings. At least, not unless they want to be famous.'

* * *

A pleasanter meeting by far took place between Frank and the Candidate for the Promotion of Regional Produce, whose name, he learned, was Hilary Newman. She'd phoned Frank earlier and asked if she might call round and collect her sponsorship money. Even the thought of running twenty-six miles left Frank gasping for breath, and he was so impressed with her achievement that he invited her to come over straight away.

When she arrived, he realised he'd forgotten how tall she was – about five feet nine – and he was reminded of her athletic physique, because she was wearing some kind of trendy garment reminiscent of the wetsuit trousers worn by divers and windsurfers.

'Would you like tea or coffee?' he asked.

'Where does your coffee come from?'

'Taylors of Harrogate,' he told her. 'I suppose that's as local as it can get.'

'I suppose so,' she agreed, 'and it's ethically sourced, which is why I asked you.'

Frank flicked the switch on the kettle and ground some coffee, which he measured into the filter. 'Will you run the Marathon again?' he asked, still amazed that anyone could do it even once.

'Yes, as often as I can. I've more time to train, now that I'm alone again.'

'I'm sorry to hear that, Hilary.' He was genuinely sorry on her behalf, but it made no difference to him, as he was happily involved with Sarah, and if that were not enough, there was always the 'amusical deterrent', as he thought of it.

'It happens,' she said philosophically. 'We were childhood sweethearts, and it's a bit silly, committing yourself at such an early age.'

'It rarely works,' he agreed, thinking of his old school and college friend Gavin Lowe, who'd been quite involved with Penny for years, until she dropped him in favour of Tim, her dancing partner and future husband.

Changing the subject completely, Hilary said, 'That was a lovely party you had at the Wool Exchange last Christmas.' She'd done the catering for it, and very expertly, too.

'Yes, it was a special celebration.' He told her about the healing of the rift between the orchestra and the band, and the recording for *Hey, Young Fella*.

'How marvellous. I mean that you could get everyone together again, as well as recording the music for the film.' Somewhat shyly, she said, 'I had ballroom dancing lessons when I was younger.'

'Before you succumbed to the lure of folk music?' He couldn't resist that.

'Oh, that was my husband's enthusiasm. I just went along with it.'

Recalling her attempt at singing, he had to applaud her wholehearted participation in her husband's pastime, if not her skill. 'That's quite understandable,' he said, getting up to prepare the coffee. 'Will you stand for election again?' He was vaguely aware of talk of another general election, possibly in a year's time.

'I think so. I managed to retain my deposit last time,' she said, 'by three votes.'

'Mine was one of them.'

'Oh, that was sweet of you. Thank you.'

'You were the pick of the ballot sheet, as I recall,' he told her. Most of the candidates had ruled themselves out in their various ways, but her pitch, like the food she supplied, was fresh and wholesome.

'It was very kind of you, as well, to sponsor me in the Marathon,' she said, reminding him of the purpose of her visit.

'Not at all. I'll just get my cheque book and pen.'

* * *

There was an extra practice that Tuesday, and the first person Frank met in the ballroom was Geoff Brierley.

'Hello, Frank,' he said, 'how did little Katie get on?'

Frank couldn't help smiling. Most of the musicians remembered Kate arriving with Helen after orchestra practices when she was a toddler, and she would always be 'Little Katie' in their eyes. 'She did herself proud, Geoff, and I was just as proud.'

'I'm right glad, Frank. You know, the place isn't the same without her.'

'It's good of you to say so, but you'd better get used to it, because she's another two years to do at the Guildhall, and then it'll be anybody's guess where she finds herself.'

He left Geoff to take his trombone from its case and fit the slide. Dan was coming his way, presumably to ask the same question.

'Hello, Dan. How are you?'

'Good, thanks. You?'

It still surprised Frank that youngsters could be so economical with words, but he had to accept it. 'I'm fine, thank you, Dan.'

'I wish I could have been at Kate's recital. Did it go all right?'

'More than all right, Dan. She was excellent.'

'Good. The thing is….'

'It's an expensive business, travelling to London, isn't it?'

'Yes, that was the problem. The thing is, I don't want her to think I wasn't interested. I just....'

'Couldn't afford it. She'll understand that, Dan. Tell you what.' He wasn't sure how this would go down. 'Why don't you write to her? Just drop her a note telling her you're glad it all went so well, and reminding her that trains to London take a huge chunk out of a student's income.'

Dan appeared to consider the suggestion, and said, 'Right, I'll do that.'

'Good lad.' It would be interesting to hear about Kate's response. Like most of her contemporaries, she regarded letter-writing as one of the amusing idiosyncrasies of old age.

When everyone was set up, he spoke to them. 'People keep asking me about Kate's recital,' he said. 'Just let me say that I'm a very proud parent. She misses the band and she asked me to remember her to you all.'

He was assured that they missed her too.

'Let's get started. We usually begin with 'By the Sleepy Lagoon', I know, but it's an ideal waltz to start an evening's dancing, so let's make sure we haven't forgotten it.'

9

WORKING WITH CHILDREN

The April Social Evening was a successful event, largely because it was so well supported. News that the New Albion Dance Orchestra was back in operation attracted a particularly large number of Exchange Club members and their guests. As usual, a disco was held in the assembly room below, but the ballroom was still pleasantly busy.

Frank began the evening with the waltz 'By the Sleepy Lagoon', as they had planned, and followed it with a string of numbers popular with the Club's members. At the interval, Hutch offered, as he so often did, to take the stick for the next number, so that Frank and Sarah could dance. The number was 'Love Walked in', which Frank had always regarded as the ultimate slow foxtrot, and it hadn't taken Sarah long to agree with him. The number was so enticing that they saw it through without speaking. That would come later.

They were both involved in the second half, however, that they had no time to talk until the end of the evening, when they drove back to Frank's flat.

'What was that you were saying to Hutch about *Northern Focus*?' she asked him.

'It was *Northern Scene*, actually. It's a new magazine-type show that follows *Northern Focus* at seven on weekdays.'

'I've never seen it, but I've heard about it,' she said. 'When did this happen?'

They phoned me yesterday afternoon and asked me if I'd go on the show.'

'Hey, fame at last.'

'I don't know why they asked me,' he said, parking outside the flat, 'except that I'm their second choice.'

'What?'

'The person they had down for it has given backword, so they asked me to step in.'

'At short notice, presumably?' Sarah gathered her things and got out of the car.

'A little over two weeks' notice, actually, and in that time I have to rehearse a number with the Hunslet Junior Band, who are also going to be on the programme, so I've got to get my lip in.'

'Your what?'

'My lip, for playing the trumpet.'

'Oh, I see. I've never heard of the Hunslet Junior Band.' She waited for Frank to unlock the door.

'They're based in Hunslet, but they take kids from all over the West Riding.' He opened the door and let her go before him.

While he prepared coffee, he asked, 'Have you heard of Perry Kilburn?'

'I don't think so. Should I?'

'I can't think why you should, but he's going to be on the programme, too.'

'What does he do? He sounds like someone who's been in the news for the wrong reasons.'

'It's quite possible he has. He's lead guitarist and vocalist with something called Genitus.'

'What?'

'No, not "Genitals", Genitus, trust me. Apparently, it's what the knowledgeable ones call a Retro Punk Band.'

'And they've put you on the same programme. It makes absolutely no sense.'

'Not to mention a junior brass band.' He poured hot water on the coffee. 'I hope Perry Kilburn, whoever he is, minds his language in front of those youngsters. He does have a reputation, apparently, for expressing himself in basic Anglo-Saxon.'

'I suppose that's the television company's problem. Do you know what they're likely to talk to you about?'

'I imagine it'll be about film and TV scores, but I haven't been told a thing, apart from the fact that I have to play a solo with the band, and that the dress code is "casual".'

Sarah was still wrestling with the strange mix of guests. 'I can see a connection between you and the band,' she said, 'but unless this Terry Kilburn has a few surprises up his sleeve....'

'*Perry* Kilburn. It's important, because he's sensitive about it, for some reason.'

'Ah, but then, I'm not going to be on the show, so I don't have to be so careful.'

'Be thankful for that, darling.' He poured coffee for them both.

Sarah accepted hers and said, 'I believe you said the buffet lady had been to see you.'

'Yes, she came to collect her money. I sponsored her in the London Marathon.'

'You said so. What's she like?'

'Physically, or what?'

'I know what she's like physically. I saw her running. I meant, what kind of person is she?'

'It's difficult to say, really. She's very active – I mean in every respect. She thinks she might stand again in next year's election, and she'll certainly run the Marathon again.'

'Incredible.'

'Laudable, I'd say.'

Remembering a detail from a previous conversation, she said, 'You mentioned that she and her husband were together again.'

'Apparently.' He thought it wise not to say too much. He knew there was nothing doing, but Sarah didn't, and he remembered that her previous relationship had ended badly, so she was allowed, very occasionally, to feel ever so slightly insecure.

Sarah's thoughts were apparently back with the TV show, however, because she said, 'How do you feel about going on a TV programme absolutely cold?'

He had to think about that. 'I'm set in mind,' he said, 'of the time I emerged from the hairdressing salon minus most of my hair. I remember looking at myself in the bathroom mirror and deciding that my beloved lawman's moustache had to go as well, so I shaved it off. It left me feeling naked and vulnerable, and that's how I feel about being on the *Northern Scene* programme.'

'I have complete faith in you.' She reflected briefly and said, 'I think *"Northern Scene"* sounds like a disagreement on *Coronation Street*. Don't you?'

'It does, rather. Shall we finish the coffee and go to bed?'

'Let's.'

* * *

Another viewing was booked for Monday and, busy though Frank was, he made sure he was at the house before the viewers arrived, if only to deny admittance to the pestilential pair, should they decide to defy him. It was unlikely, but he had to be sure.

In the end, there was no sign of them, and the viewing proceeded smoothly, with particular interest shown in the fourth bedroom, which had served at one time as Frank's studio. The woman saw its potential as a hobby room for her, whilst her husband had it earmarked as his art studio. Happily, Helen was able to suggest an acceptable solution. 'It's a large room. In fact, it used to be a double bedroom,' she told them. 'Surely there'd be room in it for both of you.' After some thought, they agreed and went happily on their way, saying that they would be in touch with the agency. It was a pleasant experience, and it prompted Helen put the kettle on and offer Frank a cup of tea.

'You really got my mum worried,' she said.

'That was the idea.'

'Don't be awful. She's started taking the *Herald* so that she can see if your friend's written anything about her and my dad.'

Frank couldn't help smiling at the thought of Medusa leafing anxiously through the local rag each Thursday, but he was conscious of Helen's awkwardness, so he changed the subject and gave her his news instead. 'I've been invited on to *Northern Scene*,' he said.

'Have you?' Helen took out two mugs, demonstrating her loyalty to her mother, who had always had plenty to say on the subject of how tea should be served. 'Do they want to talk about the band?'

'I don't know. They haven't said, but they do want me to play a solo with the Hunslet Junior Band.'

'Right, when is it?'

'A week on Friday. Someone apparently gave backword, so they asked me.'

'Well, I never.' She poured hot water into the mugs, and as she moved the teabag in one mug and transferred it to the other, Frank could almost see the wheels turning in her mind. She would tell as many people as possible, insisting that her interest was only to be expected after so many years, even though they were no longer married.

'Are you going to tell your parents?'

'I don't know.'

'Go on, Helen. Give your mother an opportunity to say, "Some folk just have to show off." Then she'll dig your dad in the ribs with her elbow and say, "Don't they, Eric?" And he'll say as distantly as only he can, "Yes, they do." One of these days, she'll give him another nudge and tell him to say it once more, with feeling.'

'Don't be awful, Frank,' she said, putting a mug of tea in front of him. 'He can't help being quiet.'

'He's not allowed to be anything else. I reckon the last time he got excited about anything was when you were conceived, and she placed an embargo on excitement after that, in case it got out of hand and gave rise to an encore.'

'You just have to say these things, don't you?'

'I don't know why people want sex,' he mimicked. 'Doughnuts and chocolate eclairs give me all the excitement I need.'

Helen took a seat opposite him and said, 'Be serious for a minute. I have something to tell you.'

'I'm serious.'

'All right. I'm seeing someone else at the weekend.'

'That's your freedom, Helen. You're a free agent, now.'

'It's someone I met through the library,' she told him, evidently feeling that a full disclosure was necessary.

'My goodness. Courtship in hushed whispers behind the Newspapers and Periodicals.'

'Don't mock.'

'All right.' It was time to be positive. 'I hope he's an improvement on the Sheriff of Nottingham.'

'I hope so, too.'

'And I hope you've got your check list ready.'

Helen frowned. 'What checklist?'

Counting on his fingers, he listed various attributes. 'He must have a proper job – nothing daft, like writing music. Two, he must be careful with the cash – no more silly spending on trendy rubbish like I used to buy. Three, he must be satisfied with instant coffee – none of that foreign muck. Four, he mustn't have a moustache, especially one that belongs in a cowboy film. Six, and this is me talking, not your mother, you need a man who's kind and loving and, importantly, he must be a considerate lover. Don't let yourself be shortchanged between the sheets, Helen.'

Half-amused, half-embarrassed, she said, 'You're awful, Frank.'

'No, I mean it. I don't want an ex-wife of mine given duff treatment beneath the duvet. I didn't bring you up to be frustrated.'

Smiling in spite of herself, to let him know she hadn't forgotten, she said, 'Between ourselves, 'Robert was a dead loss, but there is more to life, you must admit.'

'Yes, there are doughnuts and chocolate eclairs.' He finished his tea and stood up to go. 'But they're bad for your figure. Thanks for the tea, Helen.' Because he was in a good mood, he kissed her on the cheek before he left.

Walking down the drive to his car, he allowed himself a smile, secretly pleased that the Sheriff of Nottingham had turned out to be less than entrancing in the bedchamber.

* * *

He was impressed from the start with the Hunslet Junior Band and their conductor Neville Foster. He listened to them playing 'All in the April Evening' and congratulated them on the quality of their tone.

'I think we might play 'The Girl With the Flaxen Hair' on the programme,' said Neville.

'A good choice,' said Frank. 'It's soft and warm. Will they play it as written, in concert G flat?'

'Yes, they're comfortable with that.'

'It's a lovely rich key.'

'Would you like to hear them play it?'

'Yes, I would.'

The band played the piece for him and, for the second time, Frank was captivated by the tone the youngsters produced. The prelude by

Debussy was originally written for piano, but it translated readily into a piece for brass instruments.

At the end, he said, 'Thank you very much for playing that. You performed it beautifully, and *Northern Scene* viewers will be entranced when they hear you play.'

'It's kind of you to say so, Frank,' said Neville, 'but it's time to agree on a solo for you.'

'Yes,' said Frank. 'I hope you have something in mind.'

'Oh, we have.' Neville winked at the band. 'We know you're a very able trumpet player, and there must be a range of cornet solos you could play with us, but we have in mind something a little bit different.'

10

A MATTER OF PRACTICE

There was an extraordinary gathering of band members in the Wool Exchange Members' Lounge, the occasion being the broadcast of *Northern Scene* involving Frank. Sarah was one of those who'd come to watch the programme on the large screen.

Geoff Brierley watched the *Northern Focus* team deliver the local news and said, 'I wonder what happened to that lass that came here to interview us for the programme.'

'She presents *Northern Scene* now,' Hutch told him patiently, 'the one we're going to watch.' Geoff was a good trombonist and a faithful member of the band, but he was inclined to be muddle-headed.

The weather presenter joined her two colleagues on the banquette, and the news programme ended. It was time for *Northern Scene*. As the jingle led into the programme, Geoff was rewarded when the camera zoomed in on Kirstie Edwards.

'There she is,' he announced. 'I'd recognise that lass anywhere.'

'Let's hear what she has to say,' said Hutch, 'before you get over-excited.'

'Good evening and welcome to *Northern Scene*,' said Kirstie. 'Our guests this evening include a rock idol as well as a composer who's written numerous film and TV scores, but first of all, we're going to hear the Hunslet Youth Brass Band.' The camera panned over to the band, which was playing Debussy's *Arabesque No. 2*.

'Blow me down,' said Norman Barraclough, moderating his language as usual in mixed company, 'them kiddies know how to play.'

There was a murmured chorus of agreement as the other members listened, equally impressed, and Geoff asked, 'What do they think they're playing at, putting one of them rock 'n' roll characters in a programme with clever bairns like these?'

'Listen,' said Norman, 'and happen you'll find out.'

The number came to its close, and Kirstie introduced the conductor. She asked him about the ages and background of the members, and how often they rehearsed, and it was apparent that she was completely taken with them. Next, she got up and spoke to individual band members, who responded each in their own way. Finally, she said, 'Now, you're going to play another piece for us. What's it to be?'

'Another one by Debussy,' said Neville. 'It's called "The Girl With the Flaxen Hair".'

'Lovely,' said Kirstie. 'Let's hear it for the boys and girls of the Hunslet Junior Brass Band.'

As expected, there was enthusiastic applause, and the camera roamed over the band, showing some of its players in close-up as they played the prelude by Debussy.

'By heck,' said Norman, 'I like to be impressed, and I haven't been at all disappointed.'

'And now,' said Kirstie, when the applause had died down, 'for something entirely different. With a gold disc to his credit already, here is Lead Guitarist and Vocalist of Genitus, Perry Kilburn.'

The guest walked into the studio, nodding to Kirstie, and took his seat on the banquette.

Kirstie welcomed him and went on to interview him. 'The name "Genitus" is unusual. How on earth did the band decide on it?'

'What's, like, wrong wiv it?'

'It's a few years since I was at school, but I'd say it means "begotten".'

He looked at her sharply. 'Is that right?'

'As far as I know.'

'It should have been "*mis*begotten",' muttered Norman.

Perry's surprise turned to frustration. 'I'll kill that fuckin' agent,' he said. ''E told us it was, like, same as "Genesis", but, like, different.'

'I suppose it is, really,' she said, 'but please remember, Perry, that this is peak viewing time and that there are children in the studio.' Hurriedly, she said, 'Let's change the subject. How old were you,' she asked, 'when you decided you wanted to become a musician?'

'He's not a bloody musician,' said Norman, forgetting himself and apologising hurriedly to the ladies present.

'About five, I fink, 'cause you don't, like, get to be a musician, like you said. You already have it in you, like, y'know. That's what bein' a musician's, like, all about.'

Hutch groaned, and Sarah grasped his hand supportively.

It was the longest sentence they heard from Perry Kilburn, because the rest of his answers were largely monosyllabic, although when asked how he liked the Hunslet Band, he said, 'Okay if you like that sort o' fing, but, like, they ain't all that clever, 'cause they all have to have, like, the letters writ in front of 'em so they, like, know what buttons to press, like, y'know.'

Kirstie struggled for as long as she had to, and finally, with well-disguised relief, she introduced her final guest.

'The guest I'm about to introduce,' she said, 'stepped in at the last moment, and for that we're very grateful. He's well-known for writing the theme music for *Looking Back*, *The Private Life of Daniel Defoe*, *Wings Over the Weald*, *The Droitwich Diamond*, and a great many more films and TV series. Here's Frank Morrison. Please give him a big hand.'

Frank entered to a recording of *Wings Over the Weald*, waved to the youngsters in the band, and shook hands with Kirstie, Neville, and lastly, Perry Kilburn, who looked surprised.

'Frank,' said Kirstie as he took his seat, 'it's good of you to take time out from your busy schedule to join us.'

'It's a pleasure, Kirstie. Thank you for inviting me.'

'Not at all. The last time we met, you were dressed much more formally. White tie and tails, as I recall.'

'Yes, that was when the New Albion Dance Orchestra was featured on *Northern Focus*.' He was currently wearing a suede jacket with a shirt open at the neck.

'Yes, among everything else, you front that wonderful dance band I heard in Cullington. Tell me, how's that going?'

Her reference to the band earned her a bored look from Perry Kilburn, which Frank ignored. 'Very well indeed, thank you, Kirstie. We recorded the music track of the film *Hey, Young Fella* either side of Christmas – that's due for release later this year – and we're appearing regularly at our home in the Wool Exchange ballroom in Cullington.' A little mischievously, he said, 'We'd be very happy to come over to the studio.'

'Hopefully, your offer will have been noted, Frank. Now, tell us something about your musical background. When did *you* decide to become a musician?'

'Oh, a long time ago.' He had to think about his answer. 'My sister and I lost our dad when we were very young, so it was a financial struggle for our mum, but she knew I was keen to learn the trumpet, and she found me a second-hand instrument. That was the start of everything. I had lessons at school, and that was when I met two of the most important influences in my life. They were visiting instrumental teachers, and their names were Norman Barraclough and Jack Hutchins, both of whom, incidentally, helped set up the New Albion Dance Orchestra.'

Perry Kilburn was staring at Frank, open-mouthed, possibly wondering how anyone could fit so many words into one answer. His reaction wasn't lost on the viewers.

'Just look at that gormless berk,' said Norman.

Sarah squeezed Hutch's hand again, knowing how much Frank's words must mean to him. Having made his point about Perry Kilburn, Norman reached across and shook Hutch's other hand.

'So, things were far from easy at home, but you won a scholarship to the Royal Academy of Music.'

'The Royal College, actually.'

This time, Kilburn's reaction was in the form of a visible sneer.

Kirstie ignored him. 'My mistake, Frank, but while you were in London, you led the normal student life, going to parties and such-like, I believe.'

'I worked hard as well, Kirstie. Let's not forget that.'

'Look,' said Norman, pointing to the screen, 'that useless bugger's falling asleep 'cause she's not talking to him.' If he wasn't exactly falling asleep, Perry Kilburn's thoughts seemed to be far away, because he looked profoundly bored.

'You obviously did work hard, and the results are there for all to see, but you were invited to one particular party,' said Kirstie with an air of mischief, 'at a house where they had an ornamental post horn.'

Frank had to smile. 'So that was what you had in mind.'

Neville gave him an amused nod.

'Someone bet you a pound – that's how long ago it was – that you couldn't play the "Post Horn Galop" on it.' She reached behind her seat and produced a real post horn, rather than the ornamental kind with which Frank had won his bet. 'Would you mind explaining to our viewers and our studio audience if they don't already know this, how the horn was used?'

'Not at all. In the olden days, when the mail was carried by horse-drawn stagecoach, the guard used to alert the people on the turnpike that a coach was coming, so that they could open the gate and let the mail through, and this was what they used to signal with. I'm afraid some of the guards were awful show-offs, and they used to entertain the passengers by playing tunes during the journey.'

'But how on earth is it possible to get a range of notes out of a simple tube with no valves?'

'It's no secret,' said Frank, taking the horn from her. 'By changing lip pressure, it's possible to play the notes of the harmonic series, like this.' He demonstrated for the audience's benefit.

'Thank you, Frank. That's a real eye-opener for me, and probably a few more people, eh, Perry?'

Perry's look told viewers that he was unimpressed.

'And I believe history's about to repeat itself,' said Kirstie, 'because, together with the Hunslet Junior Band, you're going to play the "Post Horn Galop" by Hermann König.'

Still smiling at the joke they'd played on him, Frank walked over to the band with Neville and waited for silence.

'I hope they warned him about this,' said Norman.

'He knew he was going to play it,' Sarah told him, 'and he rehearsed it with the band, but he didn't know why.'

The band began the piece and Frank took up his cue. The musicians knew what to expect, but Sarah had no idea. All she knew was that it was a show-piece calling for the ultimate kind of virtuosity and, judging by the expressions on the musicians' faces around her, Frank was delivering the goods.

The piece reached its end to spontaneous applause from the studio audience. Frank acknowledged the band's performance, bowed and returned to his seat.

'That was fantastic, Frank. Thank you.' Kirstie was still applauding. 'How do you play those repeated notes so quickly and evenly?'

'These?' Frank played a phrase from the piece. 'It's called "triple tonguing". You use the tip and the middle of your tongue to stop the wind like this. *Tuh-tuh-kuh, tuh-tuh-kuh, tuh-tuh-kuh.* It just takes lots of practice.'

'And you must have done lots of that. How much practice did you put in for this show?'

'That was a last-minute panic, Kirstie, but when I was a student, I used to practise for at least four hours a day. That was only on the trumpet, because music students have to play another instrument as well as doing the academic work.'

'Four hours,' she repeated. 'What do you think about that, Perry? Frank used to practise for four hours a day.'

Jerked into full wakefulness, Perry Kilburn said, 'Yeah, well, if you've got talent, you don't, like, need to practise, do you?'

Frank couldn't resist the temptation. Handing him the post horn, he said, 'In that case, let's hear you get a tune out of that.'

Perry's response prompted Kirstie to remind him once more that it was peak family viewing time, and that there were children in the studio.

'Magnificent,' said Thomas Davies, the band's First Trumpet.

'Aye,' said Norman, 'he can still do it.'

'It were a lesson to that foul-mouthed yob,' said Geoff. 'Fancy effing and blinding in front of all them kiddies.'

'Well, he cut himself down to size,' said Hutch.

* * *

A short distance away, Penny, Tim and their younger son Gary had been watching the programme.

'How did Uncle Frank get to play like that?' asked Gary.

'He told you on the programme,' said Penny. 'He worked very hard.'

'Yes,' said Tim wryly, 'the music was in him, but he had to work at it. If he hadn't done that, he might have been a punk rocker.'

'No,' said Gary, almost helpless with laughter at the idea, 'give up, Dad.'

Penny picked up the phone and dialled her mother's number. The dialling tone sounded three times before she heard her mother's voice.

'Hello?'

'Mum, it's Penny. Are you all right?'

'Yes, I'm fine, love. I've just been watching Frank on *Northern Scene*.'

'Oh, good. We recorded it in case you missed it for some reason.'

'I wouldn't have missed that for anything, Penny.'

'No, well, it's there for Kate when she comes home.'

'She'll love it. I did.' Her voice was filled with emotion. 'It was like the old days, when I used to watch you and Tim on *Come Dancing*.'

'That's what it is to have talented children,' said Penny, hoping her mother wouldn't take her as seriously as she usually did.

'Yes, what did you think of that ragamuffin on the programme? Wasn't he a disgrace with his language? I bet those kiddies had never heard anything like it.'

'They'll have heard it in the schoolyard, Mum, but that doesn't make it right for him to behave like that in public.'

'No, it doesn't. He needs a few lessons from Frank.'

'I agree, Mum. I wonder if the New Albion Dance Orchestra will be invited on to *Northern Scene*. That would be another lesson.'

11

FEVER

With no reason to feel otherwise, Frank was in a carefree mood when he arrived at the Exchange that Sunday morning. He was happy, Helen was happy and Medusa and Eric were as sour as ever, so everything was as it should be. God was in his heaven – all was right with the world. He climbed the staircase to the ballroom to find most of the band already there. It wasn't unusual, and there were ten minutes in hand, so he draped his denim jacket over a chair and leafed through the scores on his desk.

Hutch came to him to ask, 'Did you see anything of Geoff on your way up, Frank?'

'Geoff? No, isn't he here?'

'No, and he's usually one of the first to arrive.'

Frank knew as well as anyone how punctual and conscientious Geoff was. 'The traffic's no worse than usual,' he said. 'Maybe his car's playing up.' Geoff ran an elderly Ford Escort that had proved troublesome on occasions.

Norman arrived at Hutch's side. 'There's still no sign of him,' he said. 'If he doesn't show by the end of the practice I'll drive round that way and find out what's happening.'

'Aye,' said Hutch, 'it's not like Geoff to miss a band practice.'

Frank knew what they were both thinking. Recent experience had brought old age home to many of them. 'Let's get started,' he said, 'and then you can go and see if he's all right.'

* * *

Geoff's house was only a short distance away, so Norman and Hutch were there in less than ten minutes.

'His sitting room curtains are drawn,' said Hutch as Norman drew up to the kerb.

'Aye, so are his bedroom curtains,' said Norman, whose eyesight was rather better than his friend's. He pulled on the brake and stopped the engine. 'Let's see if we can raise a line.'

The doorbell was ancient and only just audible to those outside.

'He'll never hear that,' said Norman, applying the heel of his fist to the nearest panel. There was no response, so he tried again, but with no result.

Hutch tried the handle, but the door was locked. 'It was worth a try,' he said. He stepped backward to peer up at the bedroom window while Norman hammered on the door again. 'His son might have a spare key,' said Hutch, but I've no idea where he lives.'

'Neither have I.' Norman belaboured the door once more, and his efforts excited the curiosity of the woman who lived next door.

'Geoff's not answering,' Hutch told her. We're concerned about him.'

'I haven't seen him since yesterday afternoon,' she said.

There was the sound of a key turning in the lock.

'Ah,' said Norman, 'now we're getting somewhere.'

The door opened to reveal Geoff, but not as they'd ever seen him. His sweat-soaked pyjamas clung to his body, his eyes were scarcely open, and he was shivering uncontrollably.

'What's up, Geoff?' asked Hutch, stepping inside. 'You're not well, I can tell.'

'Malaria,' said Geoff. It was between a gasp and a whisper.

'Let's get you some clean pyjamas. We'd better change your bed an' all.'

'I'll run him a bath,' said Norman. 'Before I do that, though, who's your doctor, Geoff?'

Geoff stood for a moment, swaying as he gathered his wits. 'Draper,' he said eventually. 'His number's in the little book in the drawer under the phone.' A few seconds later, he said, 'Hang on, Norman. It's Sunday, isn't it?'

'You can be sure somebody will turn out on a Sunday, even if they have to pay 'em double-time,' said Norman. He opened the telephone drawer to find the book. In his methodical way, Geoff had listed everyone alphabetically, surname first, and the doctor's number was easy to find. He dialled it, and when an operator of some kind came on the line, he told her he was reporting a medical emergency. The operator put him through to the requisite department, and eventually, a woman's voice answered.

'Medical Emergencies. Who's calling?'

'My name is Norman Barraclough. I'm speaking on behalf of Geoffrey Brierley of twenty-four Moorside Road, Cullington.'

'Who is his GP?'

As patiently as he could, Norman said, 'Doctor Draper.'

'And what is the problem?'

'Recurrent malaria. He's running a high fever.'

'Can he come to the Medical Centre?'

Still containing his patience, he said, 'No, he can't. He's seventy-three or more, I wouldn't like to guess what his temperature is, and it took all his strength for him to get out of bed and come to the door.'

'Please hold the line.' There was a period of silence, and then she returned. 'Will you give me the patient's name and address again, please?'

Norman dictated slowly, 'Geoffrey Brierley, twenty-four Moorside Road, Cullington.'

'The doctor will be with him as soon as he can.'

'Can you give me a rough idea how long?'

'No, he'll be there as soon as possible.'

'Thank you.' Norman put the phone down as Hutch came downstairs carrying a bundle of laundry. 'A doctor's coming,' he told him. 'Where's Geoff?'

'He's in the bath,' said Hutch. 'I've found him some clean pyjamas, and I've changed his bed. I'm looking for a washing machine.' Looking doubtful, he said, 'There certainly isn't room for one in his kitchen.'

'If I remember rightly, I believe there's a porch at the back of the house.'

'Right.' Hutch continued with his quest while Norman put the kettle on for tea.

'Found it,' said Hutch, returning from the porch. As if to bear him out, the washing machine began its noisy cycle. 'I think Geoff needs water, rather than tea. Judging by the state of his sheets and pyjamas, he must be dehydrated.'

'He can have as much water as he likes. The tea's for us two.'

'Good thinking.' Hutch filled a jug with water and took it with a tumbler to Geoff's room, where the patient had found the strength to haul himself back into bed. 'Get some water inside you, Geoff,' he said, pouring some into a tumbler.

'It's good of you two to do this,' said Geoff weakly.

'It's no bother.' He looked out of the window. 'The doctor should be here shortly.'

'Good, he'll give me a prescription for quinine and some of that stuff they give you when you've lost a lot of fluid.'

'I'm surprised you don't keep some handy. It's not on prescription, is it?'

'The dehy… dehydro…. It's in this top drawer.'

'Why didn't you say so earlier, you daft old sod?' Hutch opened the drawer and sorted through its various contents until he found a sachet marked *Rehydration Treatment*. He read the instructions, tore open the sachet, and tipped its contents into the tumbler. 'There,' he said, 'you can make a start with this. I don't suppose it tastes like Old Brewery Bitter, but you can't have everything.'

Norman came into the room with two cups of tea, one of which he handed to Hutch. 'You're not getting any of this 'til you've had five pints of water,' he told Geoff sternly.

The sound of a car door outside brought Norman to the window. 'It looks as if the doctor's here,' he said. 'I'll go and let him in.'

While Norman did that, Hutch asked, 'When did you last eat, Geoff?'

'I don't know.'

'Yesterday?'

'Yes.'

'Last night?'

'Yes, it would be.'

Norman reappeared with the doctor. 'This is the patient,' he said. 'We're his mates. We came to find out why he wasn't laikin' out.'

'Why he wasn't doing what?'

80

'Playing out. We usually meet on Sunday mornings, you see.'

'I see.' The doctor took Geoff's temperature and listened to his heart. 'Where did you catch malaria?' he asked innocently.

'Burma,' murmured Geoff, 'Mandalay.'

'"Where the flying fishes play",' said Hutch unhelpfully.

'There's a lot of it about, they say,' said Norman.

'When was this, Mr Brierley? During the war?'

'Nineteen forty-four,' confirmed Geoff.

'He can't remember when he last ate anything,' said Hutch, 'but he's never forgotten Burma and the year he was there.'

'I'm not surprised. I'm writing a prescription. I think the pharmacy in Morrisons is your best chance on a Sunday afternoon.'

'I'll get that,' said Norman, taking it from him.

'It sounds as if you haven't eaten for a while, Mr Brierley,' said the doctor. 'I suggest something easy at first, soups are always a good idea.'

'I'll get something for him while I'm out, Doc.'

'You're fortunate in your friends, Mr Brierley.'

'Don't worry,' said Norman. 'The drinks will be on him next time we get together.'

'You should soon be much better, Mr Brierley, but if you have any problems, get one of your friends to call your GP. Goodbye.'

'Goodbye, Doc. Thank you.'

Norman said, 'I'll see you out, and then I'll go to Morrisons for this prescription.'

When Norman and the doctor were gone, the phone rang downstairs.

'Oh hell.'

'I'll get it, Geoff.' Hutch hurried downstairs to pick it up. 'Hello.'

'Hello. Geoff?'

Hutch recognised the caller immediately. 'No, Frank, it's Hutch. Geoff's poorly.'

'I tried your number and then Norman's, and I imagined you'd be there.'

'That's right. He's gone down with recurrent malaria. I imagine the mosquitos thought they were giving the Japs a helping hand. Anyway, we got the quack in, and we've got him sorted with clean sheets and pyjamas. Norman's just gone to your namesake's to get him his prescription and some bits and pieces.'

81

'Can I do anything?'

'I don't think so, Frank.' Suddenly he remembered something. 'Yes, there is one thing you could do, if you don't mind. Just so that I'm not leaving Geoff too long, will you phone Sarah for me, in case she's wondering where I am?'

'Of course I will. She's here with me now, so I don't even need to phone her.'

'Thanks, Frank, and don't worry about Geoff. He'll be as right as rain.'

'Okay, Hutch. 'Bye.'

''Bye, Frank.'

* * *

Frank put the phone down to relay the message. 'Hutch and Norman are at Geoff's place. At least, Hutch is. Norman's gone shopping. Geoff's suffering from malaria, so they're looking after him.' Smiling at the picture that came to him, he said, 'I can imagine Hutch doing what's needed, but I can't think of a less likely nurse than Norman.'

'People can always surprise us, Frank, but how did Geoff get infected with malaria, anyway?'

'He was in the Far East during the war, and malaria was rife, spread by mosquitos. Hutch says the mosquitos reckoned they were on the Japanese side, but I suspect they spread their favours indiscriminately. It can crop up from time to time, as well, as it did this morning, and with absolutely no warning.'

'Even forty-odd years later,' she mused. 'That's quite a legacy.' It was clear to Frank that she was about to change the subject, and her next question confirmed his suspicion.

'What did Helen think about your celebrity appearance on *Northern Scene*?'

'Medusa wouldn't let her watch it. I imagine she recorded it to watch later, when they're not there to impede her enjoyment.'

'How petty. How controlling.'

Frank nodded. 'Those are just two of her failings. Her great fear is that the more time Helen spends with me, the likelier we are to be reconciled, and Medusa will once again have to contend with the son-in-law from hell. Helen's told her it's out of the question, and so have I, but to no avail.'

'I just don't understand it.'

Frank patted her hand sympathetically. 'Many have tried,' he said, 'with equal lack of success.'

'Why does she dislike you so much?'

'From what I can gather, the problem is that I wasn't her choice, and that I differed so much from the ideal man she would have chosen for her daughter.' An idle thought occurred to him, and he said, 'I wonder what the reaction will be to Helen's new bloke.'

Sarah was immediately interested. 'Oh, tell me more.'

'I know very little about him, apart from the fact that they met through work. I teased her about him, but she didn't tell me anything more than that.'

'What a shame.'

'She's hoping for a big improvement on the Sheriff of Nottingham. It seems he was an all-round disappointment.'

'After you, any man would be, darling.'

'Yes, I suppose so.' He knew she was being less than serious, but as ever, he was reluctant to disagree with her. He also had it in mind to phone Hutch again, later that evening, to make sure Geoff was all right.

12

DECISION AND SUSPICION

Meetings of the New Albion Dance Orchestra were infrequent and called only when necessary. Its members insisted that their primary purpose was to play music and that when administrative matters arose they could usually be dealt with informally. Occasionally, however, a decision had to be made that affected them all, and that was best carried out the traditional way. Such a meeting was called for the second Sunday in May, immediately before band practice, and by popular acceptance, Hutch took the chair.

'As most of you are aware,' he said, 'this is just a quick meeting to discuss the question of band dress. It's been mentioned a few times recently, so I think we should make a decision and clear the air. Has any of you a suggestion you'd like to put forward?'

Somewhat hesitantly, Thomas Davies said, 'I've been looking at pictures of the bands on various CD cases, and some of the later ones wore white dinner jackets.'

'That's right,' said Bernard Taylor. 'The New Mayfair Dance Orchestra started out in black, but they changed to white jackets at one stage.'

'A few did,' said Hutch, 'and some even had a uniform made, but are you saying you'd like to see this band in white jackets?'

'Well,' said Thomas unsurely, 'it depends on how everybody feels. I just thought I'd mention it.'

Hutch looked around the meeting, clearly unimpressed by the level of enthusiasm shown so far, and asked, 'Has anybody else got a suggestion?'

Norman had been uncharacteristically quiet so far, but now he felt moved to say, 'If we all wore white jackets, we could make ourselves really useful and sell ice cream at the interval.'

'I take it you're not keen on the idea, Norm.'

'No, Hutch, I'm not. Like you, I've worn black evening dress all my life, and it's habit-forming.'

'Okay, let's see who's in favour of changing over to white jackets. Can I see a show of hands, please?'

Thomas and Bernard seemed about to raise their hands, but thought better of it.

'Just for the sake of fairness, who'd prefer to stay in black?'

The silent majority raised their hands, followed a little sheepishly by Bernard, and then by Thomas.

'Yes,' said Hutch, 'I imagined that might be the case.'

'Just a minute, Mr Chairman,' said Vanessa Wainwright, the pianist. 'I think you're forgetting us.' The female members of the band had formed a small group to one side of the gathering.

'I certainly haven't forgotten you, ladies,' said Hutch, 'and I'm very interested in anything you have to say, as I'm sure everyone else is.'

'Good, because we've been talking, and we think it's very nice that the men want to keep their black dress suits, but we're not carried away with the idea of wearing black. In fact, we're not in favour of any kind of uniform – for us, that is.'

'I can see that.' As Hutch understood it, uniform wasn't a female thing. 'What do you suggest?'

'We think it would be nice to wear something bright. Dresses don't have to be the same. In fact, it's much better if they're not, but a touch of colour would certainly brighten things up. Don't you agree?'

'The point is, Vanessa, do you all agree?'

There was a committed chorus of, 'Yes'.

'In that case, let's adopt that as your band attire. We'll all look forward to seeing you booted and spurred, although, strictly speaking, it's none of our business.'

'Oh, let's not take that line,' said Vanessa. 'What do you think, boys? Let's have a show of hands for the bright and cheerful option.'

A universal, enthusiastic show of hands settled the matter, leaving Hutch free to move on. 'If nobody else has anything else to say, he said, 'I've got one piece of information for you, and it's about the

Midsummer Ball. That's the one in June, obviously, not the next social evening. Anyway, the committee have decided, after the success of the Christmas party, to have a buffet, and they were so taken with the catering at Christmas, that they've asked the Local Produce people to do it again.'

There was a murmur of approval, and Norman said, 'Just as long as the members leave some for us.'

'It'll be just as it was at Christmas,' Hutch assured him. 'Right, so if everybody's happy, let's get set up for a practice before Frank starts wondering why he bothered to come.'

* * *

Frank ran through the programme for the May social evening, including 'I Won't Dance' and 'A Fine Romance', both of which went remarkably well. The only difficulty encountered during the practice was Geoff's absence. He was still recovering from malaria, which meant that Hutch was playing second trombone cues on his tenor sax wherever he could. Happily, Geoff's son and daughter-in-law had taken him temporarily into their home, so his friends knew he was receiving attention.

'It's no joke at his age,' said Norman, possibly forgetting he was even older than Geoff. The whole band were gathered in the Club lounge after the practice.

'Aye,' said Hutch, 'he was in a bad way when we landed at his place. He didn't seem to know what was happening or even what day it was.'

'No,' said Norman, 'but it's hard to tell with Geoff. He's not all that tuned-in when he's fit and well.'

'Even so,' said Hutch, 'as you said, malaria's no joke.'

The conversation between Frank and Sarah was of a different kind. The announcement that White Rose Cuisine would be responsible for the buffet at the Midsummer Ball had not escaped Sarah's ears, as Frank learned when they were alone.

'Did you know they'd asked the outside catering firm to do the buffet?' she asked him.

He imagined her question was less than ingenuous, so he opted for a straight answer. 'Not until this morning, when Hutch told us. I suppose it makes sense as they did such a good job last time and at very short notice.'

'I suppose so.'

The subject was better left alone. Hopefully, Sarah's unease would evaporate in time, and protesting his innocence might easily strengthen her misgivings. Instead, he said, 'Your duets with Dan went well this morning. I think they'll be popular with the members.'

'I hope so. Do you think they'll be aware of the difference in our ages?'

'Frankly, no. The difference is minimal, anyway.'

'It's twelve years.'

'Twelve years is nothing, and anyway, it's not obvious. You look younger than you think.' Responding to a sceptical glance, he said, 'Yes, you do, and another reason is that there'll be so much more going on. There'll be the music and the lyrics as well as the fact they'll all be dancing. The last thing on anybody's mind will be the few years' difference between you and Dan, which don't mean a thing, anyway.'

It was evident that she was still to be convinced. 'I hope you're right,' she said. Her attitude had changed since the journey home from London, and it wasn't difficult to find the reason.

He had other matters on his mind, as well. He was required to attend two meetings. One was in London with Frances Tichbourne of Fran-Tic Productions to discuss the score for a two-part dramatisation of *Lost in Admiration*, and the other was in Droitwich, with Anvil Productions, one of Patsy's interests. The subject of the play meant little to Frank, but that was of no consequence. What really mattered was the fee, obviously, but also the fact that Patsy had put the score his way, and she was a valued friend as well as a steady source of work.

Another development occurred the following day, when Frank was nearing the end of the score of *Not Guilty*. He was used to receiving phone calls at the most inopportune times, but common sense told him they were necessary. He reached for the phone and answered it. 'Frank Morrison.'

'Good morning, Mr Morrison. It's Denzel at Carver and Glossop.'

'Good morning, Denzel.' Frank didn't believe anyone could be called Denzel. It had to be an assumed name, but good manners had so far prevailed, and he'd kept the thought to himself.

Denzel sounded excited, and the reason was immediately evident. 'It's good news, Mr Morrison.'

'That's always welcome.'

'Yes, there's an offer on the house.'

'Excellent. Is it the Parker people?'

'No, they're still arguing about the spare room. It's a pity, because they've sold their house, and there's no chain.'

'They're a strange pair, Denzel. I can't see why they shouldn't buy the place, and then argue afterwards about who gets the spare room.'

'Neither can I, but the offer is from the people who viewed it on Saturday afternoon. They're offering fifty-two.'

'Mm.' Frank thought it was well worth the asking price of fifty-six thousand.

'Well, you'll want to discuss it with Mrs Morrison…. I'm sorry, I meant to say, "Ms Kent".'

'That's all right, Denzel. I know who you mean. All right, I'll talk to Helen and see what she thinks. Thanks for letting me know.'

'Right-ho, Mr Morrison. I'll wait to hear from you. Goodbye.'

'Goodbye.' He saved his work on the computer and dialled the number of the public library, where Helen worked.

'Cullington Public Library.'

'Hello, Helen. Is it convenient for me to come round after work?'

'I suppose so. Why?'

'I've just had a call from young Denzel. Honestly, is that his real name?'

'I don't know. What did he want?'

'The people who came on Saturday have made an offer. It's not wonderful, just fifty-two thousand, but we need to discuss it, rather than dismissing it out of hand.'

'Oh.' Her lacklustre response had probably more to do with the offer than his suggestion. 'All right. I'll be home by six.'

'Fine, I'll see you then. 'Bye.'

''Bye, Frank.'

He put the phone down, feeling sorry, as he did all too often, for Helen. All right, she'd initiated the separation and divorce, albeit with a significant degree of urging on the part of her mother, but if they came out of the house sale with twenty-six thousand each, less legal and agency fees, she would have little enough for a new home. Being the major earner, he was much better-placed to start afresh.

He continued to work on the score until it was time to call on Helen.

* * *

It was almost six-fifteen when he arrived; he saw no point in rushing her after a day's work, and he found he'd timed his visit to perfection when he entered the kitchen just as the kettle began to boil.

'Come in, Frank,' she said. 'Shall we talk in the sitting room, as we're alone?'

He went through and took a seat in what used to be his armchair, while Helen brewed the tea and brought it through with a plate of biscuits.

'You knew I was coming,' he said, taking one of his favourite dark-chocolate wholemeal biscuits.

She laughed. 'I called at the shop on the way home.'

'I'm glad you did. I haven't had one of these since… I don't know when.'

'Have you been on a diet?'

'No, it just never occurs to me to buy them.'

'I don't usually.'

He was about to raise the subject of the offer on the house, when she said, 'Fifty-two thousand isn't a brilliant offer, is it?'

'I don't think so.'

'I wouldn't be able to buy much with my share.'

'That's what I was thinking.'

Staring into her tea, she said, 'Of course, I'm still young enough to get another mortgage.'

'Don't do that, Helen. Not with interest rates as they are. You don't want another millstone round your neck at forty-one.' Suddenly he smiled and said, 'You'd do better finding a rich man.'

She gave a mirthless laugh. 'Where am I going to find one of them?' she asked.

'Just keep kissing frogs. You've only tried two, as far as I know.'

'Two?' She stared at him in confusion.

'Me and the Sheriff of Nottingham. You've hardly begun. I mean to say, most women have kissed a whole pondful by the time they're your age.'

'Same old Frank, talking nonsense, as usual.' Her observation was good-natured enough.

'Anyway, how did it go with the new man?'

'It was okay. I agreed to see him again, although I don't know why.'

'I take it he didn't impress.'

'To be honest, I found him a bit creepy.'

Frank smiled benignly and said, 'I know I take some following, but give him time to get his act together.'

'If you didn't have that mug in your hand, I'd throw something at you.'

'It's funny,' he said, 'but every time I come into this room I get threatened.

'Don't.'

'All right. What are we going to do about the offer?'

She shrugged. 'What do you think?'

'I think we should reject it. It's not as if we're in a hurry to sell, and there has been other interest shown.'

'I agree.'

'I'll phone the agents in the morning, without fail.' Almost to himself, he said, 'I'm in London on Wednesday and Brum on Thursday.'

At the mention of London, Helen asked, 'Will you have time to see Kate?'

'I could, but she phoned me on Friday, and she was okay. If she doesn't need me for anything, I leave her alone. Parents can be an embarrassment.'

'In more senses than one.'

'What do you...? Oh, are you thinking about the recital? She knows who was responsible, and so does your mother. I told her clearly enough.'

Helen looked down at her feet. 'Thank goodness they're not here today.'

'Yes,' he said playfully, 'although it means I can't invite them to the premiere of *Hey, Young Fella*.'

Helen gave a half-chuckle. 'When is it?'

'August. It's part of the London Film Festival. Your mother would have enjoyed staying at the Savoy, wearing a strapless, backless creation by Karl Lagerfeld and walking down the red carpet into the Odeon.'

'Don't be cruel, Frank.'

'Okay.' He stood up and put his mug on the low table. 'Thanks for the tea, Helen. I'll phone Denzel in the morning.'

'Yes, I keep hoping we'll hear from the Parker people.'

'You never know. 'Bye.' He kissed her cheek and walked out to the car.

13

UNWELCOME ATTENTION

Everything seemed back to normal at the May social evening. Geoff was fully recovered and back in his place as second trombone, and the band were playing as well as ever. The new members were also playing with confidence and enthusiasm.

As was their habit, Frank and Sarah escaped on to the dance floor for 'Love Walked In' while Hutch took over the stick. It was an opportunity for Frank to mention Sarah's first duet with Dan.

'"I Won't Dance" went very well,' he said.

'Do you think so?' Clearly, she didn't altogether agree.

'I do.' Sensing continued reluctance on her part, he said, 'Having said that, I'm not going to push those numbers if you're not happy with them.'

'Oh, I don't mind them, really, but I'm still conscious of the difference in our ages.'

'In that case, if you can bear to sing "A Fine Romance" with Dan tonight, we'll scrub round them both in future.'

'Really? I feel like a spoilsport, now.'

'Well, at least you won't feel miscast anymore. You can't have it both ways.'

'Either way doesn't feel right.'

Not for the first time in his dealings with women, Frank found himself caught between opposing but equally unfavourable options. He decided to change the subject. He asked, 'Have you got something to wear at the Midsummer Ball?'

'I'm working on it.'

'I'll look forward to seeing you in it.' He punctuated that by kissing her neck softly. She made no reply, but at least she wasn't arguing.

They saw out the number, and Frank returned to the stand to relieve Hutch, no less concerned about Sarah's state of mind.

* * *

At the end of the evening, they returned to Frank's flat.

'There,' he said, as he opened the door, 'you won't need to sing either of those duets again.'

'I can't say I'm disappointed, Frank, but I don't like to create difficulties, either.'

'There's no difficulty. I wouldn't dream of asking you to do something when you're obviously not happy with it.' Taking her coat, he asked, 'Coffee?'

'No, thanks. Do you mind if we go straight to bed?'

'I can't see a problem with that.'

* * *

Thereafter, the subject was avoided. Frank had a discreet word with Dan, who accepted the situation without demur, as usual, and he was free to attend to other matters.

Mr and Mrs Parker had apparently reached agreement on the use of the spare room, and had made an offer of the asking price. The housing price boom that had begun two years previously had stabilised to some extent, but it was still generating quick sales and making most buyers nervous enough to avoid bargaining, for fear of losing their desired property.

Frank's solicitor, now acting for them both, lost no time in sending the Fittings & Contents and Property Information Forms, which looked too forbidding for words.

'Are you sure you have time to bother with these, Frank?' asked Helen.

She seemed even more withdrawn than usual, and he wondered what mischief her mother had been up to. 'I'll find the time,' he assured her. 'You've had the toil of preparing the house for viewing, so it's only fair.'

'Don't let him send anything without you seeing it first, Helen,' said the voice of censure from the sitting room.

'I wish those two would bugger off on holiday,' said Frank. 'They can't have been barred from every resort. I mean, not everywhere's as exclusive as Blackpool's South Shore.'

Helen waited, tight-lipped, while Frank spoke to her parents.

'Not that it's any of your business, Medusa,' he said, joining her and her husband in the sitting room, 'but the agreement is that we divide the proceeds from the house between us, and Helen can keep or dispose of whatever furniture she likes.' Continuing before she could interject, he said, 'If I wore a black mask and a red-striped jersey, I might look a bit like a burglar, but I really wouldn't know where to begin, so leave us to attend to our own business, will you?'

Mildred was bristling, almost visibly, with anger. 'You disrespectful waster. My name's Mildred.'

'Mild-*dread*, yes.'

'Tell him, Eric.'

Eric opened his mouth to speak, but before he could, Frank said, 'Don't bother, Eric. I can usually beat you to your line.' Speaking to them both, he said, 'It's time you let Helen manage her own affairs. She's more than capable of it if you two will only stop interfering, and that brings me to another matter. You know what was going to happen to you if I caught you here when the house was being viewed, so let me make it clear that the same will happen if you're here when the buyers come visiting to measure up or for whatever reason. Do you understand?'

Mildred looked fit to explode, but instead, she said, 'Tell him, Eric!'

'Stamp your foot, Eric,' advised Frank. 'I would, especially if I had what you've got to contend with.' He returned to the kitchen before Eric or Mildred could think of an appropriate rejoinder.

Helen said hopelessly, 'I feel like pig-in-the-middle between you and them.'

'Just remember, Helen, I won't always be around. Once this business is settled, you'll only see me with Kate, and even then, only until she gets her own transport.' On a mischievous note, he said, 'You might see us on BBC News at the premiere of *Hey, Young Fella*. That's if you're allowed to watch it.'

'Don't, Frank.'

'I'm sorry. Take care.' He kissed her cheek and took his leave of her, just as the voice of doom enquired, 'Don't let him make up to you, Helen.'

'He's gone now.' She sounded dejected, and he felt sorry for her again.

* * *

The phone rang while he was battling with the Property Information Form.

'Hello, Frank,' said a familiar voice. I hope this isn't a bad time.'

'No, Hutch, it's a good time. I'm filling in forms to do with the house sale. It's mind-numbing, and I'm grateful for the distraction.'

Hutch chuckled. 'I'll try not to keep you too long. The premiere's two months away, but I'm planning the trip to London.'

'I wonder what kind of reception it'll get.'

'You'll soon find out, Frank. Anyway, I'm organising hotel accommodation again and a chara.'

'A what-a? Oh, a charabanc.' Hutch had a personal lexicon of archaic, dialect words and expressions.

'That's right, and what I need to know is, are you coming with us or making your own way there again, like you did before Christmas.'

'I'll cadge a lift with you, if I may, Hutch. Since the first session, I've been more inclined to use public transport for long journeys.'

'I don't blame you, lad. It's a lot safer.'

With the uncomfortably recent memory of driving to Essex and then to London in a state of exhaustion, Frank was inclined to agree with him.

'Katie should be home for the holidays, I imagine.'

'Yes, she'll come down with us.'

'Well, that's all I needed to know.' He seemed about to ring off, and then he asked, 'How's the house sale going?'

'We've accepted an offer of the asking price, which is the good news. Unfortunately, we're having to cope with everything in spite of the usual malicious input and interference.'

'Hold on, Frank. It won't be forever.'

'That's what I told Helen this morning.'

'Poor lass. That mother of hers has never let them cut the cord.'

'It's not a pretty picture, Hutch, but you're right. Even with everything signed, sealed and made legal, she still doesn't trust me to play fair with "Our 'Elen".'

'It must be twenty years, now, and she still doesn't know you.'

'It's been twenty-two since we met.' The dates were embedded firmly in Frank's memory. 'This year would have been our twenty-first wedding anniversary.'

'It's spilt milk, Frank. Let it lie.'

* * *

Frank was content to leave that part of his life behind, but a phone call to Helen that evening was about to lead to events beyond his control.

'Just remind me,' he said. 'Did we agree to let the Parker people have the lawn mower?'

'Yes, and the roller.'

'That's good. I've just reached that part of the form that deals with the garden, and I couldn't remember what we'd said.'

'They were quite keen to have them. They're not used to a garden the size of ours… this one.' She sounded vague, possibly preoccupied.

'Are your parents still there?' They were usually responsible for Helen's moments of unease.

'No, they've gone.'

'Something's wrong, isn't it? Have they been giving you a hard time?'

'No, it's not them.'

'Somebody has, then.' In a softer tone, he asked, 'Do you want to tell me about it?' All right, he was her *ex*-husband, but he was the only reliable ally she had, at least for the time being.

'No, it's all right, it's nothing. It's just….' Her next word was lost in a series of sobs.

'I'm coming over. I'll be with you in ten minutes.'

In fact, he arrived at the house in less than ten minutes. Helen was dry-eyed, but signs of distress were still evident.

'The kettle's just boiled,' she said.

'Okay, go and sit down. I'll attend to it.' Without waiting for agreement, he took two cups and saucers from the china cupboard in defiance of Medusa's insistence that mugs were more economical, and dropped two teabags into a teapot. If he was making tea, he would do it his way.

When the tea was scalded, he put everything on a tray and carried it through to the sitting room, placing it on the low coffee table that Medusa had called a waste of money, although it shared that description with a great many items in her estimation.

For the time being, Helen sat on the sofa, simply looking down at her hands or possibly at nothing in particular, but without speaking. Frank waited for the tea to brew, and then poured it. Helen surprised him by saying, 'You don't like teabags, do you?'

'I'm not as proud as all that, Helen.' Sitting back, he asked, 'Are you going to tell your ex-hubbie what this is about?'

A tear escaped and ran down her left cheek, but she made no attempt to speak.

'Whatever it is, we'll deal with it,' he assured her. As the possibility occurred to him, he asked, 'You're not ill, are you?'

'No, it's nothing like that.'

'Thank goodness for that. Well, I'm sure we can deal with anything else.' He pulled two tissues from a box and offered them to her. 'You'll get a red nose with these supermarket things, you know. You can't beat quality at a sensitive time, whichever end you're attending to. Any puppy will tell you that.' He waited for her to blow her nose, and when she looked more receptive, he asked, 'What is it, Helen? Who do you want thumped?'

She attempted a laugh that was more of a sob, so he put his arm round her shoulders and waited.

'I'm hopeless,' she said eventually. 'I can't even... start a... new relationship without... it going wrong.'

'Are you pregnant?' It had only just occurred to him as a possibility.

'No, it... didn't get... as far as... that, thank goodness.'

Seeing tears roll again, he waited patiently.

'Do you remember... I told you...?'

'About your new fella? The one at the library?'

'Roy, yes.'

'Right. Is he being a pest?'

She nodded, causing another tear to fall. She accepted another tissue from Frank. 'I only… went out with… him twice. I was a bit… edgy the… second time. I thought he was… quite creepy.'

Frank found himself a little short of detail. 'You said you'd met him at the library. Does he work there?'

'No, he's a borrower.'

Frank resisted the temptation to comment on tiny people who live behind skirting boards. 'And he's being a nuisance?'

'Yes, he won't accept… that I don't want to see him… again.' Her shudders were now less frequent.

'Does he make nuisance phone calls?'

'No, he doesn't know my number. I was Helen Kent again by the time I met him, and this phone's under your name.'

'So what does he do?'

'He comes into the library every day and pesters me, wanting me to change my mind about not going out with him again. Sometimes, he waits outside at closing time and catches me on the way home.' She gave what seemed to be a final shudder, and said, 'I wouldn't go out with him if he was the last man on earth.'

'As I said to you before, Helen, you'll have to kiss a few frogs before you find your prince.' And that was before seeking Medusa's unlikely approval. Now he thought of it, it would be better if Medusa kissed the frogs, preferably under water for at least half-an-hour, even though scaring the wits out of the poor things might be seen as animal cruelty, but he left that unsaid. Instead, he asked, 'Have you spoken to the Chief Librarian about it?'

'Yes, she told me to ignore him and get on with my work. She's asked him not to keep me talking, but she's so ineffectual, he takes no notice of her.'

'That's a shame. Does he come into the library at any particular time?'

'His lunch-hour, usually, but he sometimes waits outside and catches me when I leave.'

'So, what time does he usually arrive?'

Alarm showed in her eyes. 'About twelve forty-five, but Frank, I don't want any trouble.'

'There won't be any trouble.' As he spoke, he remembered saying something very similar to Kate when she and her colleague were being targeted by prurient lowlife in The Copper Kettle. 'This is where the problem ceases to be a problem,' he told her definitely. 'Leave him to me.'

14

A Warning – and a Lapse

Frank had probably driven past Cullington Public Library on thousands of occasions; in more leisurely times he'd borrowed books there and used its reference department as well. It was part of Cullington's history, having been donated to the public by a wealthy local family in the 1930s, and countless visitors to the town had expressed their admiration for its Art Deco splendour and immaculately-maintained grounds, which included a large lawn to the rear with the kind of raised apron on a steep bank with a recess that architects and knowing people called a 'ha-ha'.

It was a magnificent building, but on this occasion, Frank could have been forgiven for being indifferent to its charms, because he was there for an altogether more basic reason.

He walked up the stone steps, entered by the huge oak doors and made his way into the adult library, where Helen, who was no doubt feeling highly nervous, saw him immediately. She finished scanning a borrower's books and came over to him.

'I really don't want any fuss,' she said.

'Relax, Helen. There'll be no fuss. I'm going to browse for a while.' He located the bookcase devoted to authors whose names began with 'A'. It seemed a logical place to begin.

He'd reached *Lucky Jim* by Kingsley Amis, when he noticed a man talking to Helen. He was leaning forward, and she was quite obviously in a state of anxiety. As Frank moved closer, he guessed the man's age at about forty. He had dark, grey-flecked hair, but his sideburns were completely grey.

Joining them, he asked, 'Is this the man, Helen?'

She nodded nervously.

'Come with me,' he told the man, taking his arm. 'We're going to have a little chat.'

'Who are you?' the man demanded, trying to reclaim his arm, but finding it locked. 'What do you want?'

'I've told you. Come on, Roy, through that door.'

'How do you know my name? What's this about?'

'Let's go outside into the warm sunshine, and I'll explain everything as we go.' He pushed him through the open doorway. 'Now, mind the steps. We don't want you injured – not at this stage, anyway.'

'I want to know what this is about. Where are you taking me?'

'We're going round the back of the library, where it's nice and quiet and we can have a peaceful discussion,' he said, propelling him round the corner and along the asphalt footpath. 'Helen's a close friend of mine, and I don't like to see her upset by some pathetic moron who can't take "no" for an answer.'

'What's this got to do with you?'

'I thought I'd just told you the answer to that question.' They reached the rear of the building, where the asphalt gave way to the raised, grassy bank. Confident they were out of sight, Frank stopped quite deliberately, forcing Roy to stop, too. 'Helen's not interested in you, Roy. In fact, she'd rather you left her alone. Do you understand?'

'I don't see—'

Frank heaved him sideways so that he tumbled off the footpath, on to the hard, sun-baked surface, and rolled down the steep, grassy bank. His exclamation as he hit the ground suggested that his landing was not without discomfort. However, he picked himself up, apparently uninjured.

'I'm not... standing for... this,' he gasped, taking the short flight of stone steps that were the central point of the bank.

Frank helped him up the last two steps, and said, 'I asked you a question, Roy. Do you understand?'

'Mind your own business, whoever you are!' he panted heavily.

'You take some convincing.' Kicking his feet from beneath him, Frank gave him a shove, leaving the rest to gravity to propel him down the slope.

Coming to rest once again in the grassy ditch, Roy regained his feet and made unsteadily for the stone steps.

'I'll put it to you once more,' said Frank. 'Stop bothering Helen. Do you understand?'

'You bastard! I'm… going to… the police!'

'That's right,' said Frank, hauling him on to the top of the bank. 'You can tell them how you've been tormenting an innocent, helpless woman. I don't think they'll be very sympathetic. Do you?' He punctuated that question by pitching him again down the bank. He was rewarded by a loud cry of pain. There'd been no rain for several weeks, and the ground was as hard as concrete.

This time, Roy staggered weakly up the steps, and Frank was obliged to help him yet again, rather than let him fall backwards.

'Are you wondering why I haven't hit you yet?'

Roy's mouth was open as he fought for air, but it was evident that no reply was forthcoming.

'I'll tell you. I'm saving that for later, because, make no mistake, if you ever bother Helen again, I'll beat you senseless. Now, do you understand that?'

'All right,' he gasped.

'Are you going to leave her alone?'

'Yes.'

'You've just made a wise decision, Roy,' said Frank, brushing dust and dried grass cuttings from his victim's shirt. 'Go and sin no more.' He walked with the dishevelled Romeo as far as the carpark to make sure he didn't re-enter the library, and seeing him drive away, returned to the library desk.

Helen looked up nervously when she saw him. 'What happened?' she asked.

'Don't worry,' Frank told her. 'He won't bother you again. I explained things to him, and he saw my point of view.' Leaving it at that, he left her and drove home to complete the forms the solicitor had sent him. Once he'd done that, he could return to his proper work. Orion Productions wanted to record the score of *Not Guilty*, and sooner was preferred over later.

* * *

He was making a few adjustments when the doorbell rang. Looking at the time on the computer screen, he was surprised to see that it was six forty-four. A whole afternoon had passed without his noticing it.

He went to the intercom to answer it. 'Hello.'

'Frank, it's me.'

'Come in, Helen.' He pressed the button to unlock the outer door. It was an opportune moment, because the forms for the house sale had to be signed by them both. He opened the flat door to welcome her inside. 'Come on in, Helen. I'll put the kettle on.'

She still seemed flustered. 'I had to come,' she said.

'And you're more than welcome.'

'I couldn't tell you at the library how grateful I was for what you did.'

'I did nothing more than prevail on his better nature. Just let me put the kettle on.' He went into the tiny kitchen and filled the electric kettle.

'I hope it didn't get physical.'

'I never hit him once,' he assured her. 'Now, stop worrying about it.' As he measured tea into the teapot, he said, 'I've completed those forms and signed them. They only need your signature.'

'Where are they?'

'I'll show you.' He took her into his studio, where he'd left them ready for signing.

'I see you've still got your friends for company,' she said, referring to the pictures of Wyatt Earp, Custer and Billy the Kid. 'They'll bury them with you when the time comes.'

'Not yet, I hope. There you are.' He pointed to the places for her signature and handed her a ballpoint pen. 'You know, solicitors are so good at generating work for themselves, I'm always reminded of *Bleak House*.'

'The legacy that was lost in legal fees, yes.'

'Let's go and mash that tea.' It was a more cheerful subject than legal fees.

She gave a smile of amusement. 'Who says, "mash", nowadays?'

'Hutch and Norman, to name but two. Come and make yourself comfortable.' He scalded the tea and brought everything in on a tray.

'Even living alone, you maintain your standards,' she observed, looking at the teapot and the china cups and saucers.

'Of course. Once I let them slip, there's no telling how far I'll descend.'

Looking around the room, her eye fell on the contents of a low bookshelf. 'Your old cowboy books still have a place of honour as well,' she remarked. '*The Plains Indians, The Gunfighters, Buffalo Bill's Wild West Annual, The Lawmen....*' She laughed good-naturedly, and said, 'Maybe you'll grow up one day, Frank.'

Even in her library clothes, she looked neat and appealing. She still had the slender figure he'd admired when he first met her. He dismissed the thought and handed her a cup of tea. 'You do expect a lot, Helen.'

Changing the subject abruptly, she said, 'You can't imagine how it feels to be followed around all the time. You hear stories about women being stalked by weirdos and the awful things that happen to them.' Touching his hand, she said, 'I'm ever so grateful, Frank.'

'Think nothing of it. Any knight errant with a window in his diary would have done the same.'

'But I mean you could so easily have left me to my own devices, now that we're divorced.'

'True, but could you see me doing that? You mustn't believe everything your mother tells you about me.'

'She took against you from the start, didn't she?' Her tone was almost one of regret. It was unusual, because she usually resented his observations about her mother.

'It didn't help that I dropped you in the club, I must admit, but it's fair to say, as well, that I wouldn't have been her first choice of son-in-law.

'No.' There was no argument there.

'I fell short of her approval in lots of ways, but it doesn't matter now. I just hope she's more positive towards my successor, whoever he may turn out to be.'

'I don't want to think about that yet.' She finished her tea and said, 'I'd better go, or I shan't eat.'

'We can't let that happen.' He got up and walked with her to the door.

She said, 'I have to do battle with that outer door again.'

'It's easy enough. You just push the button and hold it while you turn the knob. Don't worry, I'll come down with you.'

They took the stairs to the ground floor, and Frank opened the heavy outer door for her.

'Thanks again, Frank.'

'Any time.' On an impulse, he took her in his arms and hugged her, pleased as he was to see her relieved of the worry and fear of the past weeks. 'You've nothing to worry about now,' he said, kissing her lightly on the cheek. Even after so long apart, it felt natural, and it was little wonder that, in such a highly-charged moment, the sight of her parted lips presented temptation of a kind he was unable to resist. He bent and kissed her, feeling her respond eagerly, and for the moment, it was as if he'd just returned from a long journey. Even as he indulged in the exquisite sensation, however, he knew it was a stolen moment that mustn't be allowed to continue. Good sense intervened, and he restrained himself.

'I really didn't intend that to happen,' he said, still holding her.

'I know.' It was clear that Helen felt the same way, although she was quite breathless. 'Let's pretend it never happened, shall we?'

'Yes, I think we must.'

They were so involved in their abatement and self-embarrassment that neither of them heard a car door being closed, followed by footsteps outside on the pavement.

A familiar voice said, 'Oh, do carry on, you two. Don't mind me!'

Frank turned and saw Sarah on the footpath. He froze for the minute, tongue-tied and disadvantaged. In retrospect, he would have challenged anyone to find anything sensible to say, and before he could, she was gone.

15

AFTER THE FALL-OUT

Having rebuffed Frank's efforts to explain his behaviour, Sarah went on to dissociate herself from the band, a decision she communicated via Hutch, who spoke to Frank as soon as he could.

'She's adamant,' said Hutch, 'and it'll take a cleverer man than me to change her mind. I suppose we'll find another vocalist eventually, but that's the least of my problems. What concerns me is her happiness and yours, and as things stand at the moment, you're the problem.'

'I know, Hutch.'

'She says she caught you and Helen hotfoot for the master bedroom.'

'That's an exaggeration. In fact, it's basically not true. Let me tell you what happened, Hutch, because although I'm not proud of it, I'm not as much to blame as Sarah believes.'

'Go on, then.'

Frank gave him a plain, matter-of-fact account of Helen's dilemma and his part in resolving it. He described Helen's elation at finding she was free of what had been a threatening and fearsome experience, and went on to describe their parting hug on the doorstep. 'I weakened for a matter of seconds, Hutch, maybe ten at the most. We weren't even kissing when Sarah arrived. As a matter of fact, we'd just agreed that the best thing was to forget it had happened.'

'Fair enough, Frank, you're only human. I'll try to talk some sense into Sarah, but I can't promise anything. I think your best course is to keep your head down until she cools down a bit.'

It was good advice, and Frank was content to follow it. 'I remember her state of mind when she first came to a band practice,' he said.

'She'd been very badly treated, and I can only imagine that colours her judgement even now.'

'I'm inclined to agree with you, Frank. Meanwhile, I think we'd better proceed with the assumption that she's unlikely to take part in the Midsummer Ball. I just hope I can get her to see reason before the film premiere in August. It would be tragic if she were to miss that after all the effort she put into the recording.'

* * *

Having explained that, for personal reasons, Sarah wouldn't be available for the forthcoming ball, Frank was confronted with another crisis that Sunday morning, involving Vanessa Wainwright, the band's pianist.

Sensing that the subject matter was sensitive, he steered her away from the others so that she could talk freely.

'You said you're going to miss the Midsummer Ball, Vanessa. Why's that?' he asked.

'I have to go into hospital for an operation. I'm having it done privately, so that I can get it out of the way, but they've asked me to go in the day before the ball. I'm ever so sorry, but it's something that has to be done.' She was clearly embarrassed.

'Don't apologise, Vanessa,' he told her. 'Your health has to come first, and we'll be all right, anyway.'

'I have to avoid driving, lifting, reaching, over-exertion and generally using the stomach muscles for six weeks after the operation, but I'm told I can play the piano if I'm careful not to overdo it.'

'Of course.' By this time, Frank had gathered that the operation was most likely to be a hysterectomy, which was no small thing. He remembered his mother's experience. 'You mustn't do anything that's likely to pull at your stitches,' he said, 'but as far as the piano is concerned, I can deputise for as long as necessary, so you mustn't worry.' One important question remained. He asked, 'Where are you going to have it done?'

'The Duke of York's Nursing Home. Why do you ask?'

'We need to know where to send the flowers and our good wishes.'

'Oh,' she said, suddenly taken aback, 'how kind that would be. I wasn't expecting anything like that.'

'You're one of us, Vanessa. Come and join the others.' He left her with Thomas Davies, with whom she had long since formed a close attachment, and who was also conscious of the upheaval her absence was likely to cause. She would be able to set his mind at rest while Frank relayed the news to Hutch.

'Poor old Vanessa,' said Hutch. 'She can't help it, and I wish her well, but what's going to happen next, I wonder?'

'It's not as bad as all that,' said Frank, who was painfully conscious that he was responsible for half of the band's difficulty. 'I can fill in on the piano for as long as it takes. I'd rather do that than see Vanessa set back after her operation.'

'Does playing the piano involve the stomach muscles?' The possibility must have seemed odd to a wind player.

'It depends how hard she hits it, I suppose. If anything, though, it's pedalling that's likely to do that, however minutely. Anyway, as I say, I'll stand in for her.' His attention was suddenly taken by two of the Exchange Club Committee, who were currently examining the large doorframe. He said, 'I wonder what those two are up to.'

Hutch turned to see where he was looking. 'They're considering redecorating part of the building, I gather, starting with this floor and including the ballroom. They'll have to box crafty, though.'

'Why?'

'The Wool Exchange is a Grade Two listed building. They can't just go around changing things according to their whims and preferences.'

'I'm afraid that's lost on me, Hutch.'

'It just means that the building has to be preserved as it was when it was listed, and that includes the interior.'

It was something to think about, and anything that distracted Frank from his current preoccupation, however briefly, was welcome. 'The ballroom's looking a bit tired,' he admitted, but it would a shame to change its appearance altogether. Do you think they'd be obliged to have it painted with the original colours?'

'I'm not sure, Frank. Maybe Julie would know.' He inclined his head towards a girl who was currently in conversation with Norman and Geoff. She was the band's lighting and audio technician, but her day job was with her father's building business.

'What's up, Hutch?' she asked, joining them at the bar.

'What do you know about listed buildings, Julie?'

'I know they're a blooming nuisance. What do you want to know about them?' She was nineteen years old, with cheerful Caribbean features and a ready smile.

'This is a Grade Two listed building, and we're wondering whether or not they're allowed to change the paintwork in the ballroom.'

'The paintwork?' She considered the question. 'I'm not sure. I know they're not allowed to change any of the structure, and that includes the staging, but I'd have to ask my dad about decorating. What's going to happen, anyway?'

'The committee want to freshen the place up, and we were wondering what might happen to the ballroom.'

She nodded. 'I'll ask my dad.' Looking at her watch, she said, 'I'll be seeing him very shortly.'

Frank asked, 'Will you have another drink?'

'Better not, thanks, Frank. I'm expected home. Anyway, 'bye, you two.'

''Bye, Julie.'

'See you, Julie.'

* * *

At home, that afternoon, Frank tried to make sense of his feelings. He sat in his studio, because that was where, beneath the sobering gaze of Wyatt Earp, George Armstrong Custer *et al*, he usually found he could think his clearest thoughts. Unfortunately, this was one occasion that failed to conform to the usual pattern, because half-an-hour later, the whirligig of fragmented notions was still refusing to hang around long enough to become even remotely coherent. He decided to fall back on the established formula, and list his ideas as they came to him.

Twenty-three or so years earlier – he arrived at that approximate sum by doodling on his blotter – his trumpet professor had prescribed listing as an aid to disciplined thought, and it had served him well on numerous occasions. He took a sheet of paper from the printer and unscrewed the cap of his fountain pen, because, in his experience, a return to civilised ways usually aided cogent and grown-up thinking.

Where Do I Stand?
I love Sarah.
It was true. She might be otherwise inclined after her shock discovery, but his feelings hadn't changed.
I'm still very fond of Helen.
That was also true. After twenty years and a largely-amicable divorce, how could he feel otherwise?
Do I still love Helen? Is that possible?
Was it possible to love two women at the same time? Man was a monogamous creature whom nature had equipped with only one penis, unlike, according to Wilbur Smith, certain species of snake, which apparently had two – what was the plural of penis? *Penes*? At all events, it wasn't a plural that was in common use, for obvious reasons. Anyway, it was possible, at least in theory, for a male snake to couple with two female snakes at any given time. It must be terribly confusing, like carrying on two telephone conversations simultaneously and being equally attentive to both parties, but who cared? Snakes were a disgusting species, anyway, with no regard for the feelings of others.

He stopped there before he became completely sidetracked. He decided he did love two women, but each in a different way. His earlier love for Helen, the kind he now felt for Sarah, had morphed into a caring kind of love. He cared about Helen's safety and happiness – he'd demonstrated that by dealing with the Roy character - but it wasn't the great welling, overpowering thing it had been. The snogging thing was driven largely by lust, albeit of an honourable kind – he realised that now – and by familiarity and the mood of the occasion.

He wondered if he were making excuses for his behaviour, and he'd just acquitted himself of that, when the phone rang. It couldn't be Sarah, could it?

'Frank Morrison.'

'Hello, Frank.' It was Helen.

'Hi, Helen. Are you okay?'

'I'm fine, thanks. I don't know if I dare ask about Sarah. I'm so sorry that happened when it did. I—'

'Stop there, Helen. It wasn't your fault. It was lots of things – I've just been making sense of it – but in all fairness, I made the first move.'

There was a pause, possibly while Helen tested her memory. 'I suppose you did. Anyway, is Sarah speaking to you yet?'

'She spoke to me this morning, but only to tell me to sod off. Not even Hutch can get through to her.'

'I'm sorry, Frank.'

He had to reassure her again. 'It was none of your—'

'I mean I'm sorry *for* you, for your difficulty, if you see what I mean.'

'Thanks, Helen, I do.'

'But we weren't actually kissing when she arrived. I'm a hundred percent sure of that. At least, I think I am.'

It was an unusual take on certainty, but one worthy of Helen. In any case, he didn't see how she could be sure. 'Whether we were or not,' he said, 'she told Hutch we were poised to dive under the duvet.'

'To be honest, I thought so too, just for a second or so. I'm sure we'd have regretted it.'

'It wasn't what I had in mind, Helen. Actually, I didn't have anything in mind. It was just the way things were after your ordeal, holding you in my arms like that, and... I must confess, I was reminded of happier times. That played its part as well.'

'Don't punish yourself, Frank. We both know it's over, and what happened was a one-off momentary slip. If I could do anything to put things right between you and Sarah....'

He couldn't let that happen. 'I think you'd do better to stay out of her sights for now,' he said. 'It doesn't help that her previous chap cheated on her in the most blatant way imaginable.'

'Poor woman. Happily, that's something I never experienced.' She paused for a moment, and asked, 'What are you going to do about Kate?'

'In what sense?'

'I gather she's very friendly with Sarah. Are you going to tell her before she comes home?'

He thought quickly. 'No,' he said, 'I'll leave it. If things are still the same when she arrives, I'll tell her then.' As the thought occurred to him, he said, 'The poor girl seems to make a habit of coming home to bad news, but I don't want to upset her at this stage, with second-year exams looming up, if they're not already in progress.'

'No, you're right, but something that won't upset her is the video of you on *Northern Scene*. I finally managed to watch it last week, and I've put it in a safe place for Kate to see when she comes home. I thought you were masterly, Frank.'

'Oh, thanks for that, Helen. I'd cringe if I ever saw it, but I'd never hear the last of it if I didn't let Kate watch it.'

'I know. Anyway, I think we've exhausted every possible topic, so I'll leave you in peace.'

'Okay. 'Bye, Helen. Thanks for phoning.'

''Bye, Frank.'

After laying his soul bare, he was more than ready to start work on the new drama set in the Midlands. After that, he had to make some adjustments to the programme for the Midsummer Ball.

16

A PROBLEM SHARED

On the 22nd June, with everyone assembled in the band room, Thomas was able to tell them that Vanessa's operation had gone ahead successfully the previous evening, and that she was comfortable as long as she didn't move too much.

'That will improve with time,' he assured them, speaking in guarded terms, as they were, after all, discussing 'women's things'.

'Excellent,' said Hutch. 'Frank's organised some flowers, so a few of us will call round some time tomorrow. When's visiting, Thomas?'

'Anytime, really, as it's a private hospital. Of course, you'll have to take pot luck, so to speak, on her not being in the bath or anything like that, but they'll warn you, so that should be all right.'

'We'll be very careful,' Hutch promised him. Hospital visiting was evidently a new experience for Thomas, and he was learning quickly.

'Time to go, ladies and gents,' said Frank as the minute hand approached the half-hour. He waited until the whole band was seated and ready before making his entrance. It was the first time in a year that they would be going on without Sarah, and he felt her absence keenly as he took his place at the piano for the band's signature number. It proved as popular as ever with the members, who greeted him enthusiastically when he approached the microphone to speak to them.

'Good evening, ladies and gentlemen, and welcome to the Midsummer Ball. This is a particularly special evening for the New Albion Dance Orchestra, as it's just a year since we first appeared here.' That earned an extra round of applause, and he went on to say, 'Let's start the evening in our usual way with a waltz by that master of melody Eric Coates. Let's dance to "By the Sleepy Lagoon".' He returned to the piano and counted the band into the number.

Now that he was concentrating on the music, his immediate preoccupation seemed to fade into the background, and he was able to give each number the attention it deserved. That was until they reached 'Love Walked In', which had come to mean a great deal to both Sarah and him, having been central to their relationship from the outset. Happily, it came shortly before the band went off for an extended half-time break, and another distraction presented itself.

He found Tim and Penny beside the buffet. Hilary was busy filling the long table with enticing and imaginative regional offerings, but she saw him and waved to him with a smile.

'It's a lovely gown, Penny,' said Frank, 'and you look perfect in it.'

'Why, thank you, kind sir. I'm quite bowled over, and what an excellent idea it was, too,' she said, accepting a brotherly kiss, 'to get this lady to take over the catering. And speaking of changing roles, where's your regular pianist? It's an important question, because I imagine you won't be able to come down to the floor and dance with me.'

'I'm afraid not, Penny. Vanessa's in hospital. She had an operation yesterday, and she'll be out of commission for some time.'

'Oh dear. What's the problem?'

'As far as I can make out, she's had the same thing mum had.'

'Oh, poor woman. Still, she'll be better for it in the long run, or so everyone says. Happily, I haven't had the experience – yet.' Changing the subject to a happier one, she asked, 'When's Kate coming home?'

'Very soon, I hope. She deputising, as usual.'

'Good for her.'

Speaking for the first time, Tim asked, 'Where's Sarah, Frank? We haven't heard her sing yet.'

It was the last thing Frank wanted to discuss, although it was inevitable that Sarah's absence would have been noted. 'No,' he said, 'she's not here tonight. I shan't tell you about it now, because it's a long, complicated story, but the fact is Sarah and I are no longer on speaking terms, and she wants nothing more to do with the band.'

'Oh, I'm sorry.'

'Yes, hard luck, Frank.'

Penny gave her husband a dismissive look and addressed Frank.

'It's no good inviting you over to talk about it, because I can't guarantee that the kids will be out of the way, so maybe we should meet somewhere for lunch.'

'I'm in London on Tuesday, but I'm free for the rest of the week.'

'How about Wednesday at the Copper Kettle? Say, one o'clock?'

'It sounds good to me, and I don't think Kate will have started work there by then.'

'When is she coming home?'

'Tuesday.'

'You're probably right.'

'I'll see you there.' He took his leave of them and returned to the band room.

* * *

The second half was easier, he reflected. After his initial difficulty, he'd been able to concentrate on the programme, and the awful business of his estrangement from Sarah had only returned to him when he made the short journey home.

He retired to bed as unhappy as ever, and when morning came and realisation took hold, he was no less miserable.

He had to explain himself to Sarah, and after waiting what seemed a reasonable length of time for Sunday morning, he dialled her number. Her phone rang only a few times before she picked it up.

'Hello.' She sounded quite cheery.

'Sarah, it's Frank.'

Her tone changed abruptly. 'I've nothing to say to you.'

'If you'll only give me a chance, I've got a lot to say to you. You got completely the wrong idea—'

'Save it. I've heard it all before.'

'It's not the same thing at—' He heard the click as the line closed, and knew his chance was gone. Utterly dejected, he replaced the receiver and sat for a while, disinclined to move, although he knew he had to get ready for the morning's band practice. It was the last thing he wanted to do, but ten innocent and deserving people would be expecting him to join them. Most of them were unaware of his problem; there was no reason why they should know about it, but after the success of the

Midsummer Ball, they would be more enthusiastic than ever to extend their repertoire.

The phone rang while he was washing up the coffee things, but he saw no point in hurrying to answer it. Whoever the caller was, it certainly wouldn't be Sarah.

Hanging up the tea towel, he went back to the studio and picked up the phone. 'Frank Morrison.'

'I was about to hang up. I thought you must have left already.' It was Helen.

'No, I'll be leaving in about five minutes.'

'Good. Is there anything to report?' Not surprisingly, she sounded tentative.

'Only that I tried phoning her this morning, but she was in no mood to listen. Her mind's made up.'

'I'm sorry, Frank.'

'Well, there's nothing I can do about it.'

'I don't suppose there is, but it doesn't make the situation any pleasanter. Actually, that wasn't my only reason for phoning you, awful though the situation is for you. Kate's coming home on Tuesday. I knew you'd want to know.'

'Of course. Thanks for telling me. As a matter of fact, I'm going to be in London on Tuesday, so if she's happy to leave it until the end of the day, she can travel back with me and save the fare. I'll be catching the six o'clock from King's Cross.'

'Oh, lovely. I'll let her know, or you can.'

'Okay, I'll try and get her on that awful payphone later today.'

* * *

After band practice, Frank and Hutch drove to the Duke of York's Nursing Home, where an obliging nurse took them to Vanessa's room and checked that she was ready to receive them. They found her happy and smiling.

'Hello, boys,' she said. 'Thank you for the lovely flowers. There they are, look.' She pointed to an arrangement in a vase on the chest of drawers. It looked most appealing, but Frank was no horticulturalist, so

116

he couldn't even begin to identify the flowers. 'Aren't they beautiful?' she asked.

'We're just glad to see you looking so well and happy,' Hutch told her.

'It'll be a while before I'm allowed to do much,' she said.

'Just concentrate on following doctor's orders and getting well,' said Frank. 'I'm filling in for you on the piano, so there's no problem there. Have you someone who can do your hoovering and things?'

'Yes,' she told him shyly, 'Tom's daily help is going to see to those things.'

'Good.' Frank tried not to smile too obviously. It was the first time they'd heard anyone refer to Thomas by a diminutive; he'd always been 'Thomas', or even 'Davies the Lip' in his native Dolgellau, but if Vanessa wasn't allowed a degree of intimacy, who was?

'How's the catering here?' asked Hutch.

'It's excellent. I'm even allowed lunch and dinner guests. You two could stay for lunch.' She looked at her watch and said, 'It's due in half-an-hour or so.'

'That's very kind of you,' said Frank, 'but I have a lot of work waiting for me.'

'Even on a Sunday?'

'Every day is a working day for me, Vanessa.' He reckoned, as well, that Thomas would be along soon, and he'd no wish to play gooseberry.

'And I appreciate your invitation,' said Hutch, 'but I'm expected elsewhere.'

They chatted with her until Thomas arrived. He'd been shopping for Vanessa, and they had things to discuss, so Frank and Hutch made their excuses and left.

When they reached the car, Frank leaned into the back and retrieved a card and a gift-wrapped package, which obviously contained a book, both of which he handed to Hutch. 'Happy birthday, Hutch,' he said. 'I remembered it this year.' He was still mortified about his omission the previous year.

'Thank you, Frank. This was unexpected, and it's much appreciated.'

'You're allowed to open it.'

'Okay. He slid his thumb beneath the folds of wrapping paper, peeling off the tape that secured them, and took out a copy of *Jerome Kern* by Gerald Bordman. 'Oh, I'm going to enjoy reading this. Thank you, Frank.' He patted Frank's arm appreciatively.

'You're welcome, Hutch.' He started the engine, and they drove off.

'I'll be seeing Sarah tonight. She's invited me over, as it's my birthday, so I'll do what I can, but I shan't make wild promises, Frank. You know how stubborn she can be.'

'Yes, I tried speaking to her this morning, but I ran into a brick wall. It's almost as if she doesn't want to know the truth.'

'Aye, that business last year left her badly scarred.' Changing the subject to a pleasanter one, he asked, 'Have you heard from little Katie lately? By my reckoning, she should be home about now.'

'Yes, she had some gigs in London, but she's coming home on Tuesday. I'll be in London, so I'm going to suggest she we travel back together. That way, she can do it first class and it won't cost her anything.'

* * *

Frank left it until two o'clock before trying the payphone number at the place where Kate currently lived.

A female voice answered, 'Yeah?'

It wasn't a good start. 'Hello. I'd like to speak to Kate Morrison, please.'

'Hang on. I'll see if she's in her room.'

Frank hung on, and the girl, whoever she was, returned.

'She's gone out.'

'Thank you. I'll try again later.'

'Right.' The phone went down without another word from the girl who'd answered his call. He decided to wait until early evening. Meanwhile, work was there to be done, so he set about it.

* * *

He was more successful with his next attempt, because it was Kate who answered the phone.

'Hello?'

'Is that Kate?'

'Hello, Dad.'

'Hello, darling. Your mum tells me you're coming home on Tuesday.'

'Yes, I've been busy since the end of term. I've been doing some session work.'

'Good for you.' It probably would be, as well. 'Listen, I'll be in town on Tuesday, and I'll be catching the six o'clock from King's Cross. If you can wait until then, we can travel home together.'

'Great!'

He wondered how many parents would enjoy such a wholehearted response, and the thought made him very happy. 'I'll reserve two seats,' he said.

'Even better.'

'Listen, darling, I'm sick of doing battle with that payphone. I've had it in mind for some time to get one of those mobile phones, like Penny's.'

'A poserphone? "Buy ICI, sell Unilever!"'

'You can mock, but I think it'll be very useful. I have it in mind to buy you one as well.'

'Oh, Dad. On reflection, thank you. Suddenly, it makes a lot of sense, and it's not at all posey.'

'Good.' Here was one person who was easy to persuade. I'll see you at King's Cross on Tuesday in time for the six o'clock departure.'

'Okay. 'Bye, Dad.'

''Bye, darling.'

He put the phone down and went on with his work, only breaking off to eat a sandwich. He knew he should eat more sensibly, but some things were more pressing, and when the door buzzer sounded, he looked up irritably. He was reminded that on Hutch's last birthday, Norman, Geoff and Vernon had called *en route* for the Coach and Horses. It couldn't be them again, surely. He went over to the intercom.

'Hello.'

'Frank, it's Norman and Geoff. We've come to take you for a pint.'

History was repeating itself after all, like the thing the Americans called 'Groundhog Day.'

'I appreciate the thought, Norman, but it's not a good time. I'm fairly busy.' As he spoke, he remembered having much the same conversation with Norman twelve months earlier.

'If you're only *fairly* busy, there'll be no harm done, so come for a pint with us or we'll feel rejected.'

'Of course you will, Norman.' Smiling to himself, he said, 'All right, I'm coming down.'

The only missing element when he saw them on the doorstep was Vernon, and that was sad but inevitable.

'Hello, Frank,' said Norman, 'we thought we'd come and take you out of yourself again.'

'Aye,' said Geoff, 'a chance to lubricate your problem.' He ignored a frown from Norman at giving away what was meant to be a secret, at least for the time being.

'Somebody's been talking,' said Frank, crouching to stroke Ida.

'Not really,' Norman assured him. 'Hutch just said you needed cheering up a bit. He's at Sarah's place tonight. It's his birthday, you know.'

'I know,' said Frank, falling in beside them. 'I remembered it this year.'

They reached the Coach and Horses, which had undergone extensive alterations since Frank was last there.

'It's gone the way of many a decent pub,' said Norman.

'Aye,' said Geoff, 'open-plan noise.' He added for good measure, 'And general buggering about.'

'That too,' agreed Norman. 'Still, there's not a thing we can do about it, short of going thirsty.' He and Ida led the way into what had been the bar lounge.

'Nothing ever stays the same,' said Frank.

'Some things are dependable,' said Norman as Anthea, the barmaid, came to greet them, 'and Anthea's as dependable as any.'

'Good evening, gents.'

'Good evening, Anthea. Three-and-a-half pints of Sam Smith's and an ashtray, please.'

'No problem.' Leaning over the bar, she said, 'Hello, Ida, yours is on its way, love.' She pulled the drinks and put a clean, glass ashtray on the bar for Ida.

'Thanks, Anthea.' Norman picked up two of the pints, and the others brought the rest, including the ashtray, to a table.

'Hutch said you were down in the dumps, Frank,' said Geoff, 'but he didn't say why. I know I'm being nosey, but has it got anything to do with young Sarah not coming to band practices?'

Norman shook his head in despair but made no comment.

'Yes, it has.'

'So the bricks are up again between you two?'

'Be fair, Geoff. The last time was a year ago, before we got to know each other properly.'

'Now that you've teased it out of him so subtly, Geoff,' said Norman, 'put your crowbar down for a minute and let him decide for himself whether he wants to talk about it or not.'

'I don't mind telling you about it.' It was actually easier than pretending everything was all right. He wondered quite how to tell the story, and settled for the bare bones. 'Helen had been through a difficult experience,' he told them, 'being pestered by chap when she wasn't interested in him, but he wouldn't take "no" for an answer. Anyway, I sorted things out for her, and she was so relieved that, as she left my flat, we had a hug – nothing naughty – but it was unfortunate that Sarah turned up just then and got the wrong idea.'

'Can't you persuade her she got the wrong idea?' asked Geoff.

'No, she won't listen. Hutch is at her place tonight, and he said he'd have a go at making her see reason, but it's odds-on he'll come away defeated. She's a very stubborn woman.'

'Just out of normal, bloodthirsty interest,' said Norman, 'how did you sort out that bugger who was being a nuisance with Helen?'

That was one thing that Frank could smile about. 'I took him round the back of the library and threw him down the slope. It was a hard landing.'

'Was that all?'

'I did it three times before he saw sense.'

'I'd have brayed the living daylights out of him if I'd been in your shoes.'

'I know you would, Norman, but I decided to save that as a deterrent. I told him that's what I'd do if he didn't stop bothering Helen, and he saw my point.'

'I wish I'd been there,' said Geoff. He wasn't particularly aggressive, but he had a soft spot for Helen.

'I wonder,' said Norman, clearly deep in thought.

'What are you wondering about?' asked Frank.

'I was just thinking, if Hutch fails to get through to Sarah tonight....'

'It's not the object of his visit,' said Frank reasonably. 'I imagine she's invited him over for his birthday.'

'Of course, but if he doesn't succeed in smoothing the path of true love, I wonder who else might be able to act as go-between.'

'Little Katie gets on well with her, doesn't she?' Geoff was at least trying to be helpful.

'No, Geoff, I don't want Kate to get involved.'

'Quite right,' said Norman. 'It's not good for a youngster to get caught in the crossfire.'

'In that case,' said Geoff, 'I'll get the drinks in.' He stood up and went to the bar.

'No,' said Norman, 'but it's worth thinking about. I mean somebody lending a hand. I mean, without interfering too much.'

'Maybe it wasn't meant to happen.'

Norman didn't answer that. Instead, he asked, 'How are things between you and Helen, if you don't mind me asking?'

'We're on good terms. Apart from the episode with the boring tax collector, we've gone through the whole thing without too many harsh words. You know what the problem was, don't you?'

'That spiteful crone of a mother-in-law, wasn't it?'

'That's right. She caused all the bother.'

'Aye, it's a shame,' said Geoff, joining them with two pints in one hand and a pint in the other. 'I didn't bring one for Ida this time,' he said. 'It looks like she's got enough to be going on with.'

'Aye,' said Norman, 'I don't like her to have too much, or it makes her daft.'

'Yes, it's a lot to ask of a little dog, to drink responsibly.'

'Speaking of love's young dream,' said Norman, moving the conversation on, 'young Mark's started seeing that lass who did the catering for the Midsummer Ball.'

'Good for him,' said Frank. 'She's really nice. I sponsored her to run the London Marathon.' He remembered that Hilary had been a bone of unspoken contention with Sarah. She needn't have worried.

'Aye well, she's running around with my grandson, now.'

Smiling, Frank said, 'When Kate saw him at the Exchange, she said he was too big to be a grandson.'

'He probably seemed so, but his dad's the same, a bit like me, really, but he lacks my reserve and sophisticated charm. When's little Katie coming home?'

'Tuesday. She's been doing some session work in London. It's all grist to the mill, I suppose.'

'She's got a rare talent,' said Geoff.

'Yes, it's something to be thankful for.' He'd been thinking about that. If things never improved between Sarah and him, he still had a lot of joy in his life, and it would still be there when Sarah was a memory. He was happier, though, when Geoff changed the subject.

'Are we staying in the same hotel as before?' he asked.

'No,' Norman told him, 'Hutch got a better deal. Apparently, we're staying at the President this time.'

It was good news for Frank, who'd not been looking forward to staying at the hotel where everything had begun with Sarah. Maybe it was time he moved on. His watch told him it was also time to buy the next round of drinks. The diversion had been good for him.

17

KIND WORDS

After a straightforward session at the studio, Frank walked to King's Cross Station, where he made himself reasonably conspicuous so that Kate would be able to find him. Soon, a queue began to form for the six o'clock, so he hung around at the back, as he had reserved seats. Kate joined him at about ten to six.

'Hi, Dad!' She rested her bag and violin case and kissed him. 'What's new?'

'I'll tell you when we're on the train.'

'Did you have a good session?'

'Yes, thanks. It went quite smoothly.'

The gate opened, and the queue began to move forward. 'At last,' said Kate, who had yet to learn patience. 'Are we travelling first class?'

'Of course. The studio's paying for it.'

'That's what I like about travelling with you.'

'And I thought it was the pleasure of my company.'

'Oh yes, but it's so much pleasanter on soft cushions.'

As they walked through the gate, he asked, 'What kind of materialist have I bred?'

'The sybaritic kind.'

They boarded the nearest first-class coach and walked through until they found their reserved seats.

'Right,' said Kate, taking the window seat, 'tell me what's been happening.'

'It's not nice.'

'Oh dear. Don't keep me in suspense.'

'The long and short of it is that Sarah and I are no longer seeing each other.'

'Oh no! Why not?'

It seemed he had to tell the story again, albeit the expurgated version. 'Your mum was receiving too much unwanted attention from her ex... boyfriend.'

'Not that Roy creep?'

'That self-same creep,' he confirmed. 'She was terribly upset by the time she told me about it, so I had words with him.'

'Was it like the time you spoke to those creeps in the Copper Kettle?' Evidently, the embarrassment she'd felt on that occasion had softened with the passage of time.

'Very similar.'

'Good old Dad. So, what happened next?'

He had to tell her now. 'She came to see me at the flat, to thank me, because she hadn't been able to say much at the library, where it all happened, and she was so relieved and emotional that as she was leaving we had an innocent hug by way of celebration, and that was just as Sarah arrived. Naturally, she suspected the worst and she won't listen to the truth.'

Kate considered the situation in silence, and then asked, 'Would it help if I spoke to Sarah?'

'It's kind of you to offer, but no, darling, I don't think so. I really don't think you should get mixed up in it. Sarah suffered badly with her last chap. He cheated on her quite blatantly, and it must have left a lasting hurt.'

'I know about that. She said you were different and she could trust you.'

'And now she feels disillusioned and betrayed. By this time, she'll be convinced your mum and I are back together.'

'And there's no chance of that, I suppose?' There was a hint of wistfulness in that question. It was only to be expected.

'No, we're still good friends, but we're not going to get together again. That would really give Medusa something to work on.' Seeing the steward with the trolley heading their way, he asked, 'Would you like cup of railway coffee to cheer you up? Have you eaten yet?'

'I'll eat later, but yes, please to the coffee. It'll make me appreciate yours so much more.'

'You're becoming a coffee snob, Kate.' She usually accused him of that.

'Guess who taught me.' Then, more as a diversion than for any other reason, she asked, 'Has anything nice been happening?'

'Let me see.' He broke off to speak to the steward. 'Two white coffees, please. No sugar in either.' He took the coffees and handed the steward the money. 'Thank you.'

'Thanks, Dad.'

'You're welcome, darling. Medusa would say I'm spoiling you, but she's capable of saying anything hurtful.'

'Agreed.'

'I spoke to your mum about food. This train gets into Leeds at eight-twenty, which is a bit late for us all to go anywhere, so we'll call at the chippie on the way home.'

'Oh, good. I haven't had fish and chips for ever. They're not the same in London.' Having made that observation, she returned to the previous topic and asked, 'What good things were you going to tell me about?'

'Ah yes, well, the first thing is that Vanessa Wainwright is recovering nicely from her operation.'

'Oh good. What has she had done?'

'Women's things.'

She nodded sagely. 'Hysterectomy, right.'

'You're more clued up than I am, Kate.'

'I should hope so. It's a woman's thing, after all.'

'The only other thing I can think of is that I'm meeting Penny at the Copper Kettle for lunch tomorrow.'

'Great. I'm not starting there until Saturday, not that it makes any difference. Penny will cheer you up, anyway. She's good at that.'

Forty years' experience told him she was right.

* * *

He arrived at the Copper Kettle ten minutes before he was due to meet Penny, and ordered coffee. The waitress was new; he hadn't seen the girl who'd worked there with Kate, for some time, in fact, since the incident when he'd warned off the two creeps, and he

126

imagined the place must have an unpleasant association for her. If they'd treated Kate the way they treated her, he wouldn't have been so restrained. On reflection, he imagined he would have been banned from the place, at least. He actually preferred not to think about it, and he was still not thinking about it when Penny arrived, remarkably early by her standards. She looked particularly cool in a simple, light-blue dress.

'Penny,' he said, leaving his seat to greet her with a kiss, 'it's good to see you anyway, but bright and early is a bonus.'

'Don't be rotten, Frank. I'm not late for everything.' She took a seat opposite him. 'How's Kate?'

'Fine. She came home with me on the train last night. She'll be starting here at the weekend. 'How are the boys?'

'Gary's getting ready for Sports Day, which matters a lot more than work in the classroom and, between "A" levels, Stephen's practising the laid-back effect. Last week he answered the door to take a delivery and leaned back so casually he missed the doorframe altogether and fell on his backside. It served him right.'

The waitress came to them, and Penny said, 'Will you give me another five minutes? I haven't decided yet.' Menu indecision was another of her foibles. Frank ordered a cafetiere of coffee for two. 'Kids go through funny phases,' he said, 'although I have to admit the laid-back effect is a new one on me.'

'Don't you ever wish you'd had a son as well as Kate? I mean a sensible one?'

'Not for one moment. Medusa has quite enough ammunition with Kate.'

'Hasn't she retired from the fray, yet, to celebrate the divorce?'

'Not for one minute. She's terrified that Helen and I will have a fairytale reconciliation.' As an afterthought, he added, 'It seems to be a popular idea just now.'

'Is it completely out of the question?'

'Yes, it is. As long as that vicious old bat is working her from behind, I doubt if Helen can have a successful relationship with anyone without emigrating, and I can't see Medusa letting her do that. She wouldn't even let her go to London to Kate's recital.'

'Poor girl. Poor Kate as well.'

The waitress brought a large cafetiere and fresh cups. She asked, 'Are you ready to order yet?

'I shall be in a minute,' said Penny, re-examining the menu.

'I'll give you a bit more time,' offered the waitress.

'No,' said Frank, 'she's at her best under pressure.'

Penny gave him an admonishing look and said, 'I'd like the prawn salad, please.'

'And I'd like the quiche Lorraine salad, please.'

The waitress made a note of their order and left gratefully.

'Okay, Frank, tell me about the row between you and Sarah.'

'It was about nothing at all. We were having a celebratory hug in my doorway when Sarah arrived and got the wrong idea.'

'Was it just a hug?' Penny was adept at decoding his occasional euphemisms.

'I kissed her as well,' he admitted, 'but that was before Sarah arrived.' He reflected, and said, 'She might have seen something from her car.'

'It was unfortunate timing, and not the best location. Am I allowed to ask what you were celebrating?'

Frank was tired of telling the story, but he felt obliged to be open with Penny. 'A chap Helen had seen a couple of times seemed to think it was the romance of the century. She didn't want to see him again, but he had other ideas, and he kept doorstepping her at the library and at home.'

'Phone calls as well?'

'No, he only knew her maiden name, and the home phone number's still in my name, but he had her worried, all the same.' He broke off when the waitress brought their order to the table. 'Thank you,' he said.

'Can I get you anything else?'

'No thanks.'

'Enjoy your meal.'

They thanked her, and when she'd gone, Penny said, 'I take it you dealt with it, hence the celebratory hug?'

'Yes.'

The situation evidently evoked memories for Penny, because she asked, 'Do you remember the time Alan Duncan insulted me?'

'Vividly.' It was impossible to forget.

'He called me "Second-Hand Rose" because he knew my school clothes were from the hand-me-down shop. I was heartbroken, mainly because it was an insult to Mum, and she didn't deserve it.'

'I know.' Frank remembered two girls – they always did things in twos – seeking him out and saying to him in the righteous and urgent way girls had, "Your Penny's really upset, Frank. She's crying because of what that horrible Alan Duncan called her." When he learned what Alan Duncan had said, he lost no time in finding him and leaving him writhing in the schoolyard. 'It cost me a caning,' he recalled, 'but it was worth it.'

She reached for his hand and gave it a squeeze. 'Oh, Frank, my knight in armour,' she said. 'Helen's, too, by the sound of it.'

'I had to warn him off, Penny. She had no one else to turn to.'

'So, Sarah put two and two together and made five-and-a-half.'

'And she's completely intractable.' Hopelessly, he said, 'I really don't think I understand women, and Sarah's harder to fathom than most.'

'The trouble is you worry about not understanding women. You might do better taking a leaf out of Tim's book. He gave up on us a long time ago, and nowadays he just settles for a life of surprises. I can't help wondering, though, if Sarah might be punishing you for what someone else once did.'

'I've wondered about that, too. Still, it's all academic, now.'

'Yes.' Penny was thoughtful for a moment, and then she said, 'I'd offer to speak to her on your behalf, but I hardly know her.'

'Thanks, Penny, but Hutch is probably the most important person in her life, and if he couldn't get through to her, I don't think anyone could. I think my best course is to draw the curtains on the whole thing and put it down to experience.'

'If you say so. Meanwhile, life goes on. When's the screening of the film?'

'August, at the London Film Festival.'

18

JULY

DEAD END

Being a man of his word, Frank took Kate to the Carphone Warehouse and signed two contracts. They each came away with a Motorola MicroTAC phone and a quantity of information, little of which meant anything to either of them. They celebrated later, however, by phoning each other from opposite sides of the road. As Frank pointed out, to do it from the same side would be silly.

They arrived at the post-marital home in time for Helen's mother to pronounce judgement on those who waste money on silly, trendy toys, and for her father to agree with her. Frank's response was so candid that they decided to leave rather than suffer further abuse.

'The point is,' said Frank when they were gone, 'that it's going to be very useful for business, and Kate's going to feel a damned sight safer in the wicked city.'

'You don't have to convince me,' said Helen as she filled the kettle, 'and I agree about Kate being safer.'

'Excellent. So, how are things with you? Have you heard from Roy Rogers since I whispered in his ear?'

'*Robinson*, actually, and no, thank goodness.' She corrected herself and said, 'Well, thanks to you, actually.'

'Good.'

'Who's Roy Rogers?' asked Kate.

'A singing cowboy. I think he's still alive, but I gather he's stopped singing.' He treated her to a few lines of 'A Four-Legged Friend'.

'I wish I hadn't asked, now,' she said, 'but I'm glad he's stopped singing.'

130

'When I was a lad, my cowboy hero was Tex Ritter. He was a singer, too. I didn't see him all that often, because the afternoon matinee cost sixpence a time.'

'Maybe you could get him on video,' suggested Helen.

'Thanks, Helen, I hadn't thought of that.'

'Is sixpence Stone-Age for "six P?", asked Kate not altogether innocently.

'No, it was... two-and-a-half P.'

'Were you as poor as that?'

'Poorer. There were some weeks we couldn't afford to go, and it always cost twice that, anyway, because Penny came, too.'

'And here you are,' said Helen, 'having lashed out goodness knows how much on two mobile phones.'

'They'll be worth every penny,' he assured her. 'Or should that be every P?'

Kate's thoughts were still with Frank's boyhood. 'If Tex Whatsit was your hero,' she asked, 'how did you come to invite Wyatt Earp and the other two into your studio?'

'Ah, Tex Ritter was a celluloid hero, whereas Wyatt, George and Billy came from the pages of various books, some more reliable than others, I have to say.'

'I'm glad you mentioned that, Frank,' said Helen. 'You've reminded me about one of your old books that you left behind when you moved out. I'll go and get it.'

'I thought I'd cleared everything out,' said Frank. 'I can't imagine what it might be.

Helen returned with his copy of *Kit Carson's Autobiography*. 'There you are,' she said. 'You can curl up with that tonight.'

'Thank you, Helen. It's like being reunited with an old friend.'

'Who was Kit Carson?' asked Kate.

'He was a famous frontiersman, fur trapper, trail scout and indian agent.'

'I don't know what he did as an agent with the *Native Americans*,' said Helen, emphasising the correct name, as she usually did to correct her politically-incorrect ex-husband, 'although I suspect the worst, but I can't see anything to admire in a fur trapper.'

'Don't worry, darling. I'm taking it away.' As he spoke, he realised he'd used the d-word purely out of habit, and both Helen and Kate had noticed it and reacted in much the same way, with the merest lift of an eyebrow. They were alike in many ways. 'Anyway,' he said, covering his slip as best he could, 'I should get back to work.'

'At six o'clock in the evening?'

'I have to make up for lost time, Helen. Thanks for the tea.' He kissed them both, picked up the book and made his departure.

* * *

He was still working a few days later, when Hutch phoned at a little after eleven. As soon as Frank heard his voice, he looked at his watch. He'd agreed to take Hutch to see Vanessa, but then he remembered that it wasn't until two.

'Hello, Hutch. I thought for a minute I was going to be late.'

'Relax, lad. She's coming home today. In fact, she may well be back now.'

'Good for her. I'm glad she's on the mend.'

'That's what I was ringing to tell you.'

'Thanks, Hutch.' Then he remembered his new acquisition. 'By the way, I've got a new mobile number.' Have you got a pencil handy?'

'Just a minute. I had one a while ago when I was writing my shopping list, and that's another…. Aye, here it is.'

Frank gave him the number, and in true military fashion, Hutch read it back to him.

'That's right. What were you saying about your shopping list?'

'Oh, just that Sarah phoned to say she's got a day full of meetings, so she can't come over. I can go on the bus, so there's no problem.'

'Don't do that, Hutch. I'll come over and take you.'

'Nay, lad, you're busy enough.'

'I'm not too busy to make a trip to the supermarket. I'll be over in a jiff.'

* * *

Shopping with Hutch was as straightforward as life could ever be. Even though he usually left the actual shopping to Sarah, he planned his list aisle by aisle, so that the whole job was accomplished in very little time.

'Do you fancy lunch at the Copper Kettle?' asked Frank. 'Kate's working there again.'

'Is she? Only if you let me pay.'

'We'll discuss that later,' said Frank opening the car to stow Hutch's shopping in the back. 'We can walk through the ginnel from here.'

'Aye, I remember.'

As they walked through the passageway between two buildings, Frank said, 'I was here on Wednesday with Penny.'

'Oh, how's she keeping?'

'Busy as ever, but always ready for a chat.'

'You know, you and Penny have the same kind of easy relationship as I always did with Phyllis.'

'I know, Hutch.' Phyllis was Hutch's only sister as well as Norman's wife. Frank didn't want to dwell on the subject, so he was relieved when they reached the Copper Kettle.

The first person they saw was Kate. There were only a few customers, so she was able to greet them properly.

'We've been shopping,' Frank told her.

'Aye, your dad took pity on me.'

'Oh, couldn't—?' She checked herself, saying hurriedly, 'He needs a break from work every now and then. What can I get you?'

'Coffee for now, please, and we'll have a look at the menu.'

'No problem,' she said, writing on her pad. 'Everything on the menu is available.' She left them and went to attend to the coffee.

'You know, Frank,' said Hutch, 'when I think of how well little Katie's doing at the Guildhall, she reminds me of you when you were at Cullington Secondary School. In fact, both you and Penny did well.'

Frank smiled at the memory. 'We were among the first there to be allowed to take "O" levels.'

'You both got "A" levels as well, didn't you? You'd need them for college.'

'That was after it turned comprehensive.'

'It's a far cry from my schooldays. We had to leave at fourteen and get our hands mucky.'

'But you did well, Hutch.'

'Aye, I never made a career in engineering, but I did all right as a musician.'

Kate came to their table, and they gave her their order. When she'd gone, Hutch said, 'It doesn't seem two minutes since she was a toddler.'

'That's what I was thinking when I went to her recital at the Guildhall.' It was a treasured memory.

'You must have been proud, Frank.'

'As proud as a peacock – and a peahen. I had to be both, because Helen wasn't allowed to go in case she fell in love with me again and disgraced the Kent family name a second time.'

'It's spilt milk, Frank. Let it lie.'

'Right enough, but they'll have something else to complain about when *Hey Young Fella* goes on general release.'

'Yes.' That reminded Hutch of something. 'All the names are in, and we've filled a chara.'

'Everybody?'

'Yes, including Vanessa. I've persuaded Sarah to go, but don't hold out any hopes of a replay.' In answer to an odd look from Frank, he said, 'I'm not daft. I know what happened at Christmas.'

Fortunately, at that point, Kate arrived with their order. 'Can I get you anything else?' she asked.

Hutch shook his head, and Frank said, 'No, thank you, darling.' He ignored a woman at a nearby table, who scowled at him.

Hutch noticed her and whispered to Frank, 'What have you done to upset that woman on your right?'

'Search me.'

Similarly at a loss, Kate went on her way. The woman was still scowling, so Frank gave her a smile, which only caused her frown to deepen.

'You don't care, do you?'

'No, Hutch, I've been scowled at by professionals, and that woman is certainly no match for Medusa the Gorgon.' Looking at the cafetiere, he asked, 'Shall we have some more coffee?'

'If you can spare the time, Frank.'

'I'm happy to, Hutch.' He caught Kate's eye as she delivered the bill to the scowling woman, and when she came to them, he asked for some more coffee.

'Certainly.'

'Thank you, darling.'

The scowling woman put her money on the plate, and spoke to Kate before leaving. When Kate returned with the coffee, Frank asked her, 'What was the problem with old sourpuss at the next table?'

'She didn't approve of you calling me "darling". I told her you were my dad, but it didn't make her any happier. Sorry, Dad.'

'Don't apologise, Kate. I'm used to it, remember?'

Hutch said, 'Yes, you must be bullet-proof by now.'

They continued to chat until Hutch said, 'I really am keeping you from your work, Frank. We should be making tracks.'

'You're probably right.'

'I'll just pay a call before we go.'

Frank waited until Hutch was out of the room before calling Kate. 'Will you give me the bill before Hutch comes back?' he asked.

'No problem.' She took the bill from the desk and handed it to him.

'Thanks,' he said, putting his money on the plate. 'That's fine.'

'Thanks, Dad!'

'Keep your voice down, darling. We don't want anyone to get the wrong idea.'

'I should think not.'

Hutch returned as Kate was taking the money to the till. 'I said I was paying,' he protested.

'Oh, yes, you did,' said Frank, feigning recollection, 'but it's paid for now.' They took their leave of Kate and returned to the car.

'I'm grateful to you for this, Frank,' said Hutch on the way home.

'Not at all. If you're ever stuck for a lift, let me know.'

'I appreciate that, but you're busy enough.'

'All right,' said Frank, 'let's not argue.'

They drove the rest of the way without disagreement, but when they entered Hutch's street, they found a familiar car outside his house.

'Let me carry the stuff in, Frank, and then you can get away.'

'No, it's no trouble.' He didn't think Sarah would keep him talking.

As soon as Hutch opened the door, Frank heard her say, 'I tried phoning you, but you were out.' She sounded terse, and Frank could only imagine it was because she'd seen his car draw up outside.

'Frank offered to take me, Sarah. Come in, Frank.'

Frank stepped into the kitchen and put the carriers down. He asked, 'Can we talk, Sarah?'

'No.' She swept past him to get to the door.

'All right, have it your own way. I shan't ask you again.' He apologised to Hutch, even though the unpleasantness wasn't of his making, and walked out to his car. Sarah seemed to be struggling to start hers, but he knew she wouldn't appreciate an offer of help from him.

19

LIMELIGHT AND REJECTION

Frank sat beside Geoff on the journey to London. Kate was with Dan, and Sarah was at the front of the coach, with Hutch, who was probably feeling as embarrassed as Frank.

Eventually, Andy, who had driven them to various gigs, and who was now a fan, dropped them at the President Hotel before parking the coach. The place was busy, as was to be expected during the London Film Festival, and Hutch had done well to make the booking. Frank heard one of the staff give Sarah the key for a first-floor room, and when he checked in, he found he was on the third floor. He imagined she would be grateful for the two storeys that separated them.

It was difficult, being in the same hotel, and he was sure others would find the situation awkward at times. To make matters worse, Frank found himself questioning his feelings again. He'd told Sarah that he wouldn't try to speak to her again, and he'd felt at the time that he was finally closing the curtains on their relationship. It seemed the wisest thing to do, but it did nothing to ease the hurt.

When they went in to dinner, he noticed that she and Hutch were three tables away, and he saw her look fleetingly in his direction several times during the meal. Fortunately, Geoff and Norman had plenty to say, and they kept him entertained with their reminiscences both during and after dinner.

* * *

The next day, in Leicester Square, was easier because there was a great deal more going on. Naturally, the producers and the director were in the spotlight along with the author of the original novel, and the star of the film, eighteen-year-old Brett Isaac. Frank wondered if his parents had foreseen a career for him in the film industry, to bless him with a name like that. He seemed a nice enough lad, though, maybe a bit full of himself, but that was only to be expected.

The procession went on, until the band were summoned. Frank understood that it was only because of the unusual nature of the music that the songwriters and musicians were invited, and he wondered if Mark and Lionel, the lyricists, also felt as honoured as the producers intended.

Before long, Kirstie Edwards of *Northern Focus* and *Northern Scene* spotted him. She was interviewing Sarah and Dan, and she beckoned him to join them. Feeling a little awkward, he negotiated the camera crew and stood beside her.

'And here is Frank Morrison,' she told her viewers, 'composer of countless film and TV scores as well as some of the songs in this film. I expect you're quite excited, Frank.'

'Yes, this kind of thing doesn't happen every day.' He hated being in the limelight and wished she'd get on with the interview and let him go.

'Now, you had to write some of the songs from scratch, didn't you? That must have drawn heavily on your creative skills.'

'It was a challenge, Kirstie, but with two excellent singers to work with and, of course, the boys and girls in the band, I was in the best company possible.'

Turning to Dan, she asked, 'How did you come to be involved, Dan?'

Looking terrified, he said, 'I'd already sung with the band, and I suppose I came with the package, really.'

'I think you're being very modest, Dan, but let's turn to Sarah, who also sang on the soundtrack. 'What's your story, Sarah?'

'I don't think anyone else was available,' she said, trying not to look at Frank as she spoke. 'I remember Frank phoning me and asking if I'd do the gig, and I was quite taken aback, having never done anything like this before, but Frank was very helpful in teaching me the songs.'

'Of course, and you're training for a career in show business, aren't you, Dan?'

'In music and drama, yes.'

'And there's a connection between you and Sarah, isn't there?'

Sarah said self-consciously, 'Dan's a student at the college where I work.'

'So you all know each other, and presumably you're the best of friends. Let's go now to someone I remember from the original news item. Here's Ida, who goes everywhere with the band.'

Frank was grateful to Ida for the distraction. 'Well done, you two,' he said. 'Enjoy the film.'

'Thanks, Frank,' said Dan, 'and thanks again for the gig.'

'Yes,' said Sarah with rather less enthusiasm, 'thank you, Frank.'

'You're both welcome.' He looked to the head of the line, where he was relieved to see the stars, the director and the producers entering the cinema. They followed on. Frank had intended finding a seat some distance from Sarah, but as soon as he'd entered the theatre, he was taken by an usher and shown to his allotted seat, which happened to be next to Sarah's. As he sat beside her, he said discreetly, 'I didn't organise the seating.'

She whispered, 'I know.'

For a moment, he considered swapping seats with Dan, who was on his other side, but Dan would probably have felt awkward about it, so he settled for the arrangement as it was.

When everyone was settled, there was a speech by one of the producers, the lights came down, and the long-awaited film began.

Remembering as he did his childhood in reduced circumstances, Frank found the film very touching, and Brett Isaac's performance was superb. There was a moment of nostalgia, at least for the band, when some children were sledging, accompanied by one of Vernon Waterhouse's glorious improvisations. But then the warm, intimate sound of Dan's voice broke the spell with its own, and Frank patted his hand to congratulate him.

The next sequence featured Frank's song 'Feeling Blue and Longing for Your Smile', sung by Sarah. It worked beautifully against the scene, and as it came to its end, he was about to congratulate her when he saw tears in her eyes. Taking a pack of tissues from his pocket, he pulled one out and placed it in her hand with a gentle squeeze. They weren't on speaking terms, but that didn't mean he couldn't be sensitive towards her.

By the time the film reached its end, Frank had donated the rest of the tissues to her. Clearly, the story, the performance or the music meant a great deal to her. As they made their way out, she said, 'Thanks for the tissues. It was silly of me.'

'Not at all. It was a very touching film.'

'I mean it was silly of me not to bring any.'

She had him there, but when he looked around again she was gone, leaving Dan as embarrassed as ever.

* * *

The journey home was easier for Frank in that he was no longer anticipating difficulty with Sarah. She was safely in the front of the coach with Hutch. Possibly overcome by the excitement of the day, Geoff was fast asleep against the window, and Frank was alone with his thoughts. One of those thoughts was that he had to stop thinking about Sarah. He had to keep reminding himself that all that was over, he was forty-two and he had much of his life ahead of him. It was easier decided upon than it was to enact, however, and he was grateful when Kate came down the coach to speak to him.

'Can I have a word, Dad?'

'Of course you can. What's bothering you?'

'It's Dan. He hasn't been asked yet to pay his contribution to the trip, and it's worrying him. You know he's living on a shoestring, don't you?'

'Yes, I do. Do you want me to have a word with him?'

'Will you?'

He eased himself out of his seat, being careful not to disturb Geoff's slumbers, and followed Kate to the front of the coach. Sarah and Hutch sat on the opposite side of the aisle and two seats further back. When she saw Frank she turned her head deliberately and looked out of the window.

'What's all this about paying for the trip, Dan?' he asked.

'Oh, hello, Frank. I was just saying I hadn't been asked to pay anything yet. Hutch told me there was a special rate for students, but he didn't say what it was.'

'All right, I'll put you out of your misery. You don't have to pay anything.'

'Nothing at all?'

'Not a farthing. Kate hasn't paid anything. Didn't she tell you?'

'I thought you'd pay hers.'

'Not a bit of it. I spoil her enough already.' Having set Dan's mind at ease, he turned to return to his seat, but Hutch stopped him.

'Was Dan asking about paying?' he asked.

'Yes, I've told him he's nothing to pay.'

'Good lad, Frank. It was kind of you.'

'Not at all. Keep it under your hat, Hutch.' Trying not even to glance at Sarah, he re-joined Geoff, who, if not exactly in the arms of Morpheus, was no doubt keeping that deity awake with his snoring.

* * *

Once more in possession of Kit Carson's Autobiography, Frank photocopied a portrait of his hero, put it into a frame and hung it beside that of Billy the Kid. In doing so, it occurred to him, not for the first time, that an excellent look-alike to play Carson's part in a film would have been Errol Flynn. Unfortunately, though, Flynn had rendered himself unavailable for the part by dying prematurely in 1959. Frank remembered checking the date when he bought the video of *They Died With Their Boots On.* In any case, he decided, films about western heroes were unlikely to be popular in the current, politically-correct climate, so any actor seeking to take on Flynn's mantle would have to look elsewhere for a role.

Another kind of correctness had been imposed by the Town and Country Planning Act passed only a year previously, and that was of current interest because of the proposed refurbishment of the Wool Exchange.

As full members of the Exchange Club, Frank and Hutch learned that the plaster mouldings and cornices must be preserved in their original form and material, and that the band platform was also protected. The only argument was about the paintwork, which could be refreshed, although some members were bored with the Art Deco colours in the ballroom and favoured a change.

'They can't change the colours,' Frank insisted. 'Anything else would be wrong.' Hutch had phoned him at a busy time, but the business of the ballroom was also important. 'I'll make sure Penny comes to the next meeting of the Exchange Club, and then she can at least offer a professional opinion. I know she's keen to preserve the Art Deco look.'

'That's a good idea, and something else we need to do, Frank, is find somewhere to practise while the work's going on and until the ballroom stops smelling of paint.'

'I suppose anywhere will do in the short term.' It seemed fairly obvious to Frank.

'I've heard one suggestion, but it might not meet with your approval.'

'I can't imagine what you mean.'

'On the way back from London, Sarah suggested Beckworth College. She doesn't think it would be too expensive.'

'Don't worry about me, Hutch. I've no quarrel with Sarah. I even gave her my tissues while we were watching the film.'

'She said you were remarkably polite.'

'Of course I was. I wasn't about to be rude to her simply because she called me a liar and a cheat. Anyway, that's old news, now.'

'I'm afraid so. I tried talking to her again, but it's no use.'

'Don't get involved any more, Hutch. I've given up.'

'Okay, I'll let you get on.'

'Thanks, Hutch. See you on Sunday.'

Frank put the phone down, wondering yet again if he and Helen could make their relationship work again in spite of Medusa. It was a seemingly endless conundrum.

20

CAUSE AND EFFECT

The agenda for the Wool Exchange Club EGM included an unusual item, which the Chairman duly announced.

'We've heard a great deal of argument about the repainting of the ballroom,' he said. 'Some of you prefer the original Art Deco colours, whereas some feel that a degree of modernisation is necessary. You've no doubt noticed some unusual impedimenta in this room,' he said, pointing unnecessarily to the screen that had been erected at the front, and then to the projector that stood in the centre aisle, 'and all of this will be explained by our next speaker, who is a fully paid-up member of our club as well as being a professional artist. Mrs Renshaw, will you please enlighten us?'

Penny switched on the projector, and asked, 'Will someone switch off the room lights, please?'

An official obliged her, so that the only illumination came from the projector. The first slide showed the ballroom as they knew it, faded, but unmistakably Art Deco.

'You'll see that the music desks were removed so as not to influence any decision,' she said, inserting the next slide, which showed the ballroom largely in the ever-popular brilliant white. One member asked, 'Do we know of any Old English sheepdogs who might want to take a turn round the dance floor?'

'That really would be worth seeing,' said another, prompting friendly laughter.

The next slide showed the same view in earthy, pastel colours. The general response was negative. 'We come here to enjoy ourselves,' complained one member.

143

'So do I, said Penny. 'I dance here regularly, and that's why I've gone to the trouble of making these slides.'

'I'm sure we all appreciate Mrs Renshaw's hard work as well as her obvious talent,' said the Chairman.

'You should,' said Penny, 'because it's not often I do things free of charge.'

There was a chorus of laughter, and Frank was reminded, although not for the first time, of his sister's propensity for giving as good as she received.

'Maybe this colour scheme is more to your taste,' she said, showing them a more adventurous combination. There were murmurs of guarded approval, and she left it a while longer for them to gain a balanced impression, while Frank waited for her to draw the rabbit from the hat.

'This is less dramatic, and it might appeal more to most of you,' she said, flicking the switch again and showing them the ballroom painted in its original, but freshened, Art Deco colours. This time, the response was more positive.

'These are the original colours,' Penny told them, 'as I imagine they would have looked when the ballroom was last painted.'

'Mr Chairman,' said one member, 'I wonder if it might be easier for us to arrive at a decision with the options printed, so that we can see them side by side.'

'What do you think about that, Mrs Renshaw?' asked the Chairman.

'It's a good idea, Mr Chairman, 'but I've done everything so far without charge because I'm a member of the Exchange Club. However, printing from slides doesn't come cheap, so if the members want prints from these slides, they'll have to put their hands in their pockets.'

'That's noted,' said the Chairman. I'm sure the committee will be happy to pay for the prints. In the meantime, I think we should show our appreciation to Mrs Renshaw for her time and expertise.' There was a hearty round of applause.

After the meeting was over, Frank got the drinks in. 'Well done, Penny,' he said. 'You haven't forgotten how to control a lively class.'

'Thank goodness those days are over. Thanks, Frank,' she said, accepting a gin and tonic. 'What bit of teaching I do now is much easier.'

'I'm just lost in admiration,' said Hutch.

'Me too,' said Norman, 'whenever I see talent like yours.'

'That's sweet of you, Norman, and you as well, Hutch, but I've grown up with it, so I rather take it for granted.'

'She takes a lot for granted,' said Tim, making a rare contribution to the conversation.

'But not you, darling. You can't say that.'

'I daren't.'

'Speaking of taking things for granted,' she said, remembering something, 'students never cease to surprise me.'

'In what way?' Hutch spoke for them all.

'Well, on Mondays, they do life studies, when models come in and sit for them. I'm not talking about glamour, though. They're normal people who do it for a couple of bob.'

'What?' said Norman. 'Strip off?'

'That's right, it's a normal part of an art course. Anyway, you'd think youngsters today would have no inhibitions, but some of the students, mainly girls, are incredibly shy about drawing male genitalia. They try to pretend it doesn't exist. I suppose I was a bit coy at their age, but that was more than twenty years ago.'

Her story appealed to Frank. 'Maybe they're destined to become hardened feminists,' he suggested, 'in denial that such things exist.'

'I'd have thought they all looked much the same,' said Tim.

'Yes, you would, wouldn't you, darling? Thank goodness they're not.' She added hurriedly, 'That's speaking from an artist's point of view, of course.'

'Of course.' There was general agreement.

Changing the subject to spare the embarrassment of the older members of the group, Frank said, 'I hope this evening's slideshow has cured the modernists of their misguided notions.'

'When they see the options side by side, they'll soon come to their senses,' said Penny. Then, as the thought occurred to her, she said, 'Of course, Kate's not a member. That'll be why she's not here tonight.'

'She's busy, anyway, getting ready to go back to the Guildhall.'

'Oh, when's she going?'

'Tomorrow.'

'Presumably she's with Helen tonight.' She narrowed her eyes in fleeting thought and asked, 'Do you think Helen will mind if I call in on the way home to see Kate before she goes?'

'Not for a minute, but I can't speak for the unspeakables if they're in attendance, and they usually are.'

Penny made a dismissive gesture with one hand, and said, 'I'll deal with them if I have to.'

Frank knew her well enough to believe she would.

* * *

The Miserymobile was on the drive when Frank arrived, so he parked on the road, admiring the latest scrape as he walked past.

Helen came to the back door, only a little surprised to see him.

'I'd like to see Kate before she goes,' he said.

'Of course.'

'Penny's going to call as well. She'll be here in a minute. You don't mind, do you?'

'Of course not.' Her thin-lipped response was presumably due to her parents' presence within. 'She's in her room. I'll call her.'

Frank heard Medusa's voice coming from the sitting room. She was saying, 'He's here again. What's he after this time, I wonder?' She never referred to him or addressed him by name. He was always reduced either to a pronoun or an unflattering description.

Kate came into the kitchen alone. Frank could only imagine Helen was doing her best to placate her parents, as usual.

'Hello, Dad.' She accepted a kiss. 'How did the slideshow go?'

'So far, so good. Penny did an excellent job. She should be here in a minute.'

'Oh good.'

As if on cue, there was a tap on the door. Frank opened it and Penny came in.

'Hi, Penny,' said Kate.

'Hello, darling. I just came to see you before you go back to London.'

'Brilliant.'

Penny gathered her into a hug, slipping something discreetly into her hand as she did so.

'Oh, thanks, Penny. You're wonderful.'

Helen returned, looking careworn. 'Hello, Penny.'

146

'Hello, Helen.'

The voice from within said, 'He hasn't brought that clever-dick sister of his, has he? What's he brought her for?'

'I'll sort her out before I go,' said Frank grimly.

'Don't trouble yourself on my account,' Penny told him. 'I just came to see Kate, so I'm off now.' She hugged Kate again and kissed her. ''Bye, darling. Take care.'

''Bye, Penny. Thanks again.'

'Goodbye, Helen. Nice to see you again.' She kissed her and then Frank. ''Bye, everyone.'

'It was nice to see Penny again,' said Helen. 'It's a pity things can't be more civilised.'

'I couldn't agree more.' Frank passed her to go to the sitting room. 'Will you excuse me for a minute?'

He found Medusa and Eric enthroned as usual on the sofa. Medusa opened her mouth to speak, but Frank silenced her with a look. 'I don't give a damn what you say about me,' he said, motioning her to be quiet again. 'It's water off a duck's back, and I've been insulted by far better people than you, but don't you ever speak about my sister in that way again. Do you hear me?'

'I'm not standing for this. Tell him, Eric.'

'Shut up, Eric. I'm talking to Medusa.'

'My name's not Medusa!'

'All right, Mildew, but the message is the same.'

'I'm not standing for this.' She made several attempts to get up, finally accepting a pull-up from Eric. 'All I did was pass a harmless remark—'

'An insulting remark fit only for you, you malevolent harpy.'

'I'm going.'

'Good. See if you can match the new dent with your nearside wing this time, but don't use my car as a tool.'

'Oh!' Seemingly unable to think of a suitable retort, she bundled Eric into the kitchen, where she delivered her account of the exchange to Helen.

A few minutes later, Helen came into the sitting room to ask, 'What did you say to my mother, Frank. She was in tears.'

'Again? Good, it'll be practice for her, because I'll have a lot more to say to her if she doesn't mind her manners. Did you hear what she said about Penny?'

'Yes, she didn't mean anything by it. She thinks Penny spoils Kate, that's all.'

'She gave me some money,' said Kate. 'She always does when I go back to London.'

'It's just a… ' He stopped and searched for the word. Finally, he asked, 'What's the female equivalent of "avuncular"?'

' "Materteral",' said Helen. 'It is,' she said in response to a questioning look. 'I looked it up for somebody in the Oxford English Dictionary. It actually refers to the mother's sister, but it has been used for a sister of either parent.'

'All right, it was an act of materteral kindness.'

Returning to her original complaint, she said, 'You'd no right, though, to upset my mother in that way.'

'Cause and effect, Helen. She offends, and retribution follows. Anyway, Kate, would you like a lift to the station tomorrow?'

'Yes, please, if it's not too much trouble.'

'It's never too much trouble. Are you catching the ten-fifteen?'

'Yes.'

'I'll be here in good time. 'Bye, darling.' He kissed her. 'See you in the morning.' He kissed Helen. ''Bye, darling. I'll see you, too.'

'What's the "darling" about?' She seemed only amused.

'I'm just sharing my favours evenly. I wouldn't want to be accused of spoiling my daughter.'

'I just hope my mother's not here when you arrive.'

'If she is, you'd better warn her not to expect me to call her "darling".'

21

NOBODY'S SWEETHEART

As Hutch retained an administrative brief for the band, bookings came to him, and when he phoned Frank two weeks after Kate had returned to London, he was particularly excited.

'I've had a phone call from a production company called Times Recalled. Have you heard of them?'

'No, but names are cropping up all the time. Some production companies just get together for a one-off programme. What's the story with this one?'

'They're filming a documentary called *Fings Ain't What They Used To Be*. Each programme in the series is about bygone pursuits currently kept alive by believers such as you and me.'

'Oh yes?' Frank gave Hutch his full attention because it sounded promising.

'It's going to be about the dancing years, the time when people did it on a regular basis, and that naturally calls for music from the Golden Age.'

'I'm listening, Hutch.'

'They're approaching the Exchange Club as well because they want to film at least part of a regular social event when we're playing, but they'll be conducting interviews before the event and showing them in between numbers.'

That sounded pretty good to Frank. 'When is the documentary scheduled to go out?'

'December. If the Exchange Club hold a social in October, they want to film that, and then they've got time to work on it.'

'Excellent, just as long as the work on the Exchange doesn't get in the way.'

'Yes, there is that, but I think we can leave it to the committee to sort out the timing details.'

* * *

Frank was finishing the score for the Anvil series about the handymen. He found the humour heavy, and he suspected viewers might have the same reaction, although there was an audience, he was told, for obvious humour and telegraphed lines and situations. He just hoped the music would be well received. He couldn't expect every job to be rewarding. Looking up at Wyatt Earp, he said, 'You must have had plenty routine, boring jobs to do as a lawman, Wyatt.' Wyatt's stony expression confirmed it. Frank shifted his attention to the newest addition to his heroes' gallery. 'I'm sure you got some uninspiring tasks, Kit.' He got some gruesome ones as well. Frank remembered reading Kit Carson's account of finding the remains of a family of settlers. In particular he recalled the great scout saying that no one had ever been able to exaggerate Commanche torture. He shuddered at the thought and applied his attention to the almost completed score.

* * *

Rather than communicate by phone, Frank arranged to meet Hutch at the Coach and Horses for lunch.
'I don't usually bother with lunch,' said Hutch as they sat down.
'And I usually forget about it. Let's make it a treat.'
'Okay, Frank.' Hutch raised his glass. 'Cheers.'
'Cheers.' Frank waited for Hutch to speak.
'So far, the Exchange Club Committee are in favour of the documentary being filmed in the ballroom. Some people just love to be famous, Frank.'
'You sound like Helen's mother, but without the snarl.'
Hutch smiled, and said, 'I can only apologise for that.'
'No need. Have you found out anything about the refurbishment?'
'Yes, I have. Because all the work is internal, they've been given permission to go ahead. The paint will be as it stands, but spruced up – we have Penny to thank for that – and the mouldings need very little

work. They should be able to get everything done by early October, and that means the place will have stopped reeking of paint when we have the social at the end of October.'

'Excellent.' He picked up the menu and asked, 'Have you decided, Hutch?'

'Yes, the haddock and chips sounds inviting.'

'I'll join you with that.' Frank went to the bar and placed his order. When he returned, he said, 'I suppose they won't be holding a social at the end of this month.'

'No, but it's a small price to pay. I think we'll all appreciate the refurbishment when it's done.' Then, reminded of something else, he said, 'I've looked into holding practices at Beckworth College, and it seems we were wrong. It's far too expensive.'

'Even in the short term?'

He nodded. 'One possibility is the Arts Centre. They're actively looking for bookings.'

That was interesting. The Cullington Arts Centre had almost been a deciding factor in Frank's deliberations in the run-up to the 1978 general election. It had been 'almost', because having ruled out most of the candidates because of their negative attitudes towards the Centre, he decided to give his vote to Hilary, the Candidate for the Promotion of Regional Produce. He had to admit, albeit to himself, that his reasons had not been entirely logical. 'I'd expect them to be expensive,' he said, returning to the present.

'Oddly enough, they charge about half as much as Beckworth College, and it's easier for some of our people to get to.'

Frank agreed with him, but he was now thinking about something else. 'They could hold a social at the end of November,' he said, 'but I wonder if they've given any thought to a Christmas party. It could never rival last year's, for obvious reasons, but it would be a shame not to hold one.'

'Aye, when they've got the services of the lass who did the last one.'

'Yes.' Now that he mentioned it, Frank had been wondering about Hilary. 'Have you heard how things are between Hilary and Mark Barraclough?'

'According to Norman, it's love's young dream.'

'I hope so. They're a nice pair.' As an afterthought, he said, 'I don't see why it shouldn't work out for somebody.'

'I know, Frank.'

'At the risk of sounding dispassionate, which you know I'm not, it's a shame we'll have to do this documentary without a female vocalist.'

'Yes, but we did the Northern Focus thing with just Dan.'

'I remember, only too well.' Frank recalled having a momentary lapse of memory when he came to announce Dan's number, and that had prompted an all-out row with Sarah.

'That was a misunderstanding,' Hutch reminded him, having read his thoughts as he so often did.

'Sarah's good at misunderstanding. I just wish she'd bloody-well listen for a change.'

'So you're still feeling the draught?'

'I can't deny it.'

Hutch paused, possibly thinking about what he was going to say next, or even whether or not he should say it. Eventually he said, 'That business with her last chap hit her harder than you possibly know, Frank.' He broke off when the waitress came with their order.

'Can I get you anything else, gentlemen?' she asked.

Frank looked at Hutch, who shook his head. 'No, thank you,' he said.

'Very good. Enjoy your meal.'

'Thank you.'

Frank was aware that Hutch had been in the middle of telling him something. 'Go on, Hutch. What were you saying?'

'I was talking about the bloke Sarah knew before you met her again. It had been going on for some time, and they were actually engaged when she learned what he was doing. I think when you trust somebody as much as that, and they betray you, the hurt must be unbearable.'

'It must, Hutch. I didn't know that – about them being engaged, I mean.'

'Sarah kept an awful lot to herself, simply because it hurt so much, I suppose, and it would possibly hurt her more to tell the story in full.'

'Bugger.'

'As you say, Frank, bugger, but it possibly explains a lot.'

* * *

152

The house sale was proceeding nicely, and noticing that Helen's drive was empty, Frank called in to talk to her about it.

'Come in,' she said. 'I can't offer you a drink, because I've nothing in the house. It's a shame, because just for once you've arrived when my mum and dad aren't here.'

'Have they been arrested?'

'Frank, please. They're visiting someone else.'

Frank was surprised anyone wanted to know them, but he kept that to himself. 'Sorry,' he said. 'I brought this as a peace offering.' He handed her a bottle of red Bordeaux.

'Oh, Frank, you think of everything.' She took out two glasses and a corkscrew. 'Will you open it? You're better at it than I am.'

'You flatter me, Helen.' Nevertheless, he uncorked the wine expertly and poured two glasses.

'Let's take it into the sitting room,' she suggested.

'Why not?' He followed her.

'I spoke to the solicitor this afternoon,' he said, 'and I gather we should be able to exchange contracts very soon.' He put his glass down on the coffee table and sat beside her. 'I thought I'd come round and tell you, in case you hadn't heard.'

'Thanks, Frank, that's good news.'

'But for some reason you're less than carried away.'

'It's a lot to give up, Frank.'

'This house?'

'Yes.' Possibly thinking she should explain, she said, 'I know it's only been possible for me to go on living here because you've been keeping it going, but it's still a wrench.'

'But it won't be ours for long. When you get your new place, you'll be independent.'

For some reason, the thought failed to excite her. 'I suppose I will,' she said.

'What's on your mind, Helen? Tell your ex-hubby.'

She smiled sadly. 'I could never keep anything from you.'

'Are you going to share it, as I believe they say nowadays?'

She hesitated for a moment, and then said, 'It must be a problem for everyone when the proceeds from a house sale have to be divided. It means that neither party is left with very much to start afresh.'

'I imagine you've been looking at various properties?'

'Yes, and it's quite depressing. By the time we've paid the solicitor and the estate agent, we'll be left with about….'

'Twenty-five thousand each.'

'Yes, and when you subtract solicitors' fees again for buying, it doesn't leave either of us with an awful lot.'

'I've been thinking about that.'

'Mm?'

He topped up her glass. 'I'm the higher earner by quite a long way.'

'Don't rub it in, Frank.'

'I wouldn't dream of it. I'm just saying that you have a bigger problem when it comes to moving on, and I realise now that a fifty-fifty split is unfair on you.'

'It's what we agreed,' she reminded him.

'But what I do with my share is up to me, isn't it?'

'Yes, but I initiated the separation and the divorce. It would have been wrong to penalise you.'

He smiled at an earlier memory.

'What's the joke?'

'Here we are, both martyrs to conscience, and a year ago, the Sheriff of Nottingham was encouraging you to screw me for everything you could get.'

'Don't remind me, Frank. That wasn't my finest hour.'

'Nor his, it seems. He couldn't even start the lawnmower.'

Now she laughed. 'He was just practical enough to open the phone book and call an expert.' Reflecting briefly, she added, 'He wasn't particularly good at anything.' Reading his expression, she said, 'Let's not get into that, Frank.'

'All right. Let's be sensible. How far short are you of what you need?'

'Being sensible, about five thousand. It doesn't sound like a lot in house-buying terms, but while this housing boom lasts, it's the difference between decent and down-at-heel.' As if she were thinking aloud, she said, 'I don't suppose a small mortgage would be too punishing.'

'Don't even consider it. Interest rates are ridiculously high, and you'd be paying the earth for very little.'

'In that case,' she said abjectly, 'it's Hobson's choice.'

'It doesn't have to be.'

'What have you got in mind?' She seemed torn between curiosity and suspicion.

'As I said, it's totally unfair on you for us to split this place down the middle, when I'm in a far more comfortable financial position than you are. Suppose I pay the legal and estate agency fees and round it up to, say seven thousand five hundred, you'd get....'

She worked out the sum for him. 'Thirty-two thousand, five hundred, but that would leave you with only about seventeen thousand, five hundred.' She had always been better than him at figures.

'I'll manage with that.'

She stared at him, open-mouthed. 'Are you serious, Frank?'

'Quite serious. I want to treat you fairly.'

For a moment, she said nothing, and then a tear rolled down one cheek. 'That's the kindest thing I've ever heard, Frank.'

'Oh well,' he said, handing her a tissue, 'that's because I'm the kindest bloke you've ever known.'

'Where am I going to find another man like you?'

He pretended to consider the question, and said, 'You've got me there, but I have to leave you.' He stood up to go. He'd nothing pressing, but he wanted to avoid the kind of situation that had developed after the Roy episode.

She asked, 'Are you going to take the rest of the wine with you?'

'No, I'll leave it for you to enjoy.' He kissed her cheek.

'Frank,' she said, holding on to him, 'thank you again.'

'As I told you, it's only fair.' He allowed her to draw him into a hug because the occasion seemed to demand it, at least from her point of view. 'Let's not get carried away,' he said, kissing her on the cheek again.

'No, we mustn't.'

'I'll see you soon. 'Bye.'

''Bye, Frank, and thanks again.'

He walked to the car, confident that they were right not to let things get out of hand. His last encounter with Medusa had convinced him finally that a reconciliation with Helen was out of the question. At least for the foreseeable future, he was nobody's sweetheart.

OCTOBER

LIFE GOES ON

With planning permission granted, work went ahead on the ballroom, and the band rehearsed temporarily at the Cullington Arts Centre, which was handy and cosy, even if it lacked the thirties atmosphere of the Exchange ballroom.

Meanwhile, Frank worked on his current projects and planned the programme for the October social evening. Vanessa was now fully recovered from her operation, so she would be back on piano, and Kate was determined to be there for the recording. The only missing element would be Sarah. He tried not to think about her, but so many aspects of his life came with reminders of things that had been. He remembered how she could be fun and loving at the same time; physically, they'd been as one, and it had seemed at times that they could communicate with each other without saying a word. There was an awful lot to miss. Fortunately, there were distractions, and one came with the interviews for the documentary, which were conducted at the Arts Centre early in October.

* * *

The interviewer was a strikingly attractive redhead called Maria, who spoke to Hutch, Norman, Dan, Julie and Zoe, and who seemed particularly keen to talk to Frank.

'Now, Frank Morrison,' she said, 'composer of numerous memorable film and TV scores, how on earth do you find time to be a bandleader as well?'

Frank hated being interviewed, but he did his best to conceal the fact. 'It's not difficult, Maria,' he said. 'The band is very important to me, some of the musicians are old friends, going back thirty years or more, and I'm happy to say that the newest members are beginning to feel like old friends, too.'

'That's lovely. Now, we've heard how the band started up, and I believe you were the main instigator. What gave you the idea in the first place?'

'It happened purely by chance. I was working in my studio, and my eye fell on a photograph of my sister Penny and her husband Tim, taken at Blackpool Tower Ballroom. I imagine you're too young to remember *Come Dancing*, Maria.'

Maria laughed self-consciously. 'Not quite.'

'Well, Penny and Tim were Northern Amateur Quickstep Champions in the late sixties, and their photograph suddenly gave me the idea. We had the instrumental line-up, more or less, and some of the musicians had played with the great bands of the Golden Age of the nineteen-thirties, so it made absolute sense.'

'Yes, I've been talking to Hutch and Norman. They must have made a gigantic contribution when the band started out.'

'They did, and they still do, Maria. They're invaluable.'

'It's wonderful to hear you talk about them in that way, Frank, and there's another invaluable member of the band, who's considerably younger than they are. I'm talking about Dan Bairstow, of course, your resident male vocalist.'

'Yes, Dan is a unique performer. He's twenty-one years old, but he sings the music of sixty years ago as if he were born to it, and he has a very intimate performing style. You can't fail to notice that he seems to be singing to an audience of close friends. They're not, but they might as well be, because he communicates with them all.'

'How wonderful. I gather also that you had a female vocalist at one time.'

'Yes.' He'd had an awful feeling the subject was going to occur. 'Sarah was excellent, a true asset, but other things got in the way, unfortunately, and she left us.'

'Is there any sign of a replacement on the horizon, Frank?'

Frank hesitated. The loss of Sarah was the last thing he wanted to discuss. ' "Replacement" is a funny word, Maria. We may well find another female vocalist, but Sarah is… irreplaceable.'

157

'And with that final, touching tribute, we say a big "thank you" to Frank Morrison, because it's time to talk to some of the members of the Wool Exchange Club, who turn up regularly at the ballroom to dance, as everyone did in years gone by.'

* * *

'Well done, Frank,' said Hutch afterwards. 'I know you're not keen on having microphones thrust under your chin, but you gave a good account of yourself.'

'It was embarrassing, Hutch. She asked me about Sarah, and I think I gave myself away with that one.'

'I don't think you did. I heard the whole interview, and naturally enough, it meant something to me, but no one else would be aware of anything.' Looking around the hall, he said, 'Anyway, now the media people have gone, shall we have a short rehearsal?'

* * *

The next day, Frank was in Birmingham, recording the score for *Jobs For the Boys*. He greeted his ensemble and waited for them to tune, enjoying, as he always did, the matter-of-fact way session musicians went about their work. When they were ready, he spoke to them.

'It's very straightforward, ladies and gents. We've got opening titles, end credits and a few bits and pieces here and there.'

The voice in his headphones asked, 'Are you ready, Frank?'

'Sorry? Oh, yes, we're ready.' He was still getting used to the Midlands accent.

'Right, we'll make a start with Opening Credits,' announced the voice.

The videotape began with Frank conducting in free time; the click track and other devices were reserved for synchronising music and action, and that would come later in the episode. They played to the end of the opening credits and left it to the music editor to fade the track.

'Are you happy with that, Frank?' asked the voice.

'Quite happy,' he replied.

'What was wrong with it?'

'Nothing, as far as I'm aware.'

'But you said you were only quite happy.' Clearly, the owner of the voice was up for an argument.

'Let's just say I'm satisfied.' English could be a tricky sod for some.

'Okay, we'll go for Jobcentre.'

The click track began, giving Frank six metronomic beats' warning, and the video began on the first beat of the music, focusing on four disillusioned men. It was hard, at first, to tell them apart from the others in the Jobcentre, as everyone seemed equally displeased with life. It was only to be expected in the circumstances. The steady beat continued until one of the four men starring in the series stopped to examine a board on which index cards listed details of jobs. The camera paused on each one; there was a vacancy for a plasterer, one for a joiner, and another for a gardener. The man's face came into view. Something was obviously going through his mind, and then a 'streamer', a line of white light superimposed on the videotape, ran from left to right. As it reached the end of its travel, a circular 'punch' of light flashed, and Frank gave the cut-off signal.

'Thank you, Frank,' said the voice. 'That was spot on. Let's go on to The Pawn Shop.'

The videotape started with the four men redeeming the carpenter's tools at a rate of interest that prompted a lively argument. The sequence was followed by Postcards in Shop Windows, as the four began advertising their services.

Because of a hitch with the click track, they only managed to record the first two episodes and part of the third, but they had a day in hand, so no one was particularly perturbed.

* * *

Frank was digesting dinner at his hotel when Patsy phoned. She was now a director of both Orion and Anvil Productions, so it was expected that she should want to keep herself informed of developments.

'I gather there were problems this afternoon,' she said.

'Yes, I don't pretend to understand it, but they say they'll have it running again for tomorrow's session. Failing that, I can always conduct it in free time.'

'I'm sure you could, Frank. Otherwise, I gather it went well.'

'Yes, it's straightforward enough.' He thought that was a polite enough way to describe a particularly uninspiring series.

Fortunately, Patsy's thoughts had moved on. 'Did you read the notices for *Hey, Young Fella*?'

'Some of them.'

'They were very encouraging. It's just a pity the film hasn't taken off with the public as well as it might.'

'It was unfortunate timing, Patsy. When people are struggling to repay their mortgages, they can't be expected to get excited about a story set in the depression years. There are precedents for it.'

'I'm sure there are. I imagine you're about to cite one of them.'

'*Swing Time*, starring Fred Astaire and Ginger Rogers. It was a box-office flop because in nineteen thirty-six people wanted escapism. They didn't enjoy seeing Fred's character down on his luck.'

'There were some wonderful songs in it, though.'

'Yes, there were.' Unfortunately, when Frank thought of 'A Fine Romance', it made him think of Sarah, and he was trying hard not to do that.

'How's your daughter faring at the Guildhall, Frank?'

'Going from strength to strength. I'll be seeing her soon.'

'Oh?'

'She's coming home to take part in the recording—' He realised Patsy might not be aware of the band's involvement in the documentary. 'Do you know about *Fings Ain't What They Used to Be*?'

'I know Times Recalled, and I know the series. What's the story?'

'They're making a programme about the dancing days, using the October social evening at the Wool Exchange as its backdrop. They've done all the interviews, the music and dancing will be recorded on the twenty-sixth of October, and then I suppose they'll have to put everything together for screening on the second of December.'

'Just a minute while I make a note of that.' She was silent for a few seconds, and then she said, 'That sounds wonderful, Frank. I'll look forward to it.'

Frank was looking forward to it, too. The band deserved the recognition, and if the occasion turned out to be less than he would have liked, such was life. And life, with all its ups and downs, had to go on.

23

HOME AGAIN

There was an atmosphere of celebration at the ballroom. For one thing, the redecoration was complete, and everyone agreed that it was a huge success. The original Art Deco colours were now fresh and vibrant, and the white mouldings and cornices provided a bright contrast. The chandeliers had been thoroughly cleaned, and now they sparkled. The New Albion Dance Orchestra was home again.

The other reason was, naturally, the filming of the social evening for the documentary. At the production company's request, the committee had resisted the temptation to make the evening a ball. Instead, the emphasis was on dancing as a regular pastime, so dinner jackets, as they were called in times gone by, were in, and tails were out, except in Frank's case. After all, if the bandleader wasn't dressed for the part, how would anyone recognise him?

Vanessa went up to the platform to sound an 'A', enriching it, as she always did, with a 'D' minor chord, and the band tuned. When he was satisfied, Frank nodded to convey the fact, and one by one, the musicians made their way up the short flight of steps to the platform. He waited for the shuffling to cease, and followed them, briefly acknowledging the applause that greeted him, and counted the band into 'The Sun Has Got His Hat On.' It was the perfect signature number, setting the mood for dancers and musicians alike.

'Thank you, ladies and gentlemen,' said Frank when the applause ended, 'and welcome to the Wool Exchange Club Ballroom for our monthly social evening. Let's start with a waltz. Let's dance to 'By the Sleepy Lagoon'.' He counted the band into the immortal Eric Coates number, and the floor was taken by members and their guests, all prepared to enjoy the music and dancing from the beginning of the evening to the end.

Several numbers later, he announced a band number: 'Limehouse Blues'. Viewers were about to experience a treat. The number began in its excitedly breathless way, and taking his cue, Mark went into his virtuoso break, giving way then to Thomas, who held a high concert 'G' for four bars, to usher in the brass and reeds for the final chorus. The applause, when it came, spoke of universal delight.

'Ladies and gentlemen,' said Frank, 'you just heard Mark Barraclough, First Reed, and Thomas Davies, First Trumpet.' The enthusiastic applause was renewed. 'Let's have something a little calmer.' He waited for the laughter to fade, and said, 'It's a classic by the great Ray Noble. It's 'Love is the Sweetest Thing', and here to sing it for us is Dan Bairstow.'

Dan was a favourite with the members, and they greeted him with a barrage of applause. He went on to sing the vocal refrain with characteristic sensitivity and was rewarded by more applause at the end.

'Dan Bairstow, ladies and gentlemen, the man with the velvet voice and our regular male vocalist.' The members knew who Dan was, but Frank hoped he would benefit from his exposure on television. He was reminded briefly and painfully of the awful misunderstanding with Sarah over the way he'd introduced Dan on *Northern Focus*, but he put it out of his mind to announce the next number. 'A quickstep, ladies and gentlemen, 'All I Do is Dream of You.'' He counted the band in and concentrated on that. It brought the first half of the evening to a close, and the band left the platform for a well-deserved break. Frank headed for the bar, where he'd seen Maria from Times Recalled and also Penny and Tim. He greeted his sister and brother-in-law and signalled to Maria to join them.

'The band's absolutely wonderful, Frank,' she said.

'Thanks, Maria. I'd like you to meet my sister Penny and her husband Tim. It was their photograph at Blackpool, if you remember, that gave me the idea of starting a band.'

'And you two were... was it foxtrot champions?'

'Northern Amateur Quickstep Champions,' Penny corrected her.

A man of quiet deeds, Tim said nothing but handed Frank a vodka and tonic.

'Thanks, Tim.'

'I thought you both looked remarkably at home in the last number.'

'That's very kind of you,' said Penny.

'I wonder, would you be kind enough to do a very brief interview to camera? I think we could use it in the programme.'

As usual, Penny volunteered for them both, and Frank returned to the band room, satisfied with his work.

The second half opened with another band number, 'The Piccolino', which also proved highly popular and was applauded appropriately.

'Thank you, ladies and gentlemen. It's time to hear again from Dan, our vocalist. He's going to sing another Ray Noble classic, 'The Very Thought of You'.

Frank worked his way through the programme until the party eventually broke up. He was in the band room when Penny came to see him.

'Hi Penny,' he said. 'How was the interview?'

'Short and sweet, but possibly useful, we were told.' She brushed it aside and said, 'I actually came to talk to you about Mum's birthday.'

'Yes, Tuesday, isn't it? Do you think we could take her out tomorrow, while Kate's at home?'

'I'm glad you've asked me that, because I've booked a table for seven at the usual place, for one o'clock tomorrow. We can go splits, if you like.'

'Thanks for telling me, Penny. I take it the boys are coming as well?'

'Yes, it'll be a proper celebration. She'll be sixty-five, but that's close enough to a round figure to make it special.' Penny seemed to go through life making her own rules, and Frank usually went along with them.

'Close enough for me, Penny.'

Changing the subject, she said, 'Tonight went well. It'll be something else for Mum to enjoy, seeing both her offspring and her granddaughter on television at the same time. Of course, that's assuming they show the interview.'

'They should. Maria asked me how the idea came to me, and I told her about the photo of you and Tim at the Blackpool Tower Ballroom.'

'Have you still got that?'

'It lives permanently on my desk.'

She smiled. 'In that case, we're in good company, with… who are they?'

'Wyatt Earp, George Armstrong Custer, Billy the Kid, and now Kit Carson.'

'Don't ever grow up and be boring like the rest of us, Frank.' She kissed him. 'See you tomorrow.'

'We'll pick Mum up, as you've got a car full.'

'Right, we'll go straight to the restaurant.'

* * *

There was a visitor at the Sunday morning rehearsal, a smartly-dressed man of forty or so, and Frank imagined he was either something to do with the Planning Department, casting an eye over the improvements, or connected with the committee in some way. He turned out to be neither. Hutch introduced him before the rehearsal began.

'Frank, this is Paul Watson. He's a local photographer, and he's come to have a look around.'

'How d'you do, Paul? Glad to meet you.'

'When we were being interviewed,' said Hutch, 'that girl Maria asked me if we'd recorded any CDs, and I told her we were thinking about it. Now, it seems to me that when we do, we'll need a photo for the CD case, and we should have some photos of the ballroom as well. I've spoken to the committee, and they're happy enough.' He added mischievously, 'It'll be a change for Paul. He's more used to photographing aeroplanes and ships.'

'Oh, that was a long time ago, Hutch,' said Paul. 'I learned my trade in the Fleet Air Arm,' he explained to Frank.

'Good for you, Paul. I wrote the music score for *Wings Above the Waves*, so you're in friendly company.'

Suddenly Paul looked at him afresh. 'Are you the Frank Morrison who wrote the music for *Looking Back*?' he asked.

'Guilty on both counts.'

'I couldn't get that theme out of my head for days. It was a good film, but I enjoyed your music probably as much.'

'Thank you, Paul.'

'It's good to know that, isn't it, Frank,' said Hutch. 'Anyway, it's time we got started. I'll see you later, Paul.'

'Right. I'm going to stay for a while and enjoy the music.'

Hutch walked to the platform with Frank and said discreetly, 'Getting involved with this might do Paul some good.'

'Is he just starting out?'

'No, he's well established. I meant that it might bring him out of himself a bit. He lost his wife two or three months ago, and some of us know how that feels.'

'Poor bugger. He seems like a decent bloke, too.'

* * *

As usual, Frank's mother was ready when they arrived.

'I thought we'd better pick you up, Mum, seeing as Penny's never on time for anything.'

'Oh, that's not fair, Frank. Don't listen to him, Katie. He's awful to your Auntie Penny.'

Kate smiled understandingly, resisting the urge to tell her grandma that no one else called her "Katie" any longer, and that she never called Penny "Auntie".

'Where's your coat, Mum?'

'Here, behind me. I'm all ready.'

Frank helped her on with it and waited patiently while she buttoned it up. Then he gave her his arm and took her to the car.

'This is a lovely car, Frank,' she said as she took her seat. 'Oh, and I've just remembered, the seats warm up, don't they?'

'They will today. It's certainly cold enough.'

'It's lovely to see you again, Katie. Your dad told me all about your recital, and how proud he was.'

'I'm embarrassed now, Grandma.'

'Don't hide your light under a bushel, love.'

'If you tell me what a bushel is, I'll try not to.'

'It's a kind of basket— Oh, I can feel the seat warming up already. What a treat.'

Frank laughed, and said, 'It's a pity it's such a short journey.' He pulled into the restaurant drive and looked around for either Tim's or

Penny's car. There was no sign, so he parked as close as he could to the entrance.

There were very few people in the restaurant, which seemed odd until a waitress told them there was a Premier League match being played that afternoon.

'In that case,' said Frank, 'it's just as well we came. The table's in the name Renshaw, by the way, and it's booked for one o'clock.'

'Here it is, Mr Renshaw,' said the waitress, finding the booking. 'I'll take you to your table.'

Just as they were taking their seats, Tim and Penny arrived with Gary, their younger son, who went to the loo as soon as he came in. When they were settled, Penny explained that Nicholas, their other son, was playing in a rugby match. 'He left it until this morning to tell us,' she said. 'Never mind. We're here, and that's what matters.' Seeing Gary emerge from the loo, she said, 'Come and sit beside Kate, Gary.'

Being well brought up, he kissed his grandma and took his seat diffidently beside Kate, who'd been the object of his secret longing for as long as he could remember, despite the six-year difference between them.

'My turn,' said Kate, offering her cheek.

He kissed her hurriedly, blushing.

'I don't taste as bad as that, do I?' she said, taking his hand and squeezing it.

'Has Frank told you about the television programme, Mum?' asked Penny, to Gary's relief. He knew nothing about the programme, but any distraction from his mortification was welcome.

'The *Northern Scene* programme?'

'No, another one. It's a documentary series about the way we used to live, and this one's about dancing. They filmed us last night at the Wool Exchange. If they show the interview with Tim and me, that'll be four of us in the same programme.'

'When will they show that, then?'

'The second of December,' Frank told her, 'and that's not all.'

Penny looked at him questioningly, because she'd thought that actually was all. 'Go on, Frank,' she said. 'Surprise us.'

'I had a phone call from one of Pennylops's old flames,' he said, using his pet name for her from childhood.

166

'Okay, Frankenstein,' she said, 'let's hear it.'

'Do you remember Gavin Lowe, Mum?'

'Oh yes, he was a lovely boy.' She broke off when the waitress came to take their order. After some hesitation and vacillation, the order was noted, and she left them.

'What were we talking about before the waitress came?' asked Frank's mother.

'Frank was trying to embarrass me about Gavin Lowe,' said Penny.

'I was just going to say that he'd been in touch, and he's going to come to one of the social evenings at the Exchange.'

'What's he doing now, anyway?' asked Penny, who was not even mildly embarrassed.

'He's teaching piano and composition at a music college in Lancashire. You'll be all right, though, Penny, because he married someone who teaches dance at the same place. I met her about fifteen or sixteen years ago. Apparently, her father started up a dance band in Wensleydale, or somewhere like that, just after the war.'

'That's a coincidence,' said Tim. 'I remember Gavin, now I think of it.'

'He was very keen on Penny,' said her mother in her maternally clumsy way. 'I think he must have taken it hard when she started going out with Tim.'

Kate was following the conversation with undisguised fascination, whilst Gary tried to make himself invisible. After all, no teenager likes to hear about his parents' romantic past.

'She broke his heart,' said Frank matter-of-factly. 'He told me he went home all set to end it all, but he though better of it.'

'Why is he coming to a social,' asked Penny, 'when he can't dance? I mean, that's why I dropped him in favour of Tim.'

Sensitive to Gary's dilemma, Kate told him gently, 'I think it's a made-up story. It's certainly too silly to be true.'

'O hard, cruel woman,' said Frank, addressing his sister, 'he *can* dance. His wife taught him, actually before they were even an item. It was so that they could go to a function where her father's band was playing. I must say, I'd like to hear them if they're still together.'

'This is too complicated for words,' said Kate.

'Just wait 'til I start on your dad's lurid past,' Penny told her.

'Do you mean to say you only took up with me because I was your dancing partner, Penny?' asked Tim, sensitive to Gary's discomfiture and winking slyly at him.

'Of course I did. The other bits didn't begin to appeal until later, when we weren't dancing.'

Possibly to turn the conversation away from her daughter's fickle past, her mother said, 'Tell us about the girl Gavin married, Frank. I like to think he lived happily… well, not ever after, but you know what I mean.'

'If I remember rightly, her name's Leah.'

'That's nice.'

'I thought she was rather nice. Apparently, she was at the Royal Ballet School, groomed for a brilliant future as a prima ballerina, and then some lunatic ran her over and put her in hospital for goodness knows how long.'

'Oh, the poor girl.'

'It took a long time, but she recovered, although she never danced professionally.'

'Poor girl,' repeated his mother, apparently waiting for more detail, as was her way.

'What else can I tell you, Mum? She frowns on happy eating. I can tell you that.'

'What's happy eating, Dad?' asked Kate.

'It's a bloke thing, Kate. It's sausages and mash, baked beans and sausages on toast with a poached egg on top, fried egg and sausage sandwiches… ' He spread his hands in mute appeal. 'All the things that make life worth living.'

His mother was still inclined to take him seriously. 'How long have they been together, Frank?'

'About fifteen years, Mum.'

'He must love her, whatever you say, if they've stayed together all this time.'

'Ah well, he wore her down in the end, and now she lets him have bangers and mash every couple of weeks or so, sometimes with time off for good behaviour.'

'And speaking of which,' said Tim spotting the waitress, 'here comes lunch.'

24

OLD FRIENDS, NEW TIMES

F rank met Gavin and Leah at their home outside Bury in Lancashire. It was the first time they'd met for fifteen years, when Nidderdale College of Performance Arts performed a musical in the Thomas Arne Theatre in London, and they were obviously surprised to see Frank alone, although they were careful not to mention it. Conscious of their awkwardness, however, Frank explained.

'Helen is still one of my favourite people,' he said, 'but the marriage couldn't go on, and we were divorced last year.'

'I'm sorry, mate,' said Gavin.

'So am I,' said Leah. 'With my bumpy track record, I've no difficulty sympathising when I hear of a relationship hitting the rocks. What would you like to drink, given that you're staying the night?'

'Am I?'

'That was one of Leah's compulsory invitations,' explained Gavin. 'She's like the Mafia in that respect, and in case you're wondering, we've been togevver nah for fourteen years. Someone had to put a stop to her frivolous ways.'

'I'm glad. Is a vodka and tonic possible?'

'Not only possible,' said Leah, 'but on its way.' She poured him a vodka, took a bottle of tonic from the fridge and served it with a slice of lemon.

'Thank you, Leah.'

'How's… Katherine?' asked Gavin, remembering her name.

'She insists on being called "Kate" now, and she's in her third year at the Guildhall.' Realising that so much had happened since their last meeting, he said, 'She's studying violin, and she gave her first lunchtime recital this year.'

'You're right to be proud of her, Frank,' said Leah, 'and you obviously are. Our two are somewhere about. They've been swimming, but you'll meet them later.'

Gavin's memory was making its own journeys. He asked, 'Do you remember winning that bet about the Post Horn Galop, Frank?'

'Do I remember it? It follows me around like a tin can tied to a cat's tail. I had to play it recently on an antique post horn with Hunslet Youth Band in hot pursuit.'

'What was that about?' asked Leah.

'We were at a party in London, where they had an ornamental post horn,' explained Gavin, 'and I bet Frank a quid that he couldn't play the Post Horn Galop on it.'

'A whole pound,' said Leah, remembering the days when a pound was worth a great deal more. 'How did you come to play it with…? What were they called?'

'Hunslet Youth Band. It was on Northern Scene. They invited me because someone had dropped out at the last minute. I shared the programme with the youth brass band and a clueless, inarticulate, tone-deaf, foul-mouthed Punk Rock genius.'

'I'm sorry we missed that,' said Leah, laughing. 'Unfortunately, Gavin's a BBC addict, so we never see Northern Focus or Northern Scene. We just hear about it.'

'That's not fair,' said Gavin, 'blaming it on me.'

'At all events, I'm terribly impressed, Frank. The last time we met, you were dressed in denims and you had a moustache and hair that swept the floor.' The memory evidently still amused her.

'My last memory of you was altogether different. I'll never forget that scene, Leah, when you danced the part of the doomed queen. It was too beautiful for words, and so were you.'

'Oh, Frank, that's really sweet of you. Thank you.'

'Okay,' said Gavin, bringing the conversation down to earth, 'tell us what happened to the hair and the Wyatt Earp moustache, Frank. I didn't recognise you when you arrived.'

'I grew up. The lads persuaded me to have a trim before the band's first gig, and it coincided with my first pair of glasses. None of the frames I tried went with the long hair, at least not without making me look silly, so I sacrificed the mane. The lawman's moustache went later, before it died of loneliness.'

There was a noise in the back porch, and a boy and a girl appeared a few minutes later. The girl was possibly eleven or twelve, and the boy was maybe a couple of years younger.

'This is Emma, and this is Mark,' said Leah. 'Mr Morrison is an old friend of your dad from school and college. He's a composer.'

'Like you, Dad?' asked Mark.

'No, he's better than me. He makes money out of it.'

Emma was staring at Frank.

'What's the matter?' he asked.

'My mum said you had long hair and a moustache,' she told him shyly.

'She was right. I had,' he admitted, 'but some things are too good to last. I slipped with my razor when I was shaving, and off came the moustache. After that, I had to have a haircut, or I'd have looked daft.'

'Don't go away, you two,' said Leah. 'We'll be having dinner shortly.' She looked at the clock. 'In about twenty minutes.'

It was Frank's turn to be inquisitive. 'Has your father still got his dance band, Leah?' he asked.

'Oh yes. Freddy Hinchcliffe and the Dalesmen are a permanent feature in Wensleydale.'

'I'd like to hear them sometime.'

'I think we can arrange that.'

'Also, I'd like you and Gavin to come over to Cullington as often as you like, as my guests. There's a social evening on the thirtieth of November, and a Christmas Ball on the twenty-first of December. If it's anything like last year's, it'll be well worth the journey.'

'How kind. Thank you, Frank.'

'Now I think of it,' said Gavin, 'in all the time I lived in Cullington, I never once saw the interior of the Wool Exchange. It was far too exclusive for the likes of me.'

'It's worth a visit,' Frank told him. 'They've just had the ballroom refurbished, but the Wool Exchange is a Grade Two Listed Building, so its Art Deco style is still intact. It's perfect for what we do.'

'It sounds wonderful,' said Leah.

'I gather you've learned to dance, Gavin.'

'That's right, Frank,' Leah told him. 'I taught him the waltz, the foxtrot and the quickstep, and my mum taught him the rhumba.'

'I'm brilliant at the rhumba,' said Gavin matter-of-factly, 'but I'd no choice in the matter. I had to do exactly as Leah's mum said, but not because she's at all fearsome. Far from it, she's the last person you'd ever want to displease.'

'He fell for my mum long before I got so much as a look-in,' said Leah with a straight face.

'You must bring your mum and dad down to the Exchange sometime. I'd like to meet them.'

They continued to fill in the past fifteen years over dinner, when Gavin asked, 'How did you come to form this band, Frank?'

Frank told them about the morning at the Exchange, when he and Kate had arrived to find a dozen despondent old men cast aside and robbed of their way of life. 'Kate was heart-broken, too,' he said, 'and I think that spurred me on to do something for them. I think they were too close to the problem to find their own way forward, but I could see the possibility of a dance band in the line-up available. That was when I phoned Hutch and asked him to set up a practice.'

'Is Hutch involved?' asked Gavin with new interest. 'He taught me clarinet and sax,' he told Leah.

'I know. You introduced me to him at the theatre.'

'Hutch, Norman and Geoff are all in the band,' Frank assured him. 'So are a few others you may not know.'

'Do you see much of Ellie and Phyllis?'

'I'm afraid Ellie died four years ago, and Phyllis followed her a year later. It was a double tragedy for Hutch as well as Norman.'

'Oh, no.'

Leah was quick to lighten the conversation. 'What was it we heard about a film, Frank?'

'That's right, we recorded the music for a film called '*Hey, Young Fella*.'

'That was a Nat Gonella number, wasn't it?'

Frank looked at Leah in surprise. 'It certainly was.'

'I was brought up with it,' she explained. 'If people danced to it before the war, I had to know about it.'

'Well, it should be out on video early next year, and we've recently been filmed for a documentary that's going to be screened on the second of December, as part of the *Fings Ain't What They Used to Be* series.' He realised uncomfortably that he'd been talking rather a lot about himself. 'What about you two?' he asked. 'What have you been up to apart from bringing up two lovely children?' The children in question had been following the conversation, possibly not understanding everything, but nevertheless with complete fascination.

'I keep knocking out musicals,' said Gavin, 'for as long as I can hold the pressure for pop music at bay, and Leah choreographs and drills the dance students.'

' "Drill" isn't a nice word, darling. 'What I do is much subtler than drilling.'

'Of course it is. You're the very soul of subtlety.'

She added modestly, 'I do some examining as well.' She turned to the children. 'What did you two get up to this afternoon?' she asked.

'I went off the high diving board for the first time,' said Mark proudly.

'He wasn't very good,' said Emma. 'He was a bit untidy, really, but he'll get better.'

'Just as you did, Emma,' Leah reminded her.

'Leah taught them to swim,' said Gavin. 'She's a much better swimmer than I am.'

'It's just practice,' said Leah, 'and I had no shortage of that between operations.'

'Watching you at the Thomas Arne,' said Frank, 'I had no idea about your accident. I learned about that later, but honestly, I'd never have known, because you were just incredible.'

'Thank you, Frank.' She reached across the table and squeezed his hand. 'That means a lot to me.' She looked up at the clock and said, 'Emma and Mark, bedtime beckons.' They both appeared to be drooping.

Almost as a duet, they said, 'Thank you for dinner. Goodnight, Mum. Goodnight, Dad.'

'Kiss-kiss.' She accepted a kiss from each of them. 'Night-night.'

Emma looked at Frank awkwardly, and said, 'Goodnight, Mr....'

'Frank,' he told her. 'Goodnight, Emma. Good night, Mark. I'll see you both in the morning.'

'Good night, Frank.'

'They always thank me before they leave the table,' said Leah. 'It's the way I was brought up, and it seems right to me.'

'I can't argue with that.'

'But now they've gone to bed,' said Gavin, 'tell us what's been happening since the divorce. I mean, some lucky girl must be walking round with a smile on her face.'

'Oh, Gavin.' Leah shook her head in mock-despair.

'I'd like to tell you a heartwarming story,' said Frank, 'but what was to have been... fell on its backside. I shan't bore you with it.'

'Nonsense,' said Gavin. 'The cheese and the wine are both holding up, and we're waiting to be bored. Go on, Frank, tell your old mate and his missis all about it while I top you up.'

'All right, Gavin. You asked for it. I was seeing a lot of... well, more than that, really. She's Hutch's granddaughter.'

'I didn't know he had one.'

'Be quiet, Gavin,' said Leah. 'You'll stop the flow.'

Frank thought that was a strange thing for a woman to say, but he was sensible enough to keep that to himself. 'Her name's Sarah Hutchins. I'd met her on two occasions, but I really got to know her through the band. She came to advise us on presentation – I should explain that she teaches dance and stage management at Beckworth Performing Arts College.'

'I know her,' said Leah, 'from examining at Beckworth College.'

'Now who's interrupting?' asked Gavin.

'Be quiet, Gavin.'

'It was going ever so well, and then she saw the most innocent thing happen, and she got the wrong idea.' He told them about Helen's problem, how he'd been able to put an end to it, and about Helen's show of gratitude. 'That's all it was,' he said, 'a hug of relief and a kiss between two people who'd been married for twenty years, but it must have seemed much more than that to Sarah.' He told them about Sarah's past experience. 'Unfortunately,' he said, 'I seem to be paying for the deeds of a predecessor.'

Leah asked, 'Won't she listen to you?'

'Not for a minute.'

'You know,' she said, 'in a way, it doesn't seem all that strange to me. Before Gavin and I met, it seemed that I'd known one bastard after another, and I know how easy it is to stereotype and believe the worst.'

Frank hadn't intended telling the story, but he wasn't sorry he'd shared it. It wasn't a problem halved, but at least it had received a sympathetic hearing.

25

NOVEMBER

WATERSHED

Frank was surprised to receive a phone call from Dan.
'Hello, Dan,' he said. 'What can I do for you?'
'I'm phoning to apologise, Frank.'
'Why? What have you done?'
'It's nothing I've done, Frank. It's to say I can't be at the next band practice, I'm afraid.'

That was unusual. As far as Frank was aware, Dan had never missed a practice. 'We'll miss you, Dan, but don't worry about it.'

'It's good of you to say that. Actually, it's because the course is coming to its end next month, and I'm starting to look for shows to audition for.'

'I didn't realise that, Dan. Somehow, I had an idea your course ended next summer.'

'No, it runs from January to December. The finals start at the end of this month and go into December.'

'Well, in that case, I wish you well in both the finals and your audition. I imagine it's in London?' Most of them were.

'Yes.'

'That'll be a bit expensive for you.'

'It is, but I've been able to save a bit. That's why I couldn't go to Kate's recital.'

'I remember now. Well, thanks for letting me know, Dan. Break a leg.'

'Thanks, Frank. 'Bye.'

''Bye, Dan.'

Frank thought about the money that had just come into his bank account from the solicitor. It seemed obscene when Dan was probably struggling to travel to auditions. He looked at his watch and decided to try phoning Kate.

He heard her mobile ring several times, and then she answered. 'Hello.'

'Kate, it's Dad.'

'Hello, Dad. What's up?'

'Did you know that Dan's course is due to end in December?'

'Yes, I've known that for a while.'

'Oh, it was news to me. He's just phoned me and told me he can't be at the practice on Sunday.'

'No, he's auditioning for a show. I said he could sleep on the floor at our place.' She sounded a little awkward. 'In case you're wondering, Dad, Dan and I are no longer, but that doesn't mean he can't save a few quid by dossing down here occasionally.'

Frank had felt relieved that Dan was going to sleep on the floor, and now the news that it was over between them was another surprise. 'I see. Look, have you got Dan's address?'

'Yes, of course I have.'

'Well, will you give it to me, please?'

'Oh, I see what you mean. It's thirty-six, Sevastopol Terrace, Beckworth, BD... something or other. Have you got that?'

'Yes, thank you.'

'What else is happening up there, Dad?'

'Your mum's moving in temporarily with Medusa and your grandad—'

'Oh, no.'

'Just until she can move into the new house. It'll only be a couple of weeks or so. The money came through today, so that's not a problem.'

'I hope she can move in before Christmas.'

Frank hoped so, too. Christmas in Medusa's labyrinth would be too awful to contemplate. 'Speaking of Christmas, Kate, you will try to be back by the twenty-first, won't you?'

'What's on the twenty-first?'

'The Christmas Party at the Exchange.'

'Too right I'll be there.'

'Good.'

'Must go, Dad. Love you. 'Bye.'

'Love you, darling. 'Bye.'

He wrote a quick note and placed it in an envelope with some money. Then, with Dan's address in his hand, he went out to the car.

* * *

An hour or so later, he arrived at the labyrinth, where Eric came to the door. He regarded Frank uncertainly, but said nothing.

'Hello, Eric. I've come to see Helen. She'll be pleased to see me.' Eric stood aside, and he walked in to find Medusa enthroned in an armchair.

'What do you want?'

'I've come to see Helen. Surely you didn't think I'd come to see you, did you?'

Hearing his voice, Helen came out of the kitchen. As wary as ever when her parents were around, she said, 'Hello, Frank.'

'Have you checked your bank account today, Helen?'

'No.' Her expression changed from uncertain to excited. 'Have they paid the money?'

'Yes, and I paid the extra into your account. Come into the kitchen and I'll tell you about it.'

'Hey, what are you after? What's he after, Helen?'

'Be quiet, Medusa.' He took Helen into the kitchen and said, 'I've paid you what I said. You should be all right now, but if you have a problem, let me know.'

'Oh, thank you, Frank.'

'You've nothing to thank him for.'

'Mind your own business, Medusa.'

'How dare 'e? In our 'ouse an' all. Tell 'im, Eric.'

'Don't bother, Eric.' Taking Helen in his arms, he said, 'Thank you for all the good things about our marriage, Helen, because it was good when it was allowed to be. Good luck in your new home.' He hugged her tightly, partly out of affection, but also because he felt desperately sorry for her. She was still in her mother's clutches, and he knew she'd never break free.

'Goodbye, Medusa. Goodbye Eric.' He ignored Medusa's sour

178

riposte and went on his way, confident after his round trip that Helen could afford her new home and that Dan had enough funds to buy a few return train tickets. At some time, they would need to find another male vocalist as well as a female one. He'd told Maria from Times Recalled that Sarah was irreplaceable, and Dan was, too, although not in quite the same way.

* * *

With Dan back in the fold, unfortunately after an unsuccessful audition, the November social evening went ahead. Penny and Tim were there, as were Gavin and Leah, who came to the band room at half-time to see Hutch and Norman.

After a happy reunion, they were about to leave the band room, when Leah spotted Dan.

'Hello,' she said, 'Where did you learn to sing so beautifully? I loved your solos.'

Modest as ever, Dan mumbled, 'Thank you. I'm at Beckworth College.'

'Are you really? Well, they're to be congratulated, because you're an excellent performer.'

'Leah's a lecturer at East Lancashire College, Dan,' explained Frank. 'She knows what she's talking about.'

'It's very kind of you to say what you did,' he said.

'Not at all. It's lovely to meet you. I'm looking forward to the second half.'

'Take a break for a few numbers, Frank,' said Hutch. 'Now we're not being filmed, they won't mind not having a young, handsome fella in front of the band.'

'Thanks, Hutch. I'll take you up on that.' He went down to the bar with Leah and Gavin. 'What are you both drinking?' he asked.

'G and Ts, please, Frank,' said Gavin, but I'll get the next round.'

Frank got the drinks in and joined them at their table.

'Thanks ever so much for inviting us, Frank,' said Leah. 'It's the most wonderful thing you've got going here.'

'And the band is superb,' said Gavin.

'Thank you both.' The musicians were returning to the platform, so Frank said, 'Gavin, do you mind if I ask Leah for the next dance?'

'Not in the least, mate.'

With the band in place, Hutch came out and stood in front of them. 'Let's start the second half with a foxtrot,' he said. 'It's "The Very Thought of You", and here's Dan to sing it for us.'

'Leah, may I have the pleasure?'

'Of course, Frank.'

He led her on to the floor and they joined the line of dance. Leah followed every move as if she were a part of him, and the whole experience was a glorious surprise. 'You're a wonderful dancer,' he said.

'Thank you. It's all down to my mum, and if you danced with her you'd see why.' They saw out the number, with Leah almost melting at the sound of Dan's voice.

'He's wonderful,' she said. 'I imagine he's going to try for some stage shows, but if he ever decides to do some teaching, point him towards Gavin and me.'

'I'll remember that.' He took her back to Gavin and thanked them both. 'I'm going to find Penny,' he said.

'Is she here?'

'She's been here all along.' He caught sight of her and made his way over.

'Hello, Frank. Are you going to dance with me?'

'Of course.'

'Let's have a waltz, now,' said Hutch. 'Let's dance to "Love's Last Word is Spoken".'

'That's us,' said Penny, following Frank on to the floor. 'Who were you dancing with just now? She's a heck of a dancer.'

'Leah Lowe, Gavin's wife.'

'I didn't realise they were here.'

They joined the line of dance. 'I'll introduce you to Leah later. Gavin's madly in love with her, so you'll be all right.'

'Don't be silly.'

Partners from an early age, when Penny was still learning to dance, they enjoyed the rest of the number, and then Frank took Penny and Tim to meet Leah and Gavin while he returned to the platform.

* * *

At the end of the evening, Leah, Gavin, Penny and Tim went back to Frank's flat, where Frank showed his guests where to put their bags, while Penny prepared coffee.

'Are you really giving up your lovely bedroom for us?' asked Leah.

'You'd find it a bit of a squeeze in Kate's single bed,' he told her, 'and that's where I'm sleeping, complete with teddy bear, panda, woolly monkey and Kevin the Kung-fu-Saurus.'

'It's a shame we couldn't meet Kate,' said Gavin.

'Come to the Christmas Ball, and you shall. She'll be playing with the band. It could be interesting, though. She's just broken up with Dan.'

'Oh, no,' said Penny. 'They made a lovely pair.'

'Seriously, they've decided amicably to go their separate ways. It makes sense, even though Dan's kipping on Kate's floor when he goes to auditions.'

Leah didn't understand it either. 'When I grew up, I stopped trying to fathom young people,' she said.

'I'm just happy he's sleeping on the floor,' said Frank.

'You'll have to let go one day,' Penny told him.

'Just let him enjoy the fact that Dan sleeps on the floor,' said Tim. 'I'm thankful I haven't got daughters to worry about.'

'Even if you had,' said Penny, 'you'd leave the worrying, like everything else, to me.'

It was a cosy gathering after an enjoyable evening. There was only one person missing, and Frank could do nothing about that. Even so, he planned on making the Christmas Ball a special evening for everyone else.

26

December

Straight Talk

As was the custom when a major event appeared on television, the members of the band gathered in the club lounge at the Wool Exchange to watch it on the large screen. The event was the week's episode of *Fings Ain't What They Used to Be* and, whilst they tried not to show it, everyone was excited. Frank was reminded of the news item on *Northern Focus*, the previous year, although he was trying hard to forget that occasion.

'Here it is,' said Hutch. He was thrown for the moment, as everyone else was, because the screen was filled with people dancing, but in black and white. The clip was taken from, possibly, an old newsreel. Then the title came up, with a recording of Max Bygraves singing the song that lent the programme its title. A voice-over said, 'The local *Palais* that became a bowling alley and is now all manner of things was once the focal point of weekly entertainment for most people. Now, however, it's a thing of the past – or is it?' The picture changed to a scene from the Wool Exchange, where people were dancing to 'Love is the Sweetest Thing', with Dan at his unquestionable best. 'This recording was made recently in the ballroom of Cullington Wool Exchange in West Yorkshire, where the club's members seem unaware that ballroom dancing has faded from fashion, as they dance to the music of the New Albion Dance Orchestra. We spoke to one of the instigators of the regular social evenings here. His name may not be well-known nowadays, but Jack Hutchins played with some of the top dance bands of the pre-war years.' Suddenly, Hutch appeared on screen, being interviewed by Maria.

'Tell us how you came to be involved in music in the thirties, Hutch.

You don't mind my using the name the band have given you, do you?'

'Not at all, Maria. I was an engineer in a worsted mill until nineteen thirty-five, when the mill closed, and I was made redundant. That was when I picked up my clarinet and sax, and went to London to look for work. I was lucky enough, and I mean "lucky", to find work as a musician. It was a wonderful time to be in popular music.'

'So it was, and here's another musician with a similar background. Norman Barraclough is First Trombone with the band. I believe your story is similar to Hutch's, Norman.'

'Yes, we worked at the same mill, but I left a few months before Hutch, and I went to work in the First-Class Ballroom of the RMS *Duchess of Lancastria*.'

'So you played for the wealthy passengers travelling first-class. How did that feel, working at that level?'

Those who knew Norman could see immediately that he thought it was a silly question, but he answered politely. 'The important thing was that we were playing the music of our choice, and that amounted to luxury at any level.'

'And who is this, Norman?' The camera panned downward to Ida, who sat quietly, as usual, between Norman's immaculately-burnished Oxford brogues.

'This is Ida. Wherever the band goes, Ida goes, and she loves every minute of it, don't you, flower?'

The cameras returned to the ballroom, where, incredibly, Frank was counting the band into its signature number 'The Sun Has Got His Hat On'. Slowly, the camera zoomed in on Ida, who seemed unaware that the attention was on her.

Back in the Arts Centre again, Maria was interviewing the Chairman of the Exchange Club.

'Arnold Wilson,' she said, 'you're Chairman of the Wool Exchange, aren't you?'

'The Wool Exchange Club,' he corrected her.

'And you meet each month for the kind of social evening we've been watching. How long has that been going on?'

'Only about a year and a half. Believe it or not, we hardly ever used the ballroom until Frank and the others formed the band, and now we can't imagine life without it.'

After a few more questions, the programme returned to the ballroom, where Dan was singing, 'The Very Thought of You'. Members danced the gentle foxtrot, seemingly mesmerised by the music and Dan's singing. The number reached its end, and Frank came on screen.

'Now, Frank Morrison,' said Maria, 'composer of numerous memorable film and TV scores, how on earth do you find time to be a bandleader as well?'

Watching the programme, Frank groaned. It was the longest of the interviews, which made it all the more embarrassing for him, and he was relieved beyond belief when the interviewer passed on to other members of the band, and finally, Penny and Tim.

* * *

At her home in Beckworth, Sarah watched the programme with contrasting feelings. The band had been part of her life, and it was wonderful to hear Hutch's part in it celebrated as well. She watched the members dance to 'The Very Thought of You', and part of her longed to be there, whilst the rest of her wanted to forget the episode of her life that had caused her so much pain.

She smiled at the interviewer's reaction to Ida and at the clip of her in the band, and poured herself a drink during the interview with Arnold Wilson. The next part regained her attention, though, because Dan was doing what he did best. She was going to miss him when the course ended, but she was a little fearful for him as well. She'd worked very hard with him on the dance component, his one weakness, and she was crossing her fingers for him in the final assessment.

Thoughts of Dan were interrupted, however, in the worst possible way, at least from Sarah's point of view, when the programme moved to an interview with Frank. She listened to his modest responses, noting that, as usual, he was keen to highlight the contributions of the others, and then the interviewer mentioned Dan.

'Yes,' said Frank, 'Dan is a unique performer. He's twenty-one years old, but he sings the music of sixty years ago as if he were born to it, and he has a very intimate performing style. You can't fail to notice that he seems to be singing to an audience of close friends. They're not, but they might as well be, because he communicates with them all.'

Sarah was glad, but not all that surprised to hear Frank give a fulsome tribute to Dan. It could do his future career no harm at all— Suddenly, her attention was arrested when the interviewer mentioned a female vocalist. She listened to Frank's assessment of her and squirmed.

The interviewer asked, 'Is there any sign of a replacement on the horizon, Frank?'

Sarah saw Frank hesitate, and then he said, ' "Replacement" is a funny word, Maria. We may well find another female vocalist, but Sarah is… irreplaceable.'

Sarah could no longer see the screen for tears. Trust the sod to say something like that, she thought, and just when she was trying to force all thoughts of him out of her life. It was too awful for words.

* * *

Leah and Gavin watched the programme to the end, having enjoyed the whole of it, and seeing people they knew made it particularly exciting.

'Frank was always painfully modest,' said Gavin.

'Even when he played the Post Horn thing on that ornament?'

'He was three-parts drunk when he did that. We both were.' Seeing Leah reach for a tissue, he asked, 'What is it?'

'Just what Frank said about Sarah Hutchins. It's very sad.'

'Yes, Frank's had a lot of aggro in his life. I hope he's found a lot of pleasure as well.'

'You'll be able to ask him at the Ball. I've got my new ballgown.'

'Oh?' It was the first Gavin had heard about that. 'Can I see it?'

Leah considered the request, and said, 'All right. Wait there.' She disappeared upstairs, leaving Gavin to think about the programme, and then about his long friendship with Frank. Leah was right about his break-up with Sarah. It was very sad.

Leah came downstairs in a long, dark-blue, sleeveless gown that accentuated her slender, ballerina's figure.

'Oh, Leah,' said Gavin seriously, 'looking at you just now, I could fall for you all over again.'

'I hope you don't need to.'

'No,' he said, 'once is enough.' He kissed her, being careful not to crease her gown.

'I'm glad you like it, but I must take it off,' she said, looking at the clock. 'I've an early start and a final assessment in the morning.'

'Where are you going?'

'Of all places, to Beckworth College, where Sarah Hutchins is.'

* * *

Frank was aware that Penny had recorded the programme for Kate's benefit. Their mother, he knew, would have watched it avidly as well as recording it for posterity. For his part, he'd recorded it as a house-warming token for Helen, knowing that her mother would never let her watch it in peace while she was staying with them. He was still embarrassed about the interview, but he had no doubt he would get over that.

* * *

Leah took the temporary identity badge from the receptionist and clipped it carefully to her dress, taking care to trap only the seam on her neckline. She approved of security where young people were concerned, quite naturally, but to hell with damaging a perfectly good dress. She took a seat and waited.

After a minute or so, Sarah came to greet her. 'Good morning, Mrs Lowe.' They shook hands.

'Leah,' she corrected her.

'Of course. Would you like coffee, Leah?'

'To be honest, I'm gagging for one. Yes, please, Sarah. The M-Sixty-Two was its usual foul self this morning.'

'Let's go to my office, and I'll organise it.'

Leah followed her to her office and took a seat while Sarah switched on the kettle.

'I always think the end of a course is a sad business,' said Sarah. 'We get to know the students so well, as you know, and it's hard to let go.'

'I know,' said Leah. 'We shouldn't have favourites, but we can't help it. Some students will always make their mark more than others, for various reasons.'

Sarah made the coffee, and they chatted until the time came for them to meet the students.

Leah sat with the list of students and a clipboard and assessed them individually and in ensemble. When the time came to watch Dan's individual test piece, he recognised Leah, but being aware of his natural shyness, she spoke first. 'Hello, Dan. Fancy meeting you here.'

'Hello, Leah— I'm sorry. I mean Mrs Lowe.'

'That's all right. I saw you on the box last night. You sang as beautifully as ever.'

'Thank you. It's kind of you to say so.'

Sarah gave her an odd look, but said nothing.

'Not at all, Dan. Now I'd like to see you dance. Take it away.' She was aware of Sarah tightening her lips, and wondered about the reason for it until Dan performed his piece, and everything fell into place. He was competent, without being at all inspired, but she had to give credit where it had obviously been earned. At the end, she said, 'Thank you, Dan. Take a well-earned break.'

With the students out of the studio, Sarah said, 'Dan has had to work very hard on his dance. He's not a natural dancer, as you could see.'

Leah finished writing her comment, and said, 'Well, you can stop worrying, and so can he, because he did enough to get through.'

'Oh, that is a relief.'

Leah put her clipboard down and returned her pen to her bag. 'I can confirm your five distinctions and seven passes, Sarah. You're to be congratulated, and so are they.'

'Oh, thank you, Leah. I'm particularly relieved about Dan.' Clearly unable to contain her curiosity, she asked, 'How do you know him?'

'I heard him sing last month, in Cullington.' She saw Sarah's eyes flicker, and went on mischievously. 'You know all about the social evenings at the Wool Exchange, of course.'

'Yes, I do.' Sarah was unable to disguise her unease.

'My husband and Frank have known each other since... I believe since they started school, if you can imagine such a thing, and they were at college together, but I only met Frank about, oh, sixteen or seventeen years ago. It was shortly after I met my husband, actually, and Frank had come as a guest to talk to the composition students.'

Sarah made no reply, neither did she react when Leah placed her hand on hers, and said, 'I know about you and Frank, and, believe me, you got that one completely wrong.' She saw Sarah open her mouth to speak, and said, 'No, Sarah, listen. What you saw was touchingly innocent.'

'They were—'

'Sarah, you must listen. I know I'm an outsider, and I sometimes wish I'd inherited my mum's gentle diplomacy, but if I'm honest, I prefer straight talking, and I'm telling you now that you were mistaken. Frank could no more cheat on you than fly to Mars. Let me tell you why you caught them in what must have looked like a passionate embrace.' She told the story of Helen and Roy, as Frank had told it to Gavin and her. 'What was he to do, Sarah? Helen had no one else to turn to, so Frank got tough with the horrible man and made sure he never bothered her again. Can you imagine what a relief it must have been for her? He'd been catching her at odd times when she least expected it, sometimes at the library and usually when she was on her way home, and he was determined not to take "no" for an answer. Now she was free of all that, and so relieved, she gave Frank a hug out of immense gratitude. If I'd been in her situation, I'm sure I'd have done exactly the same, as I'm sure you would, and if he kissed her, it was because he'd been married to her for… I think, twenty years, and it must have seemed quite natural to do that in those peculiar circumstances. She's moving shortly to a new home, apparently, and as far as I know, Frank's still at his flat. *Finito*. There's absolutely nothing happening between them.'

'I'd no idea…' Tears were welling in Sarah's eyelids.

'Here.' Leah gave her a tissue. 'Don't let the students see you like this. They'll think I've failed them all, and I don't want that on my conscience.'

* * *

Frank had just finished talking to his mother on the phone. She was naturally overjoyed to have seen Penny, Tim, Kate and him on television, and she told him that several times. He put the phone down, glad to have given her so much pleasure, and then it rang again.

'Frank Morrison.'

'Frank, it's Sarah.'

Taken completely by surprise, he said, 'Hello, Sarah, how are you?'

She made no reply, but said, 'Can I come over? I need to talk to you.'

'Of course you can. Have you eaten?'

'Yes.'

'All right.' That made it easier, as he'd very little in the flat. 'Come over when you're ready.'

27

FINISHING THE WINE

Sarah stood on the doorstep, huddled in a thick coat, but still looking cold.

'Come in, Sarah.' Frank held the door until she was inside, and then closed it behind her. He went up the stairs ahead of her to open the door to the flat, saying, 'Come inside and let me take your coat.'

'You're still a gentleman, even after everything that's happened.'

'I'm not aware anything has happened, at least for quite some time,' he said, helping her off with her coat and hanging it on the coat stand. 'Take a pew. I've got some red wine opened. Would you like some?'

'Yes, please. It's been a hectic day.' She perched on the sofa, looking around the room. 'You've acquired some more furniture,' she remarked.

'It's from the ex-marital home, now sold to two appreciative owners. I took the bits Helen didn't want.' He handed her a glass of wine. 'What have you been up to today?' he asked.

'Final dance assessment. Dan got through, I'm happy to say.'

'Good for him, although I daresay you had quite a lot to do with it.'

'Yes, but I was still on tenterhooks until I got the result. Apparently, the external assessor's a friend of yours, by the way.'

'Oh?'

'Leah Lowe.'

'Oh, Leah. Yes, she told me she does some examining. I stayed with them recently. Gavin's an old mate of mine.'

'I know.' She seemed very ill at ease.

'Did you see us on television last night?'

'Yes, it was a good programme, and I imagine it won't have done Dan's prospects any harm.'

'No, he tells me he's looking for work now.'

She nodded, still far from confident. 'He told me you'd helped him out with his travelling expenses.'

'It seemed only right.'

'I'm glad you did. He and Kate have drifted apart. Did you know?'

'Somewhat belatedly, yes. Mind you, it doesn't prevent him from sleeping on Kate's floor when he's in London.'

'That's nice.'

He was quick to agree. 'Long may it continue to be nice,' he said cryptically, at the same time wondering when Sarah was going to get to the point. He could only imagine she was there in response to a shove of some kind from Leah, and that was a surprise in itself.

'Frank….' She hesitated.

'What?'

'I'm feeling a bit lonely over here, almost as if I'm being interviewed.'

' "When Did You Last See Your Father?" I'm sorry. That was ill-chosen.' He knew about Sarah's unhappy childhood, but he'd spoken without thinking. 'Would you feel less lonely if I came over there?' he asked. He realised it was a silly question, so he didn't wait for an answer, but joined her on the sofa. 'Is the wine all right?' It was Beaune Villages 1985, and it was quite good.

'It's very…. It's lovely, thank you.'

'I like Leah. She's so… the current vernacular, according to Kate, is "in your face", but I don't care for that expression. Let's say she's very direct.'

'She's certainly that.'

'Gavin thought she was a lesbian when he met her.'

'What on earth made him think that?'

Frank topped up her glass. 'One of the drama people had tried his luck with her and got nowhere, so he put it about that she turned out for the other side. She soon disabused Gavin of that idea.'

'Frank?'

'Mm?' It seemed she was about to change the subject, and he waited to hear what she had to say.

'Why do I make such a fool of myself where you're concerned?' She sounded utterly disconsolate.

'I don't think I had much to do with it,' he said. 'I just served as a handy punch bag.'

'That's awful.'

'Maybe I didn't put that too well.' He thought again. 'When we met, you were still reeling after your treatment at the hands of the bloke you were going to marry.'

She asked, 'How do you know that?'

'It was just an idea I formed when you told me about it. Maybe I was wrong.' It would be awful if she learned that Hutch had told him.

'No, you were right. That was what made what he did so awful.'

'And your dealings with me were influenced by that experience. As I see it, when you felt the tightrope wobble, you were revisited and tormented by the horrors of the past, so that you saw me as no better than him, or anyone else who'd let you down.'

'There was only him, but essentially, I'm afraid you're right.' She wiped away a tear with her thumb. 'I should have been able to work it out for myself.'

He passed her a box of tissues. 'I don't think so,' he said. 'It seems to me your powers of reasoning were probably buried under a mountain of emotional detritus still waiting to be bulldozed away and loaded into a skip after your experience with whatever his name was.'

'Jeremy.'

'Very fitting. I haven't known many by that name, but never liked any of them.'

She blew her nose and said, 'Until you said that, you were sounding quite erudite, give or take your mixed analogies, the tightrope and the building site.'

'I'm the very soul of erudition. I went to classes in the psychology of music when I was a student, although I have to say this is the first time I've been able to find a purpose for it.'

Looking completely dejected, she said, 'I suppose this visit was worth making, if only for the post mortem.'

'You'd have been welcome to that some time ago, but you wouldn't listen to me.'

'I know. I'm… sorry.'

Her tears were flowing freely now, so he passed her the box. 'Help yourself,' he said, 'I've got plenty more. You do realise now that what you saw on my doorstep was quite innocent, don't you?'

Unable for the moment to speak coherently, she nodded her head.

'You'd been unsettled for some time, though, hadn't you? I couldn't help but notice it.'

'I was... feeling inse...cure.'

'But what had I done to make you feel insecure?'

'Nothing... I realise... that now.'

'Just to set the record straight, you were concerned about Hilary, the outside caterer, although I lost all carnal interest in her last year while Norman was in hospital and I was looking after Ida.' He brought the waste paper basket from his study and put it down to serve as a receptacle for used tissues. 'Hilary is now in the throes of second-time-around romance with Mark Barraclough, and I wish them the best. As for Helen, she's about to move into her new home, about which she's very excited, and whilst we're still on friendly terms, we are divorced and likely to remain so.'

'I dow,' she sniffed. 'It wad all by fault.'

'No, it wasn't. We've already established that.' Eyeing the growing mountain of used tissues with some surprise, he put his arm round her shoulders and drew her towards him. 'Don't mind me,' he advised her. 'Have a bloody good cry. The tissues are holding up, and the waste bin's only seven-eighths full. I imagine you came tonight to see if we could mend the puncture.'

She nodded again.

'You should have said so.'

'I... thought you'd... gived up od it.'

'You were the one talking about a post mortem, and there's nothing deader than the subject of a post mortem.'

She blew her nose again and said, 'If there's half a chadce, I really wadt to make it work agaid.'

'To make it work, we have to trust each other. I trust you, but you'll have to do the same.'

'I will.'

'In that case, go and have a wash, and blow your nose so that we can have a normal conversation with "n"s and "m"s in it. Off you go, and then we'll finish the wine when you come back.'

'I have to drive hobe.'

'We'll see.' He made himself comfortable to wait for her, but then his mobile phone rang, so he answered it.

'Frank Morrison.'

'Hello, Dad.'

'Kate, how are you?'

'Pretty good, thanks. How about you?'

'Shaping up. Sarah's here.'

'Oh, have you got the bricks down?'

It always amused him when Kate trotted out one of her old-fashioned expressions. It also made up for some of the silly modernisms she picked up. 'It's heading that way,' he said. 'She's in the bathroom, tidying up and blowing her nose.'

'Ah, an emotional tumult, eh?'

'You could call it that.'

'Well, it's brilliant news about you and Sarah, although it was about time, if you ask me. I'm just phoning to tell you that I'm playing in a performance of Bach's *Christmas Oratorio* on the nineteenth – it makes a change from Handel's *Messiah* – but I'll be back for the ball, easily, on the twenty-first.'

'Excellent. Thanks for letting me know.'

'It's okay. 'Bye, Dad. Love you.'

''Bye, darling. Love you too.'

Sarah reappeared as he spoke those words, so to avoid any further misunderstanding, he said, 'That was Kate.'

'I thought it must be.'

'Come and sit down. Now that you've had a good blow, can you say, "Naughty Norma from Nun Monkton wore neither mauve nor maroon knickers between May and November"?'

'I imagine so, but not without a script.'

'In that case, you've earned a drink.' He topped up her glass.

'Have you told Kate it's on again?'

'Yes, and she said, "About time, too".'

'Are you going to kiss me?'

'No, you have to kiss me to make up for being a pain in the hindquarters.'

'All right.' She leaned towards him and kissed him slowly and with much feeling. Afterwards, she asked, 'Did you know Leah Lowe was going to speak to me this morning?'

'No, I hadn't a clue. According to Gavin, Leah is an independent spirit and an endless source of surprises. She also learned matchmaking at her mother's knee.'

'I was a bit miffed at first, about her interfering, but now I'm glad she did. I really should thank her.'

'They'll be at the Christmas Ball, so you'll be able to do it then. You are coming to that, aren't you?'

'I think I'd better, seeing as I'm irreplaceable.'

He winced. 'You heard that, then?'

'I did, and it meant a lot to me.'

He kissed her on the strength of it, and said, 'You're not serious about driving home, are you?'

'Maybe not.'

'Good. That means we can finish the wine.'

'You horror.'

'And then go to bed.'

'Now you're talking.' More seriously, she said, 'I love you, Frank.'

'So you damn' well should.'

28

NEVER SAY NEVER AGAIN, AGAIN

Rather than impose on Frank's hospitality again, Leah and
Gavin booked the Royal Hotel for the night of the ball, and
Frank took Sarah to meet them there.

'I'm glad you two have got your act together,' said Leah, dismissing
their thanks in her familiar, candid way, as tea was served in the lounge.

'I used to be unembarrassable,' said Gavin, 'but I learned to cringe
when I met Leah.'

'Nonsense,' she told him. 'When two lovely people like Sarah and
Frank get together, someone has to make sure their path runs true.'

'And no one is better-qualified to do it than Leah, who learned the
art from her lovely mum.' More seriously, he said, 'Every deserving
person should meet Sylvia at some time, as a pick-me-up, or maybe
simply as a treat.'

'If my dad hadn't been in the way,' explained Leah, 'he'd have
married her instead of me.'

'But, as things turned out, I got the best of both worlds.'

'Good for you, Gavin,' said Frank, for whom the concept of the
mother-in-law evoked an entirely different reaction. 'What more could
you wish for?'

'Actually, I've been wondering about joining the Wool Exchange
Club. How do you go about it?'

'There's an official form to fill in, and your application needs to
be supported by two full members. I'd be happy to do it, and I'm sure
Hutch or Norman would. In the meantime, though, you're always
welcome as our guests.' Looking at his watch, he said, 'I'll be going
across there shortly, so I'll pick up a form for you.'

'Thanks, Frank.'

'What's happening at the Exchange?' asked Sarah, whose enthusiasm for the social evenings was now rekindled after her absence.

'Hutch and I arranged to meet a photographer, who's going to take some pictures tonight. I think he's also going to make a video to promote the band.'

'A local photographer, presumably?'

'He's from over your way. Welsden, I believe.'

'Who is he?'

'His name's Paul Watson. He seems like a decent sort of chap, and he's going through a tough time, so it's good that he's working. I understand he lost his wife quite recently.'

'Poor man.' For Sarah, the course was obvious. 'If he's going to be there tonight,' she said, 'we should ask him to join us.'

* * *

Frank came to Gavin's and Leah's table before the ball was due to commence. 'I'm redundant for the evening,' he announced. 'I was half-expecting it.'

'It was the same last Christmas,' said Sarah, 'but we had a wonderful time.'

'Who's going to do your job?' asked Leah.

'Hutch. He wants to make sure I don't let Sarah escape this time.'

Vanessa came discreetly on to the platform to give the band an 'A', and the musicians could be heard tuning in the band room. Presently, they made their way on to the platform and took their places. There was a flurry of applause for Ida as she appeared beside Norman, and when everyone was settled, Hutch walked on and counted them into 'The Sun Has Got His Hat On', prompting a huge welcome from the members and their guests.

'Thank you, ladies and gentlemen,' said Hutch, turning to the microphone, 'and welcome to our second Christmas Ball, here at the Wool Exchange Ballroom. Let's begin with a waltz, "I Can Give You the Starlight".'

Frank and Gavin got up to lead Sarah and Leah on to the floor. Sarah watched the other two, and said, 'Leah moves like a dream.'

'She's been doing it a long time.'

'I know, but ballroom's completely different from ballet.'

'Her parents taught her ballroom from an early age. I imagine it was compulsory, with her dad having a dance band.'

'I'd like to meet them,' she said, still watching Leah. 'They sound fascinating.'

'I've basically invited them.'

'Basically?'

'By proxy.'

'Good. I love you, Frank.'

'What prompted that?'

'I've decided to tell you that every day for the rest of our lives. Will you join me?'

'I think I'd better. I love you, Sarah.'

'You're welcome to, Frank, as much as you like.'

They danced to the end of the number and returned to the table. Sarah said, 'I have to leave you soon.'

'So soon?'

'I'm singing the third number, silly.'

'I didn't know. Hutch must have made a substitution since I chose the numbers.'

'That's because you didn't know I was going to be here.'

To be sociable to their guests, they sat out the quickstep, and Sarah left them shortly before the end.

'A calmer number now,' announced Hutch. 'It's "Dream a Little Dream of Me", and here to sing it for us, I'm *more* than happy to say, is Sarah.' He counted the band into the number as his granddaughter took her place beside him.

Sarah sang the number Frank had heard her sing many times, but this time was special, as his guests probably realised as well. At the end, Leah said, 'That was absolutely lovely.'

'Yes,' said Gavin, 'quite magical.'

Frank made no comment, being lost in his own thoughts, until Sarah joined them again. 'That was beautiful,' he said.

'I'm glad you enjoyed it.'

They all danced the next number, which was 'September in the Rain', and then it was Dan's turn with 'Stay As Sweet As You Are'.

'Oh,' said Leah, 'my favourite foxtrot and my favourite singer!'

Rather than wait for Gavin to get to his feet, she towed him on to the floor.

'Leah told Dan that if he ever feels like doing some teaching, he must get in touch with Gavin and her at East Lancs,' said Frank. 'It's worth knowing, in case he ever needs a safety net.'

'I've no doubt he will at some time, and that's good news.'

As they circled the floor, Frank spotted Paul with a video camera. 'There's Paul,' he said. 'Let's invite him over when we see him.'

'Yes, we must.'

There were several more numbers before the break, and then Frank went in search of Paul Watson. He found him packing his equipment, having got the shots and film he needed.

'Hello, Frank,' he said, 'I expected to see you in front of the band.'

'I'm having an evening off, Paul. Are you going to come and join us? The buffet's quite spectacular.'

'I'm not a member.'

'It makes no difference. The rude mechanicals are allowed to eat,' he said, indicating the now empty platform, 'and I speak as one of the rudest and least mechanical.'

'Well, if you're sure.'

'My girlfriend will leave me again if I turn up without you. She's been watching you work hard, and she's determined to make sure you eat and have a drink with us.' He led him to the table. 'This is Sarah,' he said. 'You've seen her up there, and Leah and Gavin are our friends.'

'Sarah,' he said, taking her hand, 'you sing beautifully.'

'Thank you.'

He shook hands with Gavin and then Leah, who said, 'We're going to get something to eat. Come with us.'

They went off together, and Frank said, 'Something else Gavin told me about Leah is that she doesn't respond well to argument. He says he has the marks to show for it.'

'I don't believe a word. I can tell they're absolutely devoted.'

'Oh well, Gavin has been known to exaggerate. Are you singing later?'

'Yes, just one number.'

'What is it?'

'Wait and see.'

Gavin, Leah and Paul returned from the buffet, and then it was the turn of Frank and Sarah.

'Just look at these things,' said Sarah.

'It's all good, local stuff as well.'

'Hello,' said Hilary, joining them. 'Are you enjoying the evening?'

'Very much,' said Sarah, and I know we're going to enjoy the buffet.'

'I hope so. I'm also hoping Hutch will give Mark a rest so that he can dance with me. He said he would.'

'If Hutch said he would, you can bank on it,' said Frank, 'but not until they've played "Limehouse Blues".'

'Why not?'

'Because it calls for a virtuoso clarinettist.'

It was clear that Hilary's grasp of music went no further than the kind of folk offering that had led Frank to have second thoughts about her a year or more earlier. 'What does that mean?'

' "Virtuoso"? It means "brilliant".'

Hilary beamed with pride. 'Help yourselves to anything you fancy,' she said.

They did, and they returned to the table to find Paul, Leah and Gavin chatting like old friends.

'Paul dances as well,' Leah told them.

'I'm not in your class,' he said. 'I've only done it for amusement.'

'We don't do it out of masochism,' she told him.

'Funnily enough, I learned to dance when I was in the Navy.'

'The Navy?'

'That's how I learned my trade, as a photographer in the Fleet Air Arm.'

'My dad was in the Fleet Air Arm,' she told him. 'He was a telegraphist air-gunner. You probably speak the same funny language.'

'I shouldn't be surprised. I imagine he was in the war?'

'Briefly. He ditched in the Mediterranean and spent three years as a prisoner of war.'

'Bad luck.'

'It was in a way, but my mum wrote to him, and they met when he came home, and they've been potty about each other ever since.'

'What a marvellous story.'

The musicians were taking their places once more, and Hutch came on to announce the first number of the second half, which was 'Bye Bye Blues'.

Leah asked, 'Are you going to ask me to dance, Paul?'

'Well, I'd like to....'

'You've no choice,' said Gavin, straight-faced, 'it's compulsory.'

They went on to the floor, and Frank said, 'Leah evidently had no difficulty in drawing him out.'

'She could draw a boil out of a wooden leg,' Gavin told him. 'She's a forceful version of her mum.' He considered that, and said, 'She lacks her talent for diplomacy, though.'

'She's lovely,' said Sarah.

'She's that as well,' he agreed, 'but I'm a shade biased.'

Sarah left them towards the end of the number, because the next item was hers.

' "I'll Never Say Never Again, Again",' announced Hutch, 'with vocal refrain by Sarah.'

His announcement was greeted in such a way that left no doubt about Sarah's popularity among the members.

'She's excellent,' said Paul. 'Where did you find her?'

'She's Hutch's granddaughter.'

'Really?'

'I should know.' They listened to the number, and Frank was wondering a little about her choice. When she returned, he asked her about it.

'I chose it to let you know that I really will never say, "Never again" again.'

He squeezed her hand because it meant everything to him to hear that, and he was pleased when the next number turned out to be one of their favourites, which was 'Love Walked In.' They danced to it blissfully and without a word.

'Another Gershwin number,' announced Hutch. "A Foggy Day".'

Sarah reached for Paul's hand. 'Come on, Paul,' she said. 'It's my turn.'

Frank nodded his smiling approval, and they went on to the floor.

'He's not bad at the foxtrot,' said Leah. 'He just needs a bit of refinement and a lot of practice.'

'She just can't help marking everyone out of ten,' said Gavin, miming a disarming kiss in his wife's direction.

'I believe the next number's for you, Leah,' said Frank recalling the programme he'd planned.

He was right. Paul and Sarah returned happily to hear that the next dance was a quickstep. It was 'All I Do is Dream of You', and the vocal refrain would be provided by Dan.

As Gavin took Leah's hand and led her on to the floor, a familiar voice asked, 'Do you mind if we join forces?' Tim pulled out two spare chairs for Penny and himself.

'This is Paul,' said Frank. 'He came to take some pictures, but he's one of us now. Paul, this is my sister Penny and her husband Tim.'

'I filmed you both earlier,' said Paul. 'You were so impressive, I had to.'

'They have form for it,' Frank told him as they thanked him for the compliment.

When Leah and Gavin returned, Gavin said, 'You've climbed a hell of a steep hill with this band, Frank. I take my hat off to you.'

'Thanks, Gavin, but that's what hills are for, isn't it?'

'I was conceived on a hill,' said Leah quite matter-of-factly.

Gavin looked like someone who'd heard the story before, and when Leah continued, it turned out he had.

'End the suspense, Leah,' entreated Frank.

'If you have to,' muttered Gavin.

'Lady Hill is a wonderful place surmounted with Scots pines, on the road between Leyburn and Hawes in Wensleydale. It appealed to my dad as an enchanted place, like the one in *The House At Pooh Corner*, and that was what gave him the idea. What do you think about that?'

'Apart from being deeply embarrassed,' suggested Gavin.

'I think it's a lovely story,' said Sarah.

'It was a novel idea,' said Frank thoughtfully, deciding that Leah's dad was a man of imagination, and wondering about the feasibility of a similar event.

'A moment of poetry,' added Paul diplomatically.

Hutch announced the waltz 'Lovely Lady', and Penny asked, 'Do you dance, Paul?'

'Well, yes....'

'Come on, then.'

Frank smiled to himself as his sister innocently made herself Paul's third dance partner of the evening. He said to Tim, 'Paul's coping with the loss of his wife, and we didn't want to see him slope off on his own.'

'I thought there must be something like that,' said Tim, understated as ever, 'but I think Penny still wants a dance with you before they start the tinsel Christmas numbers.'

'It's an old tradition, Tim, going back to the days before you showed up, and I was the only sparring partner she could find.'

Penny and Paul returned as Hutch announced 'Embraceable You.' Immediately, Penny asked, 'Do you mind if I borrow Frank for just one dance, Sarah?'

'Feel free. Paul, will you join me?'

'Of course.' By this time, Paul had settled into his role as one of the group, a development that Leah had noticed with some satisfaction.

'Paul's enjoying this evening as much as anyone,' she said.

'This is a special place,' Tim told her. 'I'm not at all fanciful, being an electrical engineer and as hard-headed as they come, but I've seen the effect this ballroom has on people.'

Leah and Gavin watched Paul and Sarah, and had to agree with him.

Eventually, the moment came for Hutch to announce 'Rudolph, the Red-Nosed Reindeer.' 'You can please yourselves whether you treat it as a foxtrot or a quickstep,' he told them. 'It's just a bit of fun, and if we can't have fun at Christmas, when can we?'

Penny and Tim and Paul sat the number out, while the others flocked to the floor.

'I never expected it to be like this,' said Paul. 'To be honest, I'd been dreading the job, but it's been quite magical, thanks to you people.'

'Make a habit of it,' said Penny. 'We do, and it's never let us down.'

'Come as our guest, or Frank's,' said Tim. 'It's all the same, and you'll always be welcome, just like Leah and Gavin.'

Frank had told Penny about Paul, and she squeezed Tim's hand discreetly.

'Winter Wonderland' proved as popular as ever, now that the ball was approaching its end, and Frank was pleased to see Mark and Hilary together on the floor. Mark wasn't a natural dancer, but he was, after all, a virtuoso clarinettist, and he couldn't be expected to be brilliant at everything. In any case, Hilary didn't seem to mind, and she was the one who mattered most to him.

After a few closing words, Hutch announced 'Goodnight, Sweetheart', and Frank felt a touch of sadness at the absence of Fred Adams's guitar introduction, but everything else was there, and he and Sarah danced happily to the familiar closing number. Sarah was back, the band was back to full strength, the ballroom was functioning again after its refurbishment, his old friend Gavin and the lovely Leah were back in touch, and to make the occasion complete, the ballroom had been able to do something for Paul when he most needed it. Happier than he'd been for some time, Frank kissed Sarah's cheek and whispered the time-honoured message in her ear. It was for the third time that day, but neither of them was counting.

The End

www.ingramcontent.com/pod-product-compliance
Lightning Source LLC
Chambersburg PA
CBHW020841260626
47169CB00003B/1077